QUESTIONER'S SHADOW

MARK FASSETT

QUESTIONER'S SHADOW

MARK FASSETT

RAVENSTAR PRESS
MONROE, WA

Published 2011 by Ravenstar Press
Monroe, WA
http://www.ravenstarpress.com

Trade paper edition designed by Mark Fassett
in Scribus

Electronic editions designed by Mark Fassett
using StoryBox software
http://www.markfassett.com
http://www.storyboxsoftware.com

Cover art by Joe Slucher
http://www.joeslucher.com

ISBN: 978-0615594194

For my parents,
They bought me books
as a reward for good grades.

Too bad it didn't work in high school.

CHAPTER 1

In his service to the Empire, Petyr had seen any number of dead bodies. Most often, they had a bullet through the skull or a knife wound in the belly. He'd never seen anything like the body of the woman that hung naked from the trunk of a tree in front of him.

A pair of iron spikes held it there, driven through the body just above her breasts and just below her shoulders. A third spike protruded from her gaping mouth.

The spikes weren't the source of the bile that threatened to erupt from his stomach. The woman seemed young, perhaps sixteen or seventeen. Her hair, dark but not quite black, fell mostly down onto her shoulders, framing high cheekbones that had once supported her eyes, and would still, but for the fact that her killer had removed those eyes leaving empty sockets.

That wasn't all. Whatever monster had done this to the young woman had managed to pull her arms off.

Petyr had to turn away. He bent over and took a few deep breaths. They seemed to help for a moment, but the bile wouldn't stay down. The contents of his stomach emptied onto the forest floor.

He heard footsteps coming toward him, but he didn't turn around. He pulled a handkerchief from his pocket and started wiping at his mouth. *I wish I had some water.*

"Are you all right, Petyr?" Alec asked from behind him.

No. "I'm fine."

Petyr finished wiping his mouth, stood up, and checked his clothes to make sure he hadn't splashed vomit on them. When he was satisfied they were clean, he wrapped up the handkerchief as best he could so the contents of his stomach were safely inside, then turned back to face the body.

"Whoever she was," Alec said, "I can't imagine what she did to deserve this."

Petyr looked at Alec. His friend's face was pale. *Apparently Alec has never seen anything to compare, either.*

"She didn't do anything to deserve this, Alec. Some of the towns on the edge of the Empire have some brutal forms of justice, but this, the Empire wouldn't tolerate."

"How would you know, Petyr?"

How would I know? He didn't have an answer for Alec.

"Well, I'm going back to the carriage," said Alec.

Petyr looked away from his friend and back to the woman on the tree. His stomach still felt uneasy, but it had quieted. For better or worse, he was getting used to the sight.

"Go on," he said. "I'll be right along."

Alec turned and left. His footsteps, muffled in the soft loam of the forest, soon faded to nothingness.

Petyr moved within arm's reach of the woman's corpse. Blood stains descended from her wounds and empty eye sockets, the blood long washed away in the rain.

What color eyes did she have?

Her cheeks were thin and hollow, but the ghost of fullness lingered. Her nose sloped down to a petite point. From the tightness of her belly, it was clear she'd never borne children.

Petyr examined the stumps where her arms had been. The flesh ran ragged around the wounds. The holes in her chest were larger than the spikes rammed through them, the skin around the edges torn. His first impression was accurate. Her arms had been pulled off, not cut or sawn or chopped. *Who would, or even could, do such a thing?*

Something odd struck him. The body didn't smell. No hint of putrefaction lingered in the air. He could smell the dampness of the forest, the aroma of the blackroot trees, the cloying scent of the moss that seemed to cover everything, but the stink of death was curiously absent. Judging by the lack of fresh blood, the body had hung from the tree long enough it should have started to decompose. It should have been ripe, crawling with bugs. But other than the wounds and the stains, it looked like a fresh kill.

He shuddered. Something or someone committed evil here. He could feel it. Something so vile, even the agents of decay wouldn't touch the body.

He walked back to the carriage with careful steps, avoiding the shrubs and dead branches that lay across the path. Alec had already climbed up to the driver's bench and had his head bowed down, studiously watching the pair of horses as they fidgeted in their harness. They apparently didn't like waiting anywhere near that horror. Petyr wondered if they smelled something he couldn't.

"Alec," he said as he approached. "What's the nearest town?"

"Dunsriver, I think. We passed it earlier today."

"Take us back there."

"Why? If we go back, we won't make Rocktree by nightfall."

"We're not going to Rocktree, Alec."

Alec jumped down from the driver's bench and confronted Petyr. "What do you mean we're not going to Rocktree? We have to keep moving."

Petyr sighed. Alec was right. They couldn't afford to linger, not with the Empire on their trail. *On my trail. Is this really any of my business, anyway? If I just went on to Rocktree, who would know besides Alec?* He looked at his friend. *Alec wouldn't tell anyone. If I stay and put this town to Question, the Tribune will most definitely hear.*

But the vision of the girl on the tree haunted him. He had to know the truth. It wasn't just his job.

"It's who I am, Alec. I have to find the truth of this. I promise, no more than a day or two. It shouldn't take long."

They stood staring at each other for a few more moments, before Alec turned away without saying anything more and climbed back onto the bench.

Petyr opened the door of the carriage, stepped up and in, then shut the door behind him. He took a seat on the hard bench, its velvet covered cushion long since compacted to a layer that felt more like stone than anything else.

As the carriage started to move, he had a mind to lean out and tell Alec to keep on to Rocktree, but the vision of the woman's body still haunted him. No matter how close his pursuers, he couldn't let a crime like that go.

Instead of reversing his decision, he leaned back and worked at committing everything he'd observed to memory.

A threat existed here, and it was his job as Lord Questioner to root it out. *Even if I am no longer a Lord Questioner.*

⩗ ⩗ ⩗

Dunsriver, it turned out, lay off the main road down a thin track barely wide enough for the carriage. When Alec turned the carriage down that track, the trees crowded in brushing the sides with their branches. For several minutes, Petyr worried that a branch would break through the windows of the carriage to shower glass upon him. The scraping of the branches ceased, however, before his worry became reality.

When he looked out, Petyr saw they'd emerged into a great clearing, littered with stumps. In the distance along the wood-line, men sawed at the base of a tree. Farther along the wood-line he found other groups, also working to fell trees. He heard a shout. One towering monster slid off its stump, then toppled to the ground in a crash of branches and mud. Men quickly moved in and hacked away at its branches, beginning an apparently long process of preparing the tree for transport.

He watched them until he noticed a change in the clearing. The stumps gave way to empty, barren fields. This late in the season, he suspected the harvest was complete, and the fields would wait for winter to pass before seeing activity again.

As the carriage followed a slight bend in the track, Petyr caught his first sight of Dunsriver. What he saw surprised him. The town was fronted by a wall that stood more than two men tall. It appeared to be a recent construction and made with haste out of wood cut from the forest. The tops of the logs ended in shaped points, and the wood still looked green.

The carriage came to a stop outside the wall.

"State your business." A gruff voice.

"My Lord Questioner Ocyna seeks entrance and lodgings," said Alec. His voice was muffled through the walls of the carriage.

"There are no lodgings for his sort here."

"There are always lodgings for a Lord Questioner." Alec's voice sounded cold to Petyr's ear.

Petyr heard someone spit. He assumed it was the owner of the gruff voice. "We have no use for Empire... justice."

Petyr swung the door of the carriage open, and stepped down onto the road. The mud squelched out around his shoes. He ignored it and strode, with a purpose that he'd had drilled into him during his training, toward the man blocking their way. The man topped Petyr by only a hand or so, but stood as wide as two men. Spots of gray stained the beard that covered much of his face, but his eyes tracked Petyr, bright and wary.

The gate to the town stood open, but only wide enough for him to see the crowd that was beginning to gather on the other side.

"Good sir, there is always need for Empire justice." Petyr stuck out his hand, but the man hardly even glanced at it. He shifted his eyes to scan the crowd on the other side of the gate. "However,"

Petyr continued, "I'm not here to dispense justice. I am merely passing through, and my driver informed me that we would not make Rocktree by nightfall. I'd appreciate it if you could spare a bed for myself and my driver. I have no wish to spend the night on the side of the road."

The man shook his head. "We have no beds to spare. Sleep in your carriage."

"There are no free beds at all?" he asked while watching a woman in the crowd whisper into a man's ear. She was well past childbearing, and so was the man. "No hospitality for a servant of the Empire?"

The man on the receiving end of the woman's whisper stepped out of the crowd and through the gate. He approached the man impeding Petyr's way. "What are you about, Roderick?" he asked in a quiet voice, an obvious attempt to keep Petyr from hearing him. He didn't seem aware it was futile. Petyr pretended to not hear anything.

"We don't need him here, Sim. What if he finds out? We don't need the attention of the Empire."

"If we don't let him stay, and something happens to him in the forest and the Empire finds out? Then where will we be?"

"There's no guarantee anything would happen. And if we did, we could feign ignorance."

Petyr saw anger on Sim's face as he stood back a bit. "And have a whole company of Questioners fall on us? The truth would out, and they would hold us responsible."

Roderick's eyes twitched back and forth between Petyr and Sim. "I don't like having him here. We can handle it ourselves."

"Three dead and another missing, and you think we can handle it ourselves?"

Petyr jolted inside. *Three? Maybe four? Is the one on the tree the missing, or one of the dead?*

"You're out of your mind, Roderick. Perhaps he's exactly the help we need."

Fury crossed Roderick's face, but his lips closed tight. His fists clenched. Sim ignored him and spoke to Petyr.

"Lord Questioner, Dunsriver does not have an inn, but you are welcome to stay in my home. We have extra beds."

Petyr held his hand out to the older man. "Thank you, Sim. You are most generous." Sim took the proffered hand and shook it. "You will ride with my driver and direct him to your home?"

"Of course."

The crowd, sensing the excitement had ended, began to dissipate. As it broke up, Petyr noticed one blonde-headed young woman staring at him. When their eyes locked, she blinked once, smiled, then ran off into the town. *She's pretty. I wonder... No, Petyr. Think of Alura. You can't let that happen to another.*

"Come," he said to Sim, and motioned for Sim to follow.

Petyr stepped back toward the carriage leaving Roderick fuming. He didn't want Petyr there, obviously, but what was he worried about? Was it just the anti-Empire sentiment that sometimes ran strong out here on the edges of the Empire? Or was there more to it? Did he really think they didn't need his help?

Petyr climbed into the carriage. The carriage rocked as Alec helped Sim up onto the drivers bench. Petyr felt sure about one thing. The town did need his help. Three dead, one missing. A wall hastily constructed to defend against who knew what.

The carriage crept forward, and he could see Roderick standing to the side of the road, anger and frustration boiling behind his eyes as Petyr rolled by.

⚔ ⚔ ⚔

"Carree!" Sim yelled as he opened the door to his home. Petyr followed behind the man as he entered. "Carree, come down here!"

Sim came to a stop in the foyer, and looked up to a walkway that crossed the rear wall of the room. A stairway with an ornate, hand carved rail climbed the wall to Petyr's left. He could see into a sitting room to his right. To his left, a dining room was visible through the space between the foot of the stairs and the front wall of the house. Two other doors in the rear wall of the foyer stood closed.

Petyr set the one case he carried down on the stone floor and wondered where the wealth came from. The home was clearly among the largest, if not the largest home in Dunsriver. He kept silent, for the moment. The time for questions would arise later. He needed to get settled in.

"Carree!"

The right-side door at the rear of the foyer opened, and a young woman stepped out. Her blonde hair was pulled back into a tail, leaving only a few strands to fall over her eyes. The eyes that had locked on him at the gate. "Yes father?"

"Where have you been?"

Her eyes flicked quickly to Petyr, then back to her father. "I've been here, in the back, feeding the horses."

A lie, Petyr knew. He would have known had he not crossed glances with her at the gate.

"Oh, dear Mother. You were not to go outside this house. Why do you disobey me?"

She walked across the room to face her father. After that first flick of her eyes, Petyr thought she made a point of not looking at him. "Father, I cannot stay in this house forever. The others..."

Sim covered her mouth with his hand. "No, we will speak of this later. Would you show this gentleman to Bran's room?" He removed his hand.

"Bran's room? Mother will have a fit."

"No, she won't. It was her idea."

Carree rolled her eyes, then looked straight at Petyr for the first time, appraising him, he thought. "Would you at least introduce us, first?" She held her hand out.

Sim sighed. "Lord Ocyna, my daughter Carree. Carree, Lord

Questioner Petyr Ocyna. You *will not* bother him."

Petyr took her hand, but just held it. She seemed to want a more intimate gesture, but he was not about grant her desire. Doing so might lead to places in his heart he feared to tread, despite the flutter in his chest as she made the offer. "My Lady, it is good to meet you."

He released her hand, and a look of disappointment flitted across her face. "It is good to meet you, Lord Questioner."

"You may call me Petyr, if you so wish. At present, I am not performing my duties, and I find it dreary to always be called by my office instead of my name."

Sim interrupted. "Show him the room, Carree, then come down and help your mother with supper." Petyr thought it clear Sim wished his daughter to have as little contact with a Questioner as necessary. Petyr didn't blame him, not with the way Questioners were often portrayed on the edges of the Empire, and even sometimes near its heart. The Emperor himself sometimes played up the darker side of the Questioners' reputation, deserved or not. *If they only knew the truth.*

Her eyes grew hard. "Yes, father."

He picked his case from the floor, and she turned toward the stairs, motioning Petyr to follow her.

"This way my L... Petyr." The way she said his name, after the initial slip, sounded like she was testing it out.

He was about to follow her, but Sim stepped in his way. "I know you think we are backward and provincial, but do not make the mistake of thinking we are stupid. My daughter is willful and headstrong and drives me to distraction. I will not, however, allow anyone to use that to their advantage. I hope you understand."

Petyr nodded. "Your daughter is safe from me, though, she would be had you said nothing." *My memories would see to that.*

"My worry is that you are not safe from her." He laughed, then, some of the tension easing from him. "I will see that your driver has the horses stabled and the carriage stowed. You will join us for supper? I will be inviting the other Elders, though they would likely show in any case."

"Of course I will sup with you."

"Good, then go with my daughter and rest if you need, and we shall see each other at supper, if not before." Sim looked at him like he wished to say something else, but whatever words he meant to say remained in his throat as he turned and stepped out into the street again.

Petyr saw Carree waiting on the second step of the stairs and moved in her direction. When she saw he was coming, she started up the stairs. He followed her up and she led him into a room at the end of the hallway.

He followed his first instinct to go to the window and look out. It let him survey most of the southern half of the town. The gate, he knew, lay to the west. To the east, the Duns River, for which the town was named, flowed past, gray and murky.

"Are you going to be here for long?"

He hesitated before answering. "Our intention was only to stay the night before moving on to Rocktree in the morning." Smoke and soot from fires lit for heating hung low over the town.

"Then you're not here to help us." The sad, spurned tone she used caused him to face her.

"Help you?" He wanted her talking, revealing things before he had to ask questions of her father and the elders that he would meet at supper.

"With the killings. That's why you're here, aren't you?"

"There have been killings? Murders?"

Her eyes grew watery. "Yes. It's why my father won't let me leave the house."

"You did, anyway. I saw you at the gate."

Her sad look became pleading in a heartbeat. "You won't tell him, will you? The killings only happen when the fog comes."

"The fog?"

Then, they both heard footsteps coming up the stairs.

"Carree?" A woman's voice.

Carree reached out and grasped his hand. "My mother. You will help us, won't you?" she asked, her voice just above a whisper.

"Carree, where are you?"

"Of course," he said, "I'll do what I can."

She squeezed his hand, then stood on her toes and kissed him on the cheek. "Thank you." Then she turned and ran out of the room. "Coming Mother."

Petyr stood, rooted, the touch of her lips still lingering in his nerves stirring memories of another kiss and another time that he'd tried to expel. He brought his hand to his face and wiped at his cheek, erasing the touch. It would not do to let those memories come out and interfere. He would have to stay as far from Carree's reach as he could.

CHAPTER 2

W hen Petyr ventured downstairs again, his nose caught the smell of baking bread and other culinary scents. Sim saw him and brought him into the kitchen where a woman, Carree, and another younger helper were cooking supper.

Petyr recognized the woman as the one who had whispered in Sim's ear at the gate. Her hands were covered in flour, and she was rolling out some dough. She looked up as Petyr and her husband approached.

"Lord Petyr, my wife Aster," Sim said. "Aster..."

Aster interrupted her husband. "I know who he is."

She looked him up and down, appraising him for something, like he was a hog at market. Out of the corner of his eye, Petyr could see Carree watching her mother. "My Lord, is your room acceptable?" Aster asked.

"Quite acceptable."

"That is good. It belonged to my son."

Petyr had a sudden insight, like he sometimes did, an answer to a question he hadn't yet asked. Bran would not be joining them, and Aster believed him dead a year past of a hunting accident.

Petyr never questioned these answers, nor did he speak of them, not since he had learned during his early years at the academy that his friends could not do the same thing. More than once, his ability had saved him from some embarrassing situations, such as asking about a woman's dead son.

"Thank you for letting me stay here," Petyr said. "I would prefer you call me by Petyr while I am a guest. I don't think there is any need to be so formal."

"Well, My Lord, I don't think I can do that. Circumstances are such that I think the formality is appropriate. Now, if you don't mind, I'll have to ask you and my dear husband to leave the kitchen. We've still got a lot of cooking to finish, yet."

"Of course, Ma'am. Good to meet you." Petyr wondered at the woman's upbringing, but his special talent did not enlighten him this time. *She sounds like she's from the center of the Empire, not its edge.*

"Come," Sim said. "The others will be here soon, and I must speak to you before they arrive." He motioned for Petyr to follow, and led him to the sitting room. Once Petyr stepped in, Sim shut the door.

"Sit, sit. Some brandy, perhaps?"

Petyr shook his head. "No, thank you. I abstain from spirits. They interfere with my duties."

Petyr did sit, though, taking a spot on a velvet covered settee, no doubt purchased from somewhere closer to the center of the Empire. The cushion supported him far better than that of the carriage he'd spent the last weeks in.

While Petyr sat, Sim went to a cabinet that stood against the wall. A pair of doors, finely carved in a wooded scene, hid its innards. Petyr thought the craftsmanship of the cabinet indicated an origin far from the logging town, but the scene it portrayed reminded him of the forest surrounding the town.

"I hope you don't mind if I have some, then." Sim opened the cabinet.

Petyr spied multiple shelves holding a number of stoppered bottles, each of them coated with a layer of dust, and most near to full.

Sim withdrew one near-empty bottle and shut the door. He triggered a catch that Petyr hadn't noticed, and a door opened on the side of the cabinet. Sim pulled a crystal goblet from the hidden compartment.

"The cabinet is an amazing piece," Petyr said. "I don't think I've seen anything quite like it."

"You wouldn't have," Sim said as he unstoppered the brandy. He lifted the bottle to his nose and sniffed.

"Why not?"

"My son made it. Come, take a closer look." He poured himself a liberal serving of the brandy.

Petyr stood, approached the cabinet, and bent down to get a better look. As he did so, the forest in the carving came alive. Blackroot trees, despite their immense trunks, bent in a wind that threatened to topple them. A river, obscured by the trees, wandered along among the roots, frothy with spray from the wind. Behind it all, a shimmery something, a wall, or a veil, or something less cohesive, exuded a calm malevolence, eternal and implacable.

He reached out and touched a tree with a finger. He felt the wood, smooth and polished under his skin. His finger slipped off the tree and brushed a portion of the veil.

The malevolence poured into him and up his arm. His arm went numb and fell away from the cabinet. His heart leapt in his chest. His whole body wanted him to leave, now. He knew what the veil had to be. The Fringe. That wall of mystical energy that cut through the forest somewhere north of the road they'd traveled. He'd heard stories of it in Genova, but never from anyone who had seen it first hand.

He stood up, unwilling to examine it so closely any longer. He wanted to ask about the veil, about the Fringe, but something told him to hold off, Instead, he asked, "You're son carved this?" He found he could hardly breathe the words.

"About a year ago. He was a fine craftsman." Sim looked into his brandy.

"You diminish him, I think. Your son was an artist."

"I would have said so, before." He lifted the goblet to his lips and took a large swallow.

"Before he died."

"Before he disappeared."

Petyr turned back to the settee and sat down again. Something here didn't fit. When he Questioned people, the answers he received were never wrong. Aster believed Bran had died in a hunting accident. He'd accepted that explanation without probing further. He wouldn't make that mistake with Sim.

"How long ago?"

Sim looked into his goblet, swirled the contents, then drained it before answering. "Just after he finished the cabinet, we went hunting. Autumn had come along quickly, and it looked to be a hard winter. I wanted some more meat salted before the snows came. He was a far better hunter than I, and he took the lead. I did not realize how close to the Fringe we had come, until it was there, just beyond Bran."

The Fringe. Petyr was glad he held off asking about it. "Is it normal to get so close?"

"No, we try to stay away from it. Strange things often happen nearby. Horses run off for little or no reason, or you lose your sense of direction and wind up traveling in circles for hours. Fires don't seem to burn as hot in its shadow. The trees often seem to be restless, or even angry."

From behind him, Petyr heard the click of the latch on the door to the room. Sim did not look up, so Petyr ignored it. "He led you right to it, didn't he?"

"That day, I think he did. I didn't think of it before, or perhaps didn't want to. He had an obsession with the Fringe since the first time he saw it, always wanting to go see it, get closer. He'd talk about wanting to see what was on the other side, but I'd always thought it idle musing."

Petyr glanced at the carving on the brandy cabinet again, and this time, even with the distance, he saw the Fringe behind it all. "What happened, then?"

"I tried to go toward him, called out to him, even, and then I tripped and fell to the ground. I swear something reached out and grabbed my ankle, but when I looked, I saw only tree roots and bushes. I lost sight of Bran in that moment. When I looked back up, he was gone." Sim poured himself more brandy and drank it dry.

"You lied to your wife."

"If she knew Bran went through deliberately, I don't know what it would do to her."

"Why is that?"

"We've been here for a long time," Sim said. "Long enough that some don't remember we weren't always here, I think. We moved here when we were young, hoping to get wealthy off the loggers, which we did. I grew to love it here." Petyr recognized a lie, but let Sim continue. He didn't feel that interrupting his host with the accusation would get him the information he wanted.

"Aster," Sim continued, "has always had an unreasonable fear of the Fringe. She's wanted to move back to Genova for many years. The day before we went hunting, Bran presented that cabinet to her, and she wouldn't have it.

"So when he died..." Sim shook his head. "I've been saying that so long it sounds like truth. When he disappeared, I told her he fell down into a ravine and was swept away by the waters."

For the first time since beginning his story, Sim looked up. His eyes went wide, and he stared right past Petyr to the hallway. Petyr turned around to find Carree standing in the doorway, tears streaming from her eyes.

"Carree," Sim said.

She stood there for a moment longer, then turned and went out the front door, slamming it shut behind her.

"If she tells her mother," Sim said, leaving the result to hang there between them unsaid. He didn't move to stop Carree, though.

Petyr waited for a long moment, waiting to see if Sim would go after his daughter, but when Sim only poured himself another spot of brandy, Petyr stood. "I'll go get her."

Sim seemed lost. His eyes were unfocused, and his hands had begun to shake. Eventually, he mumbled, "She'll be down by the river."

Petyr nodded. He took his coat from the rack by the door, then rushed out into the street.

⅄ ⅄ ⅄

Petyr stopped at the top of the slope above the river. Carree stood near the river's edge. She had picked up some stones from the river bank, and was tossing them, one by one, into the river. The current swept away the ripples each stone created, obliterating evidence of their existence almost as soon as they entered the water.

To his right, a hundred lengths away, several men wrestled a log so that it lay parallel to the river bank. They rolled it up and over the slight crown of the hill. When the log hit the slope, it picked up speed until it hit the water with a great roar of spray flying up and about it.

In that moment, Carree turned to watch. In the late afternoon dinginess, her profile against the river sparked a memory in Petyr that he tried to shake, but it overwhelmed him.

Alura stood near the lake edge, looking to her right, watching a pair of children playing in the sand.

"Petyr, come here," she said, waving him down from his perch atop a stone.

He slid off and went to her. Her face, the profile of her against the water; Alura was more than he felt he deserved.

"Do you see them?" she asked as he approached.

Of course he saw them. He smiled and feigned ignorance. "See what?"

"Those children playing in the sand."

Petyr put his arm around her and pulled her close. "Oh, those little monsters on the shore? I see them."

"When will you let us make some of our own?"

"Love," he said to her, and then paused as she looked up at him. Her deep brown eyes bored into him, penetrated him.

Almost as if she were a Questioner herself, she said to him, "Don't say soon."

Which was just what he was about to say. "The investigation, when it's done, when we're safe."

"When we're safe?" He felt the fear in her.

He'd never told her that part before, and he regretted the slip. "I'm investigating some very powerful men. If they find out before I have enough proof, before I can bring that proof to the Emperor, well, I fear what they will do."

The children began to pile sand into a mountain.

Through her shoulders, he could still feel the fear in her, but her strength, the strength that allowed her to marry a Questioner in spite of the difficulties the unions almost always brought, came out and pushed the fear aside. "When will that be, Petyr?"

"Soon," he said, grinning.

She backed away from him. She grinned, too, right before she punched him in the shoulder. "Petyr Ocyna, you are a bore and a coward."

"What?"

She leaned in close to him and whispered into his ear. "We will start making our own children this night. It takes months, you know, before they appear and you have to worry about them." She kissed his ear with her warm lips, while he watched as the little boy swung a fist into the mountain of sand and destroyed it.

Petyr shook his head again, freeing himself from the memory. His heart raced in his chest. Why, after all this time, and in this place, would he have thought of that and let it take him over? *I should never have let her talk me into it.*

The memory hadn't lasted but a moment, though. Carree still stood watching the log slide out into the river.

While he waited for his heart to slow, Carree turned and looked at him. Even with the distance, he thought he could see tears still flowing from her eyes. She turned back to the river and threw another stone.

He straightened himself up, and cleared his head. *I won't let the past rule me.* "Carree is not for me, in any case," he said, and started down the slope.

Along the way, he kicked some stones loose, and they rolled down the slope. Carree had to have heard them, but she remained facing the river. She threw her last stone as Petyr arrived at her side.

He didn't say anything. He could feel her anguish and her anger, and decided to wait on her to break the silence.

She bent down and picked up some more stones from the ground, then tossed one into the river before speaking. Her voice, when she did speak, broke and cracked. "I don't understand why he lied to us for a year," she said.

Petyr didn't really have an answer. "He feels poorly about it."

"He said Bran was dead, said it was an accident."

Petyr stood silently. Carree threw another stone, then looked at him. Despite the memory of Alura he'd just experienced, he had to resist an urge to reach up and caress her face, tell her it was all right, and wipe away her tears. *She's not for me.*

"Bran could still be alive," she said.

"Beyond the Fringe?"

"Why not? We don't know what's beyond the Fringe. It could be anything. It could just be a wall, couldn't it? And the forest could just continue on beyond it."

Petyr bent down and picked up a stone of his own. He threw it as far out into the river as he could. It felt good. "I don't know," he said. "If it were just a wall, why wouldn't he come back?"

"I don't know," she said, punctuating it with another thrown stone. "He's always been fascinated with the Fringe. He once told me he'd crept close enough to touch it."

"Did he? Touch it, I mean?"

"I don't think so. He never said."

She threw another stone. Petyr couldn't help watching her. He couldn't keep his eyes off her. *I hope Alura doesn't notice. What would she say? Why can't I control myself?*

"Why would my father lie?" she asked again.

"Why would he think it would break your mother if she found out Bran had gone into the Fringe intentionally?"

She seemed to think about it for a bit before answering. While he waited, Petyr noticed the light had faded while they talked. Night had nearly crept up on them. For some reason, he felt vulnerable by the river in the near dark.

"My mother, I think, never wanted to come here."

That's not what Sim said. He said your mother had an unreasonable fear of the Fringe. He held that information back. It wasn't his place, yet. "Your father doesn't want you to tell your mother what you heard," he said instead.

"But, he lied to us."

"He lied to you, I think, to protect your mother. Don't judge him yet."

"My father doesn't do anything without thinking about what it will cost him."

Petyr was glad to hear the spirit in her voice. He could reason with her anger. The shock of discovery was nearly impossible to reason with.

She looked thoughtful. "Should I tell her?" she asked.

"It's not my place to say."

Her hand reached out and took his, surprising him and sending a tingle through his spine. "What would you do?"

He thought for a moment before answering. In the silence, he heard footsteps near the top of the river bank, but he kept his focus on Carree. "I would probably end up causing your mother a great deal of pain."

"You would tell her."

"If she asked."

She squeezed his hand. "Then that's what I'll do."

"You'll tell her?"

"If she asks."

Out of the corner of his eye, he saw a large shadow barrel down the slope at them. Petyr pulled his hand away and turned to defend himself and Carree.

The shadow slowed to a stop near them and resolved itself into a man that couldn't have been much older than Carree. "Carree, what are you doing down here with *him*?" Petyr didn't miss the venom involved in the reference to himself.

"Willam," Carree said. "What are you doing here?"

"I came to find you after I went to your home and your father told me you weren't there."

"Well, it's none of you're business what I'm doing here with the Lord Questioner."

"He's not to be trusted." Willam apparently didn't care what Petyr thought. "You know what they do to people."

"I know no such thing. All we ever hear are stories. I'm sure most of them are wrong."

Petyr scowled, and was glad that in the dim light it probably wouldn't show. He knew fact stood behind most of those stories. Perhaps not every Questioner lived up to them, but enough did. The stories weren't just stories. Of course, until a little over a year earlier, he'd thought different.

Willam looked at Petyr. Petyr suspected Willam was gauging whether or not he could take Petyr in a fight. Willam was larger, probably a head taller than Petyr. Petyr didn't want to fight him.

Willam reminded Petyr of someone he'd met recently.

Roderick. Petyr felt suddenly sure Willam was Roderick's son. Now, he knew where the venom came from.

"I don't like it, anyway," Willam said.

"You don't own me, Willam. Go tell my father we'll be right there."

Willam stared at her for a moment, then turned and started back up the bank. Over his shoulder, he said, "I'll be watching."

Petyr watched him go. His body faded into shadow as he climbed up the slope and disappeared back into the town.

"Don't worry about him," Carree said after he was gone. "He's had this idea in his head as long as I can remember that he and I would wed."

"You're not interested?"

"No. You're far more interesting."

Petyr wasn't completely surprised by her admission, but her forwardness surprised him. "We have to go. They'll be waiting for us."

She reached for his hand and somehow found it again. He tried to pull away, but she held it firm. "Then, by all means, we should head back."

"You're not going to tell you're mother what you heard?"

He felt the little twinge that ran through her.

"Not yet."

They walked up the bank together, back to the town, as the last light in the sky finally failed and darkness settled over the town. *I will have to put her off, somehow*. He refused to admit to himself that he liked the feel of her hand holding his.

CHAPTER 3

Petyr thought supper an interesting affair. Sim had a large table made of blackroot. It had some sort of blonde wood inlaid around the edges in an intricate pattern. Petyr wondered if Bran had crafted this table, but refrained from asking. He didn't want to upset Aster any more than Carree already had.

When they returned from the river, Aster had rushed Carree at the door. She grabbed Carree's hand, and after a quick, "Thank you for bringing her home," directed toward Petyr, pulled Carree into the kitchen. A voluminous pile of words could be heard from the kitchen, all in Aster's voice. Petyr had listened for a moment before Sim approached him, a bit unsteady on his feet. Sim brought Petyr into the sitting room and introduced him to the other Elders.

Roderick sat in a seat, his lips pursed in a sour expression with a goblet in his hand. His son Willam sat next to him, unconsciously mimicking his father's expression, though Petyr suspected the two had different reasons.

Two other men were also in the room.

Sim introduced the older of the two first. "Our tanner, Eduard." Eduard's hair had turned to white, and years had carved lines in his face.

"How do you do?" Petyr asked, extending his hand.

The tanner seemed to think for a moment before extending his hand, but did so eventually. He grasped Petyr's hand and shook it. The tanner's strength did not appear to be diminished by age. Petyr had to work to avoid wincing. "I'm well. You're trip here was uneventful, I hope?"

"No more eventful than one could have expected," Petyr said. It was as close to a lie as he was willing to get.

Sim gestured to another man. His skin was sun dark and lined, but his hair still maintained the black of a younger man. "And this is Rolend. He's our Master of Farms."

"Master of Farms?"

Rolend moved forward and shook Petyr's hand without hesitation. "I manage the land that's been cleared by the logging operation. Dunsriver is what you might call a company town. It exists mostly to log the forest and send the trees downriver. The logging clears areas that, especially near the river, are ideal for farming, so we use them to grow much of our food."

So, Petyr thought, *one man actively dislikes me, another is unsure, and two are apparently enthusiastic about my presence. Better odds than I could have hoped for.*

"I saw little livestock."

"There's not yet enough room, and the hunting is still good. In time, though, that will change and we will adjust."

"Yes," said Eduard. "We always adjust. Tell me, why are you here? I've been told you said you were passing through. In my experience, no one passes through Dunsriver. They pass by it."

The question hung in the air for while Petyr tried to think of a response that wouldn't play his hand too early. He needed to discover who wanted help with the situation and who was against his help. He was saved from answering by Aster's knock at the door. "Supper is ready, come sit at the table."

"Let's eat. We'll discuss business after," said Sim. He motioned for those sitting to stand and leave.

After a few moments, they stood and started filing out of the room. Petyr caught Eduard looking at him pointedly before turning to leave. Petyr knew he would have to come up with an answer to Eduard's question. Eduard would ask it again after supper.

Thus prohibited from speaking about anything important, they sat around the table and ate in near silence. Carree had seated herself to his right, Rolend to his left. Across from him, the eyes of Eduard and Roderick bored into him. Petyr tried to pick up any stray thoughts that he could, but few of them were powerful enough to be read at a distance, especially when nothing was being said to provoke strong thoughts.

Eventually, Carree put down her fork and spoke. "What's it like in Genova? I have heard it's beautiful, that there are gardens with walkways and streams flowing through them, that the buildings are all made of marble, and that there are so many people you couldn't possibly know everyone."

"Carree," Aster hissed.

Petyr leaned back in his chair and looked at Carree. The eagerness in her eyes made them sparkle. "It's a fair question," he said. "In many places, it *is* beautiful, and there are gardens of spectacular arrangement. Also, you are correct that you couldn't possibly know everyone. However, only parts of the city are made of marble, and only parts of it are beautiful. It is like any place, I guess. Much beauty, but also much that is ugly. It's a place of power, and that power tempts all kinds of people to try to capture it. Do you not remember it from your childhood?"

"She wouldn't remember," Sim said, preempting any response from Carree. "We moved here soon after she was born."

Maybe I'll get some truth now. "You made the trip with a newborn?"

"You may be too young to remember, but circumstances were rather chaotic in Genova seventeen years ago. It was not a good place to turn a profit." Sim looked to his wife for a moment before turning back to his food.

Petyr thought it curious Sim would try to hide something from him, knowing what Petyr was. Sim wasn't lying this time, but he hadn't told the entire story. Petyr looked around the table. *But then, maybe he's not hiding it from me.* He decided he'd worry about it later. He wasn't ready to question the man that brought him in while eating.

"I wouldn't know," Petyr said. "Our early training happens far from the walls of the city."

Rolend turned to Sim. "I remember the day you and your family rolled into town. Three wagons full. It didn't appear to me you lacked for profit."

"Maybe to you, but in Genova, I'd nearly become a pauper."

Rolend laughed. "You managed to set yourself up here, rather well." He looked to Petyr. "Are you recently from Genova? We hear rumors of unrest."

Petyr chewed the bite of bread he'd just taken, slowly, then swallowed it down before answering. "I haven't been to Genova in over a year."

"Do you think the rumors true?"

Petyr had to work hard to keep a neutral set to his features. "All I can say is I've heard the same rumors. I can't vouch for their accuracy." *I hope they are true and the High Lords get their due.*

"Rolend," said Sim. "This treads far to close to business."

"It's just gossip."

"No, leave it for later. We have enough to worry about without spreading rumors."

Rolend nodded, and Petyr was glad to be off the topic.

Silence prevailed over the remainder of the meal. They all knew what would come after, and Petyr thought the four elders, each in their own way, wished the moment would not come. For some reason Petyr couldn't understand, the people in this town seemed reluctant to talk about the darkness surrounding them, the evil in their midst.

As supper finished up and they retired to the sitting room, Petyr approached Aster. "Do you know where my driver Alec is?"

"I believe he said he was going to eat at the tavern."

Petyr chided himself for forgetting Alec's penchant for finding information within the local alehouse. Of course, Alec's trip served another purpose in maintaining the fiction he was Petyr's driver. *But all you're really looking for is something to numb your mind, aren't you Alec. Drink some for me.*

"Thank you," he said. "You serve a fine meal, Aster."

She smiled at that, the first he'd seen from her. "Thank you, my Lord." Then she turned away to the kitchen.

Petyr followed the other men into the sitting room. As he approached the door, he saw Willam standing outside it, moping. Apparently, the elders had excluded him. When Petyr entered the room, he found Sim standing to one side of the door. Once Petyr cleared the door, Sim shut it behind him.

"Lord Ocyna," Eduard said, "please elaborate on why you really came here."

"May I suggest that I'll answer your question after you have told me why you are all so nervous about my presence? It's obvious that the town is on edge about something."

"There is nothing of any consequence," said Roderick. Petyr saw wariness in his eyes. If he hadn't already overheard him at the gate, it would have been easy to hear the lie.

Petyr stepped toward the middle of the room, facing Roderick directly. "Roderick. I think you forget who you're talking to. It won't do you any good to lie to me."

"We don't need you here. It's nothing you can help with, in any case."

Petyr smiled. "On the contrary, Roderick. I've always found that when a man wishes to hide the truth, there is a great need for my services."

Eduard moved to stand next to Roderick. "What we need, my Lord, are Watchers and Protectors. A Questioner is of little use in our predicament."

"Enlighten me."

"Something is murdering our daughters," said Sim from behind.

"Some *thing*?" Petyr hadn't expected that. Not entirely.

"It comes from the forest," said Rolend, "cloaked in a thick fog that rolls over the town. A night watchman saw it, or said he did. A large beast, taller than a man, with glowing blue eyes."

"Did he get a good look at it?"

"He said, other than the eyes, it was a shadow in the fog."

"Like I said," Eduard interrupted, "we need Watchers and Protectors."

Petyr could see his point. He wasn't likely to stop a beast. Not by himself. The whole thing was just too strange, though.

He was about to open his mouth when anger suddenly boiled out of Sim. "Eduard, we need more than Watchers and Protectors. We need to know why this thing keeps mutilating our daughters."

"Sim!" Roderick shouted. "Stop now."

Sim's face had flushed red. "I won't stop now. What this thing is doing is obscene. It is not a beast. It's something else. You've never seen a Questioner work, not one from Genova, at least. Lord Ocyna may not be able to stop the thing himself, but I'm certain he can figure out what it is."

The room fell silent. The four elders looked at each other, and Petyr watched them. Every word they'd spoken was truth, in their eyes. But it was the unspoken that Petyr needed to bring out.

"How many?" he asked after a moment.

"Three, so far," Rolend volunteered, "and a fourth has been missing for nearly two weeks."

"So this has been going on for a time?"

"Six months or more."

"Does this thing kill them in town?"

"No. It takes them out into the forest, then stakes them to a tree and..."

Petyr interrupted him. "You don't need to tell me the rest."

"Why not?"

"We had traveled half the distance between here and Rocktree when I noticed something odd in the forest and asked my driver to stop. About thirty paces from the road, a young woman was hanging from a tree in the manner you describe."

The four elders simultaneously shouted something to the effect of, "Why didn't you say something earlier?"

Petyr waited for them to calm down before speaking. "I had to be sure you weren't responsible. I had to be sure of my own safety."

The four elders stood, mollified, it seemed.

I could go. I don't need to involve myself in this. I could spend a month or more here and discover nothing. Half of them are fools. Why risk capture for them? He decided, though, to give them the choice. The vision of that woman on the tree still haunted him.

"I'm more than willing to leave in the morning, if that's what you decide. I think you need me here, though. There's more to this than is apparent. Why only women? Why the fog? Why the ritual?

"If you don't learn the answers to those questions, I fear you're likely to bring some greater doom upon your heads than already lies upon them.

"Good night, gentlemen. It was good to talk with you."

Petyr turned and went to the door.

His hand was on the latch. He expected someone to say something, but he heard nothing. He opened the door and stepped out.

Maybe they do want me to go. Can I really forget it? Is this place worth the risk?

He let the door swing shut behind him, and made his way up to Bran's room. He hoped he'd know the answers by morning.

CHAPTER 4

A lack of curtains on the window allowed the early morning light, gray as it was, to intrude and drag Petyr from a restless slumber. He'd dreamt a jumbled mess of images, and could remember little of them but the vision of the woman on the tree. He couldn't be sure, however, whether he remembered it from his dreams or from the previous day.

He had come to one conclusion. Unless they asked him to stay, he was leaving. *I'm not going to risk getting caught for people that don't want help.*

And whatever was happening between him and Carree, he couldn't allow. Whenever she got near, his heartache, his longing for Alura fled, replaced with a desire to do whatever Carree wanted. He didn't want to bury Alura's memory so soon.

He swung his legs out from under the covers so his feet touched the bare wood floor. *You deserve better than that from me, my love.*

He'd found his trunk in the room when he'd come up the previous night, and assumed Alec had brought it up before finding his way to the tavern. Petyr undid the lock and opened the trunk to reveal fresh clothes packed neatly inside. Underneath the clothes were the items he needed to lock away, the evidence he'd gathered against the High Lords. Evidence that was useless unless he could find an uncorrupted someone that cared, and a way back to Genova that wouldn't end with him dangling from a gibbet.

He pulled a change of clothes from the trunk, shut and locked it. After he dressed, he stepped out into the hallway and strode the length of it until he stood outside the door where Alec would be sleeping, if he made it back from the tavern. In a town like this, Petyr knew the taverns typically didn't stay open all night.

He knocked on the door. After a moment, he heard movement in the room and someone moaning. Eventually, footsteps approached and the door cracked open. Alec's face emerged.

"Petyr," he groaned. "Do you know what time it is?"

"The sun has come up. I need to know if you learned anything."

Alec's sleepy eyes stared out through the crack in the door for a moment, then he stepped aside and pulled the door open. "Fine," he said. "Come in."

"You learned something?" Petyr asked as he entered the room.

Alec shut the door behind him.

"I did, though I'm not sure how useful it is. The men talked of a demon."

"A demon? Interesting. The elders said it was a beast."

"Does it matter, really?" Alec sat down on the bed. "They claim it is twenty feet tall and arrives cloaked in fog. They say it steals the women away, and then days or weeks later, the women are found in the forest, displayed much like the one we saw yesterday."

"That resembles what I was able to gather." Petyr paced across the room. It was sparsely furnished. A bed, a small chest of drawers. Four paces brought him from one end of the room to the other. "Did you talk to anyone who claimed to have seen it?"

"By the end of the night, everyone I talked to claimed to have seen it, even though they nearly all fed me some variation on the same story."

"The Elders told me of one man who had seen it. I suppose I'll have to talk to him."

Alec looked up. "We're staying? You told me we'd only stay here a day or two. Any longer, Petyr, and we risk…"

"You're right. But I've got this feeling. I don't know what it is, but there are odd things happening in this town. None of the Elders lied to me, but they all seemed to work hard at hiding things."

"Related to the dead women?"

Petyr shook his head. "I couldn't tell. It wouldn't surprise me if they've all got some sort of side deals going on and are afraid I'll discover them."

"Petyr, you are going to get us captured and your neck stretched."

Petyr knew he was right. *But there's something about that woman on the tree, something under the surface of this town.* "One more day, Alec, if they don't kick us out this morning."

A quick knock on the door caused him to turn around. It was open. Carree stood in the doorway.

"You're not thinking of leaving, are you? You promised me you'd help us."

How much did she hear? "You have a habit of sneaking in on conversations."

Her hand went to her mouth quickly as her face flushed. "I'm sorry, I didn't mean to intrude. It's just… I heard you from the hallway talking about the demon, and I had to stop to listen."

Petyr tried to think back over their conversation. He couldn't remember anything either of them said, except perhaps the part about stretched necks, that might make her suspicious.

"To answer your question, we are thinking about leaving, but only because your Elders don't think my help is necessary."

She stepped into the room and walked over to him, then took his hand in hers. Her hand was soft, warm, inviting. She squeezed his hand gently. "You promised to help us. The next time the fog comes in, that thing could take me."

An urge to do what she wanted welled up from within him. She was right that he had promised her. He didn't want to break that promise.

"I wouldn't want to start breaking promises."

She jumped up and down, and her eyes opened wide with excitement. "You'll stay?"

Petyr looked to Alec, and saw Alec wore a concerned look on his face. Alec's focus was on Carree.

"Of course, Carree. We'll stop this thing."

She stood on her toes and kissed him on the cheek. "Good," she said. "Now, Mother says it's time for breakfast, if you'll be so good as to join us."

"We'll be down in just a minute. Alec needs to dress."

Carree squeezed his hand once more, then dropped it and turned to leave. "Thank you, Petyr."

When she was gone, Alec said, "Petyr, that girl is dangerous."

Petyr didn't even bother to look at Alec, instead staring after the girl that had just left the room. "I know."

"We can't stay here now. We have to get out."

"How far do you think we'd get if we tried?"

Petyr heard Alec stand. "We have to try. She's a Coercer, Petyr."

Petyr turned on Alec. "I know what she is. I felt her working on me. But I promised, Alec. I won't break another promise."

"This is nothing like before, Petyr. It's not Alura."

Rage boiled inside Petyr and he stepped right up into Alec's chest. "Don't you ever say that to me again." Alec backed up a step, and Petyr tried to calm himself. "Alura is dead because of me. I won't let that happen to someone else.

"Besides," Petyr said, allowing a smile to cross his face as he pondered the possibilities, "don't you think it could be useful to have a Coercer to help us?"

Alec grimaced. "You're risking quite a lot with her." He turned to his travel bag and started pulling out clothes.

⋏ ⋏ ⋏

Petyr made his way down to the dining room, with Alec

following close behind, and found a well set out table. Eggs, flat-bread, berries, and sausages filled the plates. Sim was already sitting and motioned Petyr to a chair across from him.

Petyr took it and started dishing sausages and eggs onto the plate in front of him. Sim didn't look ready to talk, so Petyr started in on his food, sampling the sausages first. As the peppered sausage hit his tongue, Aster stepped into the room and sat at the table. Soon after, Carree entered and sat herself down to eat.

They ate in silence. Petyr wondered if it was always like this. His meals in his own home, before he'd gone to the Academy, were a cacophony of amusement and well aimed insults spread by his brothers and sister. He wondered if the silence at Sim's table was a result of his presence, or just the general malaise that seemed to hang over the town.

Sim ate quickly, then stood.

"Meet me outside when you're finished, Petyr," he said, then left the table.

Petyr gulped down the eggs, followed it with some water, then stood. "Those were excellent sausages, Aster."

Aster nodded, but did not say anything. Petyr left the table in search of Sim.

He found the merchant out back, hooking up a large dappled draft horse to a an empty cart.

Sim apparently heard Petyr exit the house. He looked up as Petyr approached. "I'm sorry about the silence. We have a rule about talking business at meals. Unfortunately, there doesn't seem to be anything to talk about except business these days."

"It's quite all right," said Petyr. "Are you going somewhere?"

"Yes. If you or your driver would be so kind as to tell me exactly where you found the body, I'll be off with some others to retrieve it."

"A grizzly business."

Sim nodded. "Necessary, though. I'd like to be through with it before too long. I don't think the rain will hold off all day."

"Rain?" Petyr looked up and saw the cloud cover was a light gray.

"No, look over that way," Sim said, pointing, "toward the Fringe."

In that direction, Petyr did see the clouds were dark and angry with pent up moisture.

"I'll do better than tell you where it is, I'll have Alec take you there."

Sim looked puzzled. "You're not leaving?"

"I only said I'd leave if you didn't want me here, and I've heard no one yet tell me so. You didn't decide last night that we should go, did you?"

Sim shook his head and slapped a palm on the cart, causing the horse to startle a bit. "We didn't decide anything. Eduard and Roderick think you are useless, or somehow, even a danger to them."

"I *am* a danger. I'm a revealer of secrets. Once I start to work, few secrets are safe."

"After yesterday, with the truth about Bran coming out, I'm well aware of that." He started digging in the dirt with the toe of his boot. Petyr suspected he was thinking about the other secrets he held that might come out. Secrets Petyr already knew. "But I don't care. I can't lose my daughter, too. We need to understand what this thing is. The things it does to them, they're not right."

Petyr looked up at the sky again. "No, they're not."

⚏ ⚏ ⚏

After Sim left with Alec, Petyr decided to find Roderick and see if he could reason with him, or, at the very least, see if he could uncover some of the truth.

Before he left the house, he went up to his room and pulled a heavy cloak from his trunk. The sky was growing darker as the storm approached, and he figured he might wind up in it before too long.

Aster told Petyr, when he asked, that he'd likely find Roderick at the town hall. She gave him directions that amounted to walking down the street in front of their house and taking a left at the next opportunity.

He followed them as far as taking the left, then realized when he did why there weren't more directions. The hall was obvious in the distance, brooding, despite its stark white paint, over the center of the town. The hall looked to have three stories, and a bell tower to the left side. It sat at the center of a square paved with stone, which was a stark change from the packed earth roads that ran throughout the rest of the town. The closer he approached, the more it seemed to cast a threatening shadow over the buildings that surrounded the square, even without the help of any sunlight.

The moment he placed his foot on its steps, one of the doors, painted a dark green, swung open and Rolend emerged. He let the door shut behind him and hurried down the stairs, almost running into Petyr before pulling up.

"Lord Petyr, what are you doing here?"

"I'm going to talk with Roderick."

"I don't think you want to do that. He's not in the best of moods, and he doesn't want you here."

"So I've been told. What's caused the foul mood?"

"The inbound storm. The loggers will have to come in from the forest, which means fewer dollars in his purse."

"I'll have to chance it. I'm not leaving, and I need to get his support, if possible."

Rolend moved down the steps into the square. "Good luck. Come get me when he runs you out, and I'll help you where I can."

"I shall."

Petyr watched Rolend hurry away for a moment before turning to head up the steps into Roderick's lair. He wished he could just follow Rolend and get his help, but in all his time as a Questioner, he'd found one immutable principle. *The most interesting answers come from the reluctant and the adversarial.*

He put his hand on the oversized latch, pulled open the door, and stepped inside.

The doorway led into a foyer that extended the width of the building, and a dozen feet into its body. Double doors stood open in front of him, leading to a meeting hall. He looked to either side of him, and did not see anyone, so he stepped forward to peer through the open doors.

He'd guessed right. Empty benches rested in two sets of rows facing a low dais. To the right of the dais, a desk, and Roderick behind it, hunched over some papers.

Petyr knocked on one of the doors, then strode into the room.

Roderick looked up, and even from across the large room, Petyr could see the corners of his mouth turn down and his brow furrow.

"What are you doing here?" Roderick asked.

Petyr walked the aisle between the two sets of benches, approaching Roderick while trying to maintain the air of supremacy his instructors had drilled into him. *Make them think you believe you are superior, and they will come to believe it.*

"I have some questions to ask, if you don't mind."

"Of course I mind. I'm busy."

"They are but a few questions Roderick. I'm sure you can spare the time."

"No, I don't think so. You are not welcome here."

Petyr arrived at the desk and rested his hands on its edge. He leaned over it, trying to loom over the Mayor. "That's not what I've been told, Roderick. It was made clear to me that the four of you could not come to an agreement last night, which, to my thinking, leaves the burden of whether to stay on my shoulders."

Roderick leaned back, away from Petyr. "What good can you do here? You don't even have a Protector with you."

"I don't need a Protector to figure out what this thing is. You said it was a beast. The men my man Alec talked with last night claimed it to be a demon."

"It is a beast. What else could it be? Demons are fantasy, myth. They don't exist."

Petyr eased up on his looming. "I'm inclined to agree with you.

I've known many a peasant to claim fantastic origins for every crime imaginable. But ultimately, when enough people are put to Question, there is always a natural, if human, explanation."

"Putting everyone to Question isn't going to help."

"No, I don't have the time to question everyone. I would like your help, though."

"You're not going to question everyone?"

Exasperated, Petyr leaned over the desk again. "Roderick, I'm not here to persecute you. I'm not here to lay bare the petty embezzlements you're involved in. I'm here to figure out what's killing those girls and stop it, if I can." *I couldn't even turn you in if I wanted to. I'd end up in the cell right next to you.*

Roderick's eyes went wide. His hands gripped the arms of his chair, and his knuckles turned white. "You know about..."

"Of course I know. I'm a Questioner, and you've been afraid of me since the moment I arrived. Do you think I didn't notice, or couldn't figure out what you're hiding?"

Roderick frantically shook his head.

"I don't know the details on how much you skim, but those are only details. What do you think? Are you going to help me? Or am I going to have to question you and Eduard?"

"You don't have to question anyone. I'll help you with whatever you need."

Petyr relaxed. "Good. First, I'd like to see the bodies of the other girls."

"What?"

"I need to see the bodies, and talk with whoever took care of them."

"They're all buried. The first one for months, now. But you can probably find out whatever you need from the Doctor."

"Doctor? Why didn't he eat with us last night? I would think he'd be counted among your Elders."

"Oh, he is counted among us. However, he has some peculiarities, and prefers to avoid gatherings. We're just as happy to have him avoid them."

I wonder what he means by that. "I should like to meet him, then, if he was responsible for the girls interment."

"I'll take you to him then." Roderick stood up, started to step out around the desk, then hesitated. "You promise you won't…"

"If you help me, I promise I won't say a word. I just want to prevent that horror from happening to another of Dunsriver's women."

Roderick relaxed then, and even smiled for the first time. Petyr realized Roderick was turning over the idea in his head that he might avoid the stocks, or worse, the gibbet.

"Roderick. I can't prevent another Questioner from showing up and stumbling across your enterprise. You might think about cleaning that up."

Roderick's smile faltered, and then he said, "Right. Well, follow me."

Petyr followed him out of the hall and out into the square, where he immediately regretted forgetting his hat in his room. The skies had opened up while he'd been inside, and heavy rain pounded the stone at his feet.

CHAPTER 5

They hurried through the streets. The pavement of the square gave way to mud that thickened with every passing minute as Petyr followed the Mayor through a maze of turns to get to the Doctor's home.

The rain fell in thick sheets, blown by the wind. It stung Petyr's face and found its way down his neck, soaking the garments he wore underneath. His hair hung in his eyes. If he hadn't remained only two paces behind the Mayor, he had little doubt he would have lost sight of the large man.

Petyr tried to pull his coat even tighter around his neck in an effort to keep as much of the water on the outside as he could. It helped only a little. By the time they reached the low building that served as both hospital and home for the doctor, even Petyr's trousers seemed made more of water than cloth.

When the Mayor knocked, they only had to wait moments for the door to open. They rushed inside, and someone shut the door behind them.

"My, my, that's some weather. What are you doing out in it, Roderick?"

Petyr wiped the water from his eyes and looked around. He stood in a hallway of sorts, dimly lit with light from open doors along its length. A short man, the top of his head no higher than

Petyr's shoulder, stood off to the side. His white shirt was rumpled, suspenders held his pants up. He was thin and bony. White stubble covered his head.

"I brought Lord Petyr Ocyna to talk with you." Petyr stopped for a moment, surprised Roderick had used his full title.

"The Questioner, then. I wondered if you'd bring him here. Take your coats off, hang them on the rack. You're dripping all over my floor."

Petyr turned and saw a rack where the Doctor pointed. He shed his coat and hung it from an iron hook.

"Come, come. I've got a fire going. We can sit and drink brandy, and you can tell me what you need from me."

Then the doctor scurried off. *Much like a rat.*

Petyr followed the doctor and Roderick down the corridor. They passed two closed doors before stepping through a third.

Once in the room, the warmth from the fire burning in the stone fireplace comforted Petyr. He moved in close to absorb as much heat as he could. Roderick also moved as close to the fire as he dared.

The doctor had lined the walls with shelves, all filled to capacity with books. A veritable library.

The little doctor went to a cupboard, built among the book-shelves, and pulled out three glasses. He began pouring brandy.

"No brandy for me, thank you," said Petyr.

The doctor turned and looked at him, his eyes squinting a bit. "Are you sure? It's quality brandy. I made it myself."

"It interferes with my duties."

The doctor smiled. "Ah, of course." He picked up the two glasses he filled and brought them over, handing one to Roderick.

The doctor took his brandy to a chair that faced the fire and nestled himself down in it. "Now, what do you say you explain why you've come to see me."

Petyr knelt down, and turned to face the Doctor. The heat of the fire felt good on his back. "Roderick tells me you interred the girls. I'd hope you can answer some questions for me."

"I'll do my best. A vile business that was."

"The body I found in the forest..."

"You found a body? Another one?"

Roderick spoke up. "Yes, he found Aslinda"

"Poor girl."

The Doctor's eyes never wavered while he spoke. Petyr didn't think he was surprised, or all that sympathetic, despite what he said.

"The body I found, Aslinda. The killer pulled her arms off and took her eyes. Were the other girls' deaths similar?"

"Yes, very similar. Was she spiked to a tree?"

Petyr nodded.

"Then I'd say they're deaths were essentially identical."

What did that mean? What manner of creature took eyes and arms? "Was anything else taken?" Petyr asked.

"Like what? No other body parts were removed."

Petyr didn't want to ask his next question, but he had to ask. "Were they still maidens?"

"Virgins?"

Petyr nodded.

"No, but that's not so unusual in this town."

"I suppose not. Do you think you would be able to tell if the deflowering were recent?"

The little Doctor's eyes grew wide. "I understand now. You want to know if the beast deflowered them. You know, I didn't even think to pay attention."

"Wait," said Roderick. "You suspect it's a man?"

Petyr stood. The heat on his back had begun to burn more than it soothed. "I conjecture. I have to explore every possible path. In the fog, tricks of light can make a man seem taller than they are. There were things done to these girls, I cannot imagine it just a beast."

"But no man could pull their arms off."

"Not by hand, but couldn't ropes be used? Wrap them around a tree or something for leverage? No. I will rule nothing out."

"You don't suspect anyone here, do you?"

"I don't suspect anyone, yet." He turned back to the Doctor. "Do you think, when you examine Aslinda, you could check?"

The Doctor blinked his eyes rapidly. "I will. I regret not checking the others."

Roderick spat into the fire. "It's repulsive."

"The whole scenario is repulsive. Did you see any of the bodies as they were found, Roderick, or only after they were brought back?"

"After."

"Then you didn't see. These aren't normal killings. These are sadistic, brutal, torture killings that have no place in this world. However, the type of man that kills is a different type of a man than he who rapes first, or after. I need to know which type I'm looking for."

Petyr saw the Mayor's lips pinch and his nose wrinkle up. "I need to get back to my work. Is there any other thing I can do for you?"

Petyr thought for a moment. "If you could make a list of the people that came to town within the few months before the first killing took place, I'd like to talk to them."

"Do you think one of them responsible?"

"It could be anybody, but something like this doesn't happen without some sort of provocation. People new to the area, especially if they came alone, I would suspect more than others."

"I'll get your list." Roderick set his glass down, and then started out of the room. "Good day, Doctor, Lord Questioner."

The doctor chuckled. "You are a thorough man."

"I do what's necessary. Tell me, you are an Elder, correct?"

The doctor nodded and took a sip of his brandy.

"Then why did you not sup with us last night?"

"Do you have to ask? You're so observant, but you can't figure it out?"

Chided, Petyr looked closer, and realized what he'd been missing in the glow of the fire, and the dim light. The doctor was not old, like he'd assumed from the white hair. He was albino.

"Yes, you see. I grew up, hidden from the out of doors, hidden by my mother. I burn easily. Just a few minutes in the sun is enough."

"It's winter. You could wear a coat, or…"

"It doesn't matter. I have an aversion to the open air. And typically, people have an aversion to me. They fear I am a ghost, or vampiri, or some other such nonsense. Even the other Elders, who I see often, feel uncomfortable around me."

Petyr didn't know what to feel about it. "It's not right."

"You think I resent being stuck in here? I don't resent it one moment. I have my books, my brandy, and my researches, such as they are. The people come to me, or are brought, when they are hurt, and I'm not bothered. Believe me, Lord Questioner, it is better this way."

Petyr nodded, seeing, and even more, understanding in only the way a Questioner could, the doctor was telling him the truth.

"By the way," the doctor continued, "the body you found in the woods."

"Yes?"

"Was it rotting?"

Petyr stared the doctor in his slate flecked eyes. "No, why?" The eyes didn't waver.

"When the other girls were brought to me, their bodies looked as if they were freshly killed. But, over night, each body decomposed like they had spent weeks on my table. I've never seen the like."

"Why did you wait until now to tell me?"

The doctor laughed. "The Mayor, he has a weak stomach for these things. Whenever anyone is injured, he is always the last to come to help."

A silence fell across the two, Petyr standing near the fire, his clothes nearly dry, and the Doctor sitting in his chair drinking his brandy. Petyr decided he liked the man. He appeared to have few illusions about his place in the world, and accepted it. Petyr thought if he could have settled in a town, settled in this one, he could get to be long time friends with the doctor.

"Why don't you sit down, Lord Questioner, while we wait for your find to come to us. Your clothes look dry enough."

Petyr saw another chair, facing perpendicular to the doctor's chair, and took the doctor up on the offer. He didn't feel like facing the storm again.

"Just call me Petyr. Lord Questioner was another life." Petyr surprised himself with the admission.

"Then call me Ilsan, Petyr."

"That's not an Empire name."

"No. No it's not." Ilsan lifted the glass of brandy to his lips and sipped, his eyes turning to the fire. Petyr saw contemplation and longing in the dancing flames reflected in them. Ilsan obviously wasn't ready to explain, and Petyr didn't push it.

In the silence, the pounding of the rain on the roof seemed to grow louder. Petyr listened to it while trying to discern a path to follow from the crumbs of knowledge he'd collected. Nothing yet made sense.

▲ ▲ ▲

An hour or so passed before a pounding at the door echoed down the hallway and into the room where Petyr and Ilsan sat with their thoughts. They had said little, but Petyr felt like they had said all that needed saying. It was a comfortable time. He hadn't come to any conclusions, or any decisions, but Ilsan's room, his fire, his company, had been soothing in a way he hadn't felt since before Alura died.

"It seems they have returned," said Ilsan, and he rose from his chair, setting his now empty glass on the small table next to him. "Come, let's see what they have brought us."

Petyr stood, groaning. He had no real desire to see the body again. He could still see it whenever he closed his eyes. He followed Ilsan out of the room, despite his desire to remain where he was.

As soon as Ilsan opened the door, Sim and Eduard entered while holding the front end of a stretcher. The girl was mercifully covered with a tarp. Alec and another man Petyr had not met, held the other end. The four men were drenched from the storm, and all looked chilled.

Ilsan led them down the hall and through a wide doorway to the right.

Petyr followed them into the room. A raised operating table with a granite top dominated the center of the room. They laid the stretcher on it. A smaller table sat off to one side and held a number of medical implements.

The four men stood around the table, unsure what they should do. Ilsan took little time before he started making shooing motions. "Out, out. You're dripping on my floor. Get home, change clothes and sit in front of a fire. I don't need you four back here, sick with fever."

Petyr saw Alec trying to catch his attention discretely. Petyr moved close to him and said in a low voice, "Go back to Sim's and get dried out. The Doctor is right. I can't afford you to take ill. Whatever you need to tell me can wait until tonight."

"You're staying here?"

Petyr nodded, and pushed his friend toward the door. "I need to know everything I can about what happened to her. I'll be back as soon as he's done."

Alec followed the others out, and Petyr found himself alone with Ilsan and the dead girl.

Ilsan had a hand on the tarp. "Are you prepared for this?"

"I've already seen the girl, when she was spiked to the tree."

"This will be different. She has already begun to decompose. Can you not smell it?"

Petyr inhaled a little deeper, and wished he hadn't. He could smell it. Faint, yet, but the stench of death, which had been so mysteriously absent in the forest, now crept out from beneath the tarp that covered her.

"You see? So, are you prepared, or would you prefer to wait in the other room?"

"Just get on with it."

Ilsan pulled off the tarp. Petyr nearly gagged like he had at the tree. The tarp had held the stench in. Removing it allowed the foulness to escape into the room. Worse yet, the skin had loosened. Instead of looking like a fresh death, her body looked like it had been left in the rain for two days. Whatever glamour had protected her while she hung on the tree was gone.

While Petyr struggled to keep his bile down, Ilsan pulled some sort of apparatus over his head. It had a series of lenses attached to a leather head band. With what appeared to be years of practice, he manipulated the series of lenses the way he wanted, then leaned in close, moving over every inch of the body, paying particular attention to the wounds. He occasionally flipped a lens in or out, but made little noise while he examined her.

He reached over and pulled another tool from the smaller table. To Petyr, it looked like a small, thin, rod of bronze. Ilsan started poking at the wounds with the tool, lifting parts up to look underneath.

After several minutes passed, Petyr couldn't contain his curiosity. "Is there anything different with this one?"

Ilsan shook his head, but didn't look up. He was examining the spike holes. "No, it all looks the same as the others." He prodded at the left hole with the small rod.

"What about her virginity?"

"Quiet. I'll get to that." Ilsan moved to the arm sockets, and prodded at them. His lips moved as he seemingly talked to himself, but no sound escaped.

Petyr looked over her body, from the hair, splayed out wet and limp on the table, to the empty eyes where he tried to imagine what they'd looked like when she was alive, to her mouth, her neck which was long and thin, her torso, her pubic area, her legs which had length and grace to compliment her neck. His mind flashed back to a vision of Alura, as she lay on the tile floor of their home, the blood flowing from the back of her head where she'd hit it after falling from the balcony.

"Run, Petyr, run! Leave this place. Come back when you can. I'll be waiting."

He reached out and pulled her head to his, kissing her, pulling her body tight against him. He could feel the small bump of her belly against his, the baby already growing there. He didn't want to go.

"I don't have to leave. I can find a way."

She pushed at him. "Petyr, no. You know they are coming. You can't find a way if you are dead."

Then they both heard shouts followed by the feet of soldiers intruding in their home.

He pulled her close, and kissed her for what he knew could be the last time. "Take care of the baby. I'll be back for you."

Tears leaked from her eyes, the deep wells he'd lost himself in so many times. He reached up to wipe them away, but she stopped him. "Go, now," she whispered.

He turned to run down the stairs when he saw a Protector coming up, one he did not know. Alura saw him at the same time, and she ran down the stairs and blocked the way.

"Run Petyr!"

For some reason, he couldn't move, couldn't will himself to leave.

The Protector saw him, and started running up the stairs, two at a time. When he reached Alura, she stood her ground.

The Protector reached out, his hand grabbed Alura, and he pushed her roughly to the side, out and over the railing. Time slowed to a crawl as Petyr watched her fall, tumbling to the tile floor thirty feet below. The back of her head hit before the rest of her body, and the loud crunch of broken bone echoed throughout the chamber.

"Noooo!" The scream erupted from his lips unbidden, just as the first traces of blood leaked out from below her lifeless body.

"Petyr."

The voice reached into the depths of his horror and pulled him out of his past.

"Petyr, is everything all right? Do you need to sit down?"

"What?"

"You shouted. Startled me right out of my wits."

Petyr looked up and, like coming out of a fog, started to reorient himself to where he really was. The body of the girl lay on the table in front of him, Ilsan still held the tool, and he was looking at Petyr with questions, and maybe concern.

"Sorry, just a vision, a memory."

"A memory?"

"My wife." Petyr rubbed his face, trying to clear the fog. "Have you found out about her virginity yet?"

"I was just about to look when you shouted."

"Don't let me stop you."

"Right." He reached down and spread the girls legs apart and began to prod at her parts. Petyr looked away. He didn't really want to see. Somehow, with the memory of Alura so fresh, he felt looking would defile it.

"Interesting," said Ilsan after a moment.

"What?"

"There's quite a bit of trauma here. Now, I really regret not examining the others."

"Would you say she was raped?"

"I would stake my reputation on it."

"So, what about it is interesting?"

"If I had to hazard a guess, whatever raped her was larger than a man."

Petyr closed his eyes. *Larger than a man. So, if it's not a man committing these crimes, what is it? Where is it from? Maybe Roderick is right. Maybe I am useless here.*

CHAPTER 6

W hen Petyr entered Sim's home, soon after the rain storm had ended, he found Alec in a chair in the sitting room, feet resting on an ottoman, facing a fire. Sim sat in a similar fashion. They were both sipping brandy.

"Take your coat off, Petyr," Sim said, "and sit with us. Tell us what you and the Doctor discovered."

Petyr hung his coat on the coat rack in the corner of the room, then took a seat near enough to the fire that it warmed him. He sat there for a while and said nothing, pondering what he should tell Sim. *Do I even need to be here any more, promise or no?*

If he could bring Carree with them, somehow, her gift could be useful, but only if she could control herself. Otherwise, she'd be a danger to them. He didn't even know for sure if his promise was coerced out of him or not. *That's the problem with Coercer's. You don't even know the thought wasn't yours.*

He looked over at Alec, who was staring into the fire. His face looked red from the heat. Alec was right. He couldn't risk it. No, they'd leave in the morning, hopefully before Carree could wake and make him stay. All that was left was to tell Sim what he'd discovered about the girl.

"The girl, Aslinda," Petyr said, breaking the silence. "Her

manner of death was like the others. Ilsan confirmed it. I also asked him to check for any evidence that she might have been forced to engage in other activities." Petyr didn't want to say it aloud, for some reason.

"Other activities? Do you mean…"

"If she was a virgin before she was taken, she no longer was at her death."

Sim cursed. "Please, do not repeat that to others."

"I will keep it to myself. Of course, you will have to say something to Ilsan."

"I won't have to. Ilsan keeps everything to himself."

"Fine. One other thing."

Sim turned to face him.

"I no longer believe I will be of much use in finding the killer."

"Hog swill. How could you be of no use?"

"Ilsan was able to confirm from the examination that whatever killed her, it likely was not human. It was too large."

"What are you saying?"

Petyr just looked past Sim, to the fire, and watched the flames dance. He didn't want to answer the question. *I shouldn't have to.*

Sim sat back after a bit and sagged into his chair. "I see."

"Unless you have someone in the town delving into foreign magics, no one here is at fault. Anyone who could do this, I would think you would already suspect, and you would point me in their direction."

"We don't suspect a soul."

"In the morning, I think I'll take my leave. I'll put in a word at Rocktree to send for Protectors and Watchers. This seems something the Empire might want to take an interest in."

Sim sighed. "Thank you for trying, at least."

"I'm truly sorry. I wish I could help, but I don't see how I can."

"Sending help will be more than enough. At least we have Aslinda's body."

"Sim. Could you do us a favor?"

"What?"

"Could you not mention to Carree that we are leaving? I was, perhaps, a fool and promised her I'd help find the killer."

"I'll keep it quiet. I assume you'll want to leave before daylight."

"It would probably be best."

After that, they fell silent for a time. Petyr kept glancing over to Alec, and eventually Alec noticed and shook his head. Whatever Alec wanted to say to him, he didn't want Sim to hear. It couldn't be good news.

⚔ ⚔ ⚔

Petyr woke to knocking on his door.

"Petyr, wake up." Alec's voice.

"I'm awake." He still felt groggy with sleep, and had trouble seeing in the morning darkness. He wished there was a candle nearby, then caught a flicker of light under the door. "Come in."

The door opened, and Alec came in, bearing a candle.

"What time is it?"

"Just before sunrise, near as I can tell. I have the horses and carriage ready."

Petyr blinked his eyes some, then rubbed at them, trying to clean out the gunk. "You didn't wake me?"

"We don't need you stumbling about in the middle of the dark, as well. Your trunk is packed?"

"Yes, just need to put my nightclothes in it."

"Hurry up, then."

Petyr finally woke up enough to catch the sense of urgency in Alec's voice.

"What has you so agitated?" He started stripping off the night clothes, pulling the shirt over his head, first.

"I didn't get a chance to tell you last night, with Sim tethered to your side and trying to convince you to stay."

The shirt came off, and he tossed it into the trunk. He started stepping out of the bottoms. He wanted to hurry. A chill had stolen into the room during the night.

"What couldn't you tell me?"

"While I sat in the cart, waiting for them to get the body of that girl off the tree, a company rode by. Questioners, Protectors, and a Tracker."

That stopped Petyr. "A Tracker? Are you sure?"

"As sure as I can be without having stopped them to ask."

"And you think they were after us?"

"You don't really want to find out, do you?"

Petyr finished pulling off the leggings, and tossed them in the trunk, too. Then went over to the chair where he'd left his clothes and started pulling them on.

What now? What do I do?

"They went on to Rocktree?"

Alec nodded. "In that direction."

"So now they're ahead of us..."

"They wouldn't be if you hadn't made us stop." Petyr heard some anger in Alec's voice for the first time.

"You know I had to. I couldn't pass something like that without investigating it."

"You could have if you valued your life more."

"What's that supposed to mean?"

Alec stared at him for a moment, saying nothing. His eyes, in the candlelight, looked like they smoldered. "Since we've worked together, you've tried to right every wrong we've run across."

"I haven't."

"You have! You've got to stop, Petyr. We don't have time to get involved like this while we run from them. You are not a Questioner any more!"

Alec stopped, and for a moment they both said nothing.

For one of the few times in his life, Petyr heard the truth of someone's words, and wanted to refuse it, wanted to believe it was a lie. Needed to believe the lie.

He closed his eyes, not wanting to look at his friend. If he opened them, he'd have to acknowledge him, and he couldn't do that. Acknowledging he was no longer a Questioner felt tantamount to failure.

He heard light footsteps in the hallway, just before he heard Carree's voice. "What does he mean, that you are no longer a Questioner?"

Petyr sighed, sat down on the bed, put his elbows on his knees and his head in his hands. "He means I no longer hold the office of Lord Questioner."

"I don't understand."

"There's nothing much to understand. I'm not a Lord. Not any more."

She was quiet for a moment, and he looked up and saw her looking around the room. Alec had a look of fear on his face. Petyr should be angry at him, but he just couldn't find the energy. Petyr knew the reason they were in this position at all was his fault, and his fault alone.

"Why are you leaving?" Carree asked. "You promised me you'd stay and help." She'd apparently forgotten all about his not being a Lord Questioner.

"I did try to help," Petyr said. "I was with the Doctor when he examined Aslinda. We determined that it was no man that killed her or the other girls. My skill is not in protecting people from monsters. It's in finding the truth."

She looked thoughtful. She really was beautiful, and with her power, she would be formidable. He hoped she wouldn't use it on him here. Or on Alec.

"Take me with you then," she said.

"What? We can't take you with us."

"Why not?"

"You would not be safe with us."

She came over and sat next to him on the bed, then tried to slip her hand into his. He stood up quickly.

She looked up at him. He couldn't be sure in the flickering light, but he thought he saw hurt in her eyes. "Why wouldn't I be safe?"

Alec stepped close to him and whispered in his ear. "Don't tell her. You can't trust she'll keep quiet."

Petyr knew he was right. He shouldn't tell her. But he didn't want to be coerced into telling her, either. He wanted to be able to hold back what he could.

"There are some dangerous men chasing us. I'm no longer a Lord because I angered some very powerful people, and they want me dead. We've been on the run for more than a year. I'm trying to find a way to get them to stop chasing us, but they're relentless."

"Why are they so angry?"

"I told some truths they didn't like."

"Who are these people?"

"It's better, I think, that you don't know. If they come here, and they probably will, the less you know, the quicker they'll leave you alone."

The room fell silent while they all pondered the problem. Then Alec tugged at his shoulder. "Come on, Petyr, we have to go now."

Carree jumped up and put her arms around Petyr's waist, and pulled him close. She tilted her head up to look into his eyes. Her body was soft underneath her nightgown, but her arms were strong. His breath caught in his throat.

"Petyr, since you're going to break the promise you gave me, you owe me another one to replace it." Her breath felt warm on his lips.

"What do you want me to promise?" He saw Alec shaking his head, and he agreed with Alec, but he didn't know what he could do. The only way out of being compelled to hold to the promise was to promise voluntarily. He hoped she felt that would be enough.

"I want you to promise to come back for me. Come back and get me, and take me to Genova."

"I promise." He couldn't say anything else. He heard in her

voice, it was a true desire. If he didn't agree, she would compel him. She couldn't be argued out of it, not right now.

She pulled his head down and tried to kiss him on the lips, but he managed to turn slightly so that she kissed his cheek. She pulled away, and smiled.

"Come, I'll see you to the door, at least." And she left the room. He heard her footsteps on the stairs.

Petyr stepped over to the trunk, shut and locked it.

When he looked up, Alec was standing next to him.

"Petyr, you can't bring her to Genova. She's too old for training. They'll just execute her."

"I know."

Alec picked up the trunk from one end. Petyr took the other. They moved it out into the hall and down the stairs. The entire time, Petyr tried to figure out how to convince Carree to stay away from Genova.

CHAPTER 7

As Petyr stepped out into the early morning with the trunk and Alec trailing behind him, he realized he could see better than he could in the house. Dawn had come while they argued.

The horses, hitched up to the carriage, stamped their feet, restless, apparently impatient to be off. Cold mist erupted from their nostrils at every exhale.

Petyr noticed Carree off to the side, watching as they emerged, her arms wrapped around herself tight in an attempt to ward off the morning chill.

He kept his eyes facing in front of him, away from her, as he and Alec carried the trunk to the back of the carriage. They lifted it into place, and Alec set to work strapping it in.

"Petyr," Carree said, "can I at least ride with you to the gate?"

"What purpose would that serve? You're not even properly dressed."

"Someone needs to see you off."

Petyr wasn't sure what to say. If he let her ride to the gate, she might decide to make him let her ride beyond it.

Fortunately, footsteps from in the house saved him from having to answer. Soon after, Sim emerged.

"You're still here?" Sim asked. "I would have thought you far down the road by now."

Petyr let his eyes drift to Carree, and Sim followed them.

"Carree, what are you doing out here in your bed clothes? You'll catch a cold."

"I wanted to see them off."

Sim's face took on a practiced, stern look. "Carree, you weren't trying to convince them to take you along, were you?"

"Just to the gate."

"You are not going to the gate. You're not even supposed to be outside."

Carree stamped her foot. "I have to go outside at some point, or I'll turn into a rat like Ilsan!"

"Carree."

"Fine."

She started moving toward the door, then ran over and grabbed Petyr by the shoulders and pulled him down so that her lips were only a finger's breadth from his. "Please don't forget to come back and take me to Genova."

She finished pulling him toward her and kissed him, a quick, warm, passionate hint of what she might offer.

Petyr, shocked, could say nothing while she turned and ran into the house.

"I'm sorry," Sim said. "I can't control her any more, not since..." He cut himself off.

Petyr knew what he had almost said. *I have to warn him.*

"Sim, why don't you ride with us to the gate? I have something I need to tell you, but we really need to be on the road."

Sim looked puzzled, but stepped out into the yard toward the carriage.

"Are we ready, Alec?" Petyr asked

Alec nodded and climbed up to the driver's bench. Petyr opened the carriage door and motioned for Sim to climb in.

Once they were both seated, the carriage began to move. Petyr adjusted himself so he could look Sim in the eye. "I need you to listen carefully. We don't have a lot of time, and there are some things you need to know."

"Tell me."

"I know about Carree's gift."

Sim's eyes widened, but he said nothing.

"She's in a dangerous position. Untrained, but too old to go for training. You can't go back to Genova. She can't go there, ever."

"I know."

"You know?"

"Why do you think we moved here? I knew she had a gift, and I had a pretty good idea what it was."

"Why didn't you have her go through training?" Petyr could imagine any number of answers to the question.

"It's a long story. Do you think we have the time?"

Petyr sighed. "No, we don't. I have one more thing you need to know. Your daughter is in danger here. Today."

"Today?"

"Yesterday, while you were collecting Aslinda's body, Alec saw a group of Questioners and their Protectors pass by the cart, heading in the direction of Rocktree. They had a tracker with them."

"If they're going to Rocktree, why is Carree in danger?"

"They're going to double back, if they haven't already, and they're going to come here, after me."

Petyr watched Sim's fists clench and release, over and over.

"Why are they after you? What do they want?"

Petyr didn't want to tell him, didn't want to admit it out loud to anyone who didn't already know, but for Carree's sake, Sim had to believe him. "I'm a fugitive. I accused some very powerful people of some very improper actions. I'm no longer a Lord Questioner, and if they catch me, I'll be executed for treason.

"It doesn't matter, however. You have to hide your daughter. It would be better if you left altogether, camped in the forest or across the river until they leave. Go on a hunting trip. Just don't let them near your daughter, or you will lose her."

Fear and anger warred across Sim's face. "Why did you bring this on me? Why didn't you keep on running?"

"You know why, Sim. Whatever I'm accused of, I'm still a Questioner through every part of my body. When I saw the girl hanging there on the tree, I couldn't leave it alone. I had to find out what happened."

Sim's eyes had grown cold as steel, and Petyr found them unsettling as they bored in on him. Sim had every reason to be angry, but he had to get moving. Petyr slid a window open a little and yelled through the opening. "Alec, stop the carriage. Sim needs to get out."

The carriage came to a stop.

Sim sat a moment longer, then opened his door and started to step out. He turned back to Petyr before putting a foot on the ground. "Don't you ever come back here again." The man who had been nearly lost two nights ago when he told Petyr about Bran now seemed as fierce and present as a Protector.

"I won't."

Sim turned and stepped down, then stopped, his hand still on the hold. "No."

Petyr peered out past Sim, and saw a thin, light blue fog, almost like smoke, rising from the ground.

"No, no no!"

"What is it?"

"It's back. Get out of here. We don't need help from the likes of you." Sim slammed the door shut, and Petyr heard him yell. "Alec! Take your traitorous friend away from here."

The carriage started forward, and Sim ran toward the town center, yelling at the top of his lungs to hide the women.

As the carriage moved toward the gate, Petyr watched out the window and saw the strange blue fog thickening. There were swirls in it as it seemed to rise up out of the ground. It had a faint resemblance to something he couldn't place.

He yelled for Alec to stop, and when the carriage came to a halt, he climbed out and up onto the driver's bench to sit next to Alec.

"What are you doing up here?"

"I need to see this thing, if I can."

"But if we cross paths with the Questioners..."

Petyr interrupted him. "I'll climb down as soon as we're out of this fog."

I have to see what killed those girls.

Alec started the horses moving again.

As the carriage moved through the fog, Petyr kept his head turning, looking everywhere for the thing that plagued the town. He couldn't see far yet, not with the buildings in the way. But he looked down every side street they passed.

The fog thickened with each horse-length traveled toward the gate. It wasn't a moist fog, like he'd expected, but dry as smoke. A strange energy ran through it and into his skin where it was bare. For a moment, he almost thought it was searching him for something. *But that's ridiculous. It's not alive.*

"This fog is really strange," Alec said. "It doesn't feel right at all."

Petyr looked at Alec, and noticed a nervousness, twitches in his eyes, a tick at the corner of his lip, that Petyr couldn't remember Alec ever displaying.

They rounded the last corner before the gate. It was closed. Two men stood atop a tower built inside the wall, facing out toward the fields and the forest, muskets ready. Neither man turned around as they approached.

Alec yelled up to them. "Open the gate."

"Not until the fog clears," one of them yelled without turning. Petyr had heard the voice before, but at the moment, he couldn't remember who it belonged to.

Petyr wasn't surprised. He wouldn't open the gate, either, if he had a choice. He examined the tower. It had a flat platform on top and a ladder leading up to it. It could probably fit another four men with ease.

"Stay here," he said.

He jumped down from the carriage and ran over to the ladder.

"Petyr!" he heard Alec shout after him.

Petyr ignored the shout. He had to see this thing.

When he was about half way up the ladder, one of the men, the same one who had just refused to open the gate, said, "Hey, what are you about?"

"I want to see."

"Oh, it's you." Petyr finally recognized Eduard's voice. "If I'd known it was you wanting out, I might have opened it."

Roderick must not have convinced Eduard he was safe from me.

Petyr finished climbing his way up and found Eduard focused back on the fields in front of him. Petyr moved up to the wall and looked out.

The blue fog looked thicker toward the forest. He could see swirls and eddies in it, as if currents moved through it, but the air was still. No breeze touched his face. Only the cold of the morning.

"Has it always come this way?" Petyr asked.

"I don't know. We never had the wall before. Now be quiet and let me concentrate."

Petyr did as he was told, and searched the fog for something large and aggressive.

Several minutes passed in silence. The fog grew thicker, until, as he looked along the top of the wall, he could no longer see more than thirty or forty feet of it. The forest had all but disappeared, only the tops of the trees were left visible.

"I see something out there," said the other man, and Petyr immediately recognized Willam.

Of course it's Willam. I'm amazed he didn't say anything. Maybe Roderick had a talk with him.

One could hope.

"Where?" asked Eduard.

Willam pointed out into the fog, just off to their left. Petyr strained to see through the swirls. For a moment, he couldn't make out what Willam was talking about. All he saw were the movements of the fog.

"Ah, there," said Eduard, and he put his musket up to his shoulder. "Get ready, Willam."

Willam shouldered his own musket.

And Petyr saw it.

A shadow moving through the fog at a lope, easily the speed of a running man. It was big. Two men tall, at least, and it walked on two legs. It looked like a giant out of the stories his mother told him when he was a child. What he was seeing couldn't be real.

But it was.

"Now," Eduard's voice rang out, and then the sharp report of a pair of muskets firing left Petyr's ears ringing. The smoke from the explosion of gunpowder floated up into the air.

A roar answered the musket fire, carried by the fog and the chill morning air. Petyr saw the shadow break into a run, aiming straight for them. It covered the ground as fast as a horse might.

Eduard and Willam wasted no time in their efforts to reload. Petyr gauged the distance and the speed of the giant, if that's what it was, and knew they wouldn't have time.

He could see its eyes, bright and blue like he'd been told, and fierce with anger. He wanted to turn, turn and run, turn away from the terrible face that he could now see almost clearly, but it held him. Something about it drew him. He couldn't ask it questions, but maybe, if he tried, his extra gift might find some truth.

He looked into the thing's eyes, stared into them, and asked the questions in silence. *Why are you here? What do you want?*

He got nothing. A wall. Anger. Rage.

It came closer, closer, and he tried, tried to find a way in.

But it was alien. Its eyes seemed to rest on cheeks made of boulders, shrouded by thick, dirt brown hair. Its nose, flat and hidden between the boulders, hardly looked like a nose at all, with just a pair of nostrils directed nearly straight out of the face.

He thought he could feel its footsteps shaking the wall, the platform he was standing on.

He tried to turn, to look away, to slide down the ladder and escape, but the eyes of the demon wouldn't let him go.

Petyr'd been wrong. He felt Eduard lift his musket up, felt him take aim. Heard the musket fire and felt the ball leave the barrel, and felt it hit the giant demon.

The demon didn't flinch. It jumped. Jumped up onto the wall, onto the platform, swung its arms.

Petyr saw one arm swing at his head, and then he was falling, like Alura, and he felt a pain in his head. He heard an enraged scream, and then the morning became night as his eyelids shut and he lost consciousness.

CHAPTER 8

Petyr clawed his way up out of the blackness. Thoughts came to him, memories or dreams. He couldn't differentiate. Pain surrounded him, throbbing, threatening to cause him to loosen his grip.

But he had to climb out of the pit. Something urged him on, something he had to do, or should have done.

A dream pushed through the blackness, Alura poking at him. "Petyr," she said.

No, that isn't right. She's dead.

"Petyr, wake up." Not her voice this time. Alec's.

"Are you sure he's all right, Ilsan?"

"As sure of anything as I can be." Ilsan's voice.

Where am I?

"I could feel no skull fractures or anything to indicate he won't wake."

Their voices came through like they were talking in the distance through a fog.

A fog. And then the memory came, the giant, or demon, or whatever it was. Swinging. Falling.

Petyr knew where he was. Ilsan's operating room. No. He didn't lay on stone. It was softer. A bed. But in one of Ilsan's rooms.

Petyr let his eyes open slowly. The first thing he saw through the haze his eyelashes created was Alec's beak-nosed face staring down at him.

"Ilsan," Alec said. "He wakes."

"You should have more faith," said Ilsan.

"Petyr, you feel all right?"

Petyr tried to move his head a bit, and groaned when the pain went shooting into his eyes.

"Petyr?"

Petyr finally got his eyes open all the way just as Ilsan pushed Alec out of the way.

"How do you feel, Petyr."

"My head hurts."

"Do you remember what happened?"

Petyr had to search for a moment. That last dream. Did that happen? It did. He felt sure of it.

He tried to sit up again, but the pain in his head forced him back down.

"Not so fast, Petyr. Tell me what you remember."

"I—I remember that thing, that giant, coming out of the fog. They shot at it, and then it jumped up on the wall and swung at me, and then..." He trailed off. Whatever happened after was a blank.

"And then you fell fifteen feet and landed on your head. It probably saved your life."

"Why do you say that?"

"That thing," Petyr heard a hint of hysteria in his voice, "ripped Eduard and Willam apart."

Petyr let that sink in for a moment. Not that he held any love for them, but he'd seen the girl. He tried to keep from imagining the scene.

"What happened after? How is it that you are alive?"

"I don't know. Maybe it didn't see me. As soon as it was done with them, it jumped down and ran off to the center of the town, ignoring me completely."

Petyr closed his eyes. The ache in his head subsided a little. "Did it take anyone?"

"It took another girl," said Ilsan. "I'm told it destroyed the home in its effort to get at her."

"Carree?" Petyr asked. A sudden knot of fear grew in him.

"No, a young woman named Uma."

Petyr relaxed, and the knot started to break up. Another question came to him. "Did it follow her into the home, or did it know she was there without seeing her first?"

"I can't answer that."

Petyr rolled the implications around in his head. *If that thing will go into a house to get what it wants, no one is safe. And the bullets, the bullets didn't do anything but enrage it. It's after something. Something specific.* He didn't know how he knew, but he felt sure it knew where the girls it wanted were.

"Petyr," Alec said.

Petyr opened his eyes and saw Alec again. He realized then what he'd seen on Alec's face earlier was not hysteria. It was anxiousness and fear.

"Can you move?"

"I don't think he should," Ilsan said.

"We don't have much choice, Ilsan."

Like a strike from a Protector, the reason they were leaving came back to him.

"Are they here yet? How long have I been out?"

"You've been out about an hour, maybe a little more. They're not here yet."

"I can move if I have to." *I have to. As long as my head doesn't come apart.* "Help me up."

Petyr felt Alec's hand clasp his and begin to pull. Petyr helped as much as he could. After a short struggle, he was sitting up on the bed. His head swam with pain which radiated from the back of his head. He assumed that's where his head had connected with the ground.

He put his hands up to his forehead to press his skull back together. They rubbed up against a bandage that appeared to be wrapped around his head. That thing took a swipe at him. It must have caught him with a claw.

"Go get the carriage, Alec."

"It's already waiting. "

Petyr groaned. He'd hoped for a couple minutes to get used to sitting up.

"If you're going to insist on leaving," Ilsan said, "I'm going to see to my other patients. If you die, don't blame me."

"If I stay here, I'll surely die."

Ilsan blinked a couple times, then asked, "Who are these people Alec was talking about, and why do they want you?"

Petyr looked Ilsan straight in the eye. "Trust me. It's better that you don't know."

"Fine. I hope you're journey is blessed with luck."

"May your home be blessed as well, Ilsan."

Ilsan seemed to ponder him for a moment, his jaw shifting back and forth, then turned and left the room.

"I regret that I won't have more time to talk with that man."

Alec looked surprised. "Why? He's very strange."

"I don't know. Maybe it's because he's as much an outcast as I am."

"I don't see..."

"No, you don't know the whole story. I'm not sure I do. I'll explain it later, if we have a later. Help me out to the carriage."

⚔ ⚔ ⚔

The walk down the hall seemed to take an hour. Petyr's head throbbed the whole way, and the only thing that kept him upright was Alec's support.

They emerged from the home, and the light of the sun blinded him. When the fog cleared away, apparently the clouds had left with it. The sun, as distant as it was this close to winter, drove daggers through his eyes and into his skull.

He shut his eyes, as much as he could, and allowed Alec to guide him up into the carriage.

Petyr lay down on the seat while Alec closed the door behind him. Alec rocked the carriage as he climbed up onto the driver's bench. The carriage began to move, bumping Petyr's head as it hit the ruts and stones in the road.

I wonder if torture and execution might be less painful.

The rocking and bouncing of the carriage reminded him of another time, another carriage. He dove into the memory, hoping to forget the pain in his head.

"Petyr, wake up. We're home."

He opened his eyes. Home. It'd had been months since he'd seen his home. Months since he'd held Alura in his arms.

His head rested in her lap, and he didn't want to move it. But, to see his home.

"It's been so long," he said as he sat up.

"I'm glad you're home. It's been empty without you."

"Didn't you meet some friends? I left instructions that you be invited to the functions."

"I didn't want to go to any functions, not without you."

Petyr took her hand in his, feeling the delicacy of her fingers, the softness of her skin. "You need to go to the functions, introduce yourself to the other ladies."

"Why?"

"So that, when we go together, I can leave you with them if necessary. You need to know them, so that you know who to trust."

"I didn't marry you to play politics, Petyr."

"I know that. But if I ever want to gain the favor of the the Tribune, he need's to know that you can be trusted. If the wives, and his in particular, trust you, it's a good bit of influence to wield."

She sighed in that way he loved, a petite breath of air that crossed her lips and almost whistled. "All I want is to be with you. I don't care if you gain his favor or not. I don't care how far you advance. But if it makes you happy, I will attend every function I'm invited to."

"Thank you," he said, and turned to look out the window, imagining the circles he wanted to join, imagining being greeted by the Tribune as near equal.

"Petyr!" The shout from Alec brought him out of his dream, and back to the pain in his head.

"What?"

"Stay down. I think I see them in the distance."

His heart nearly stopped, and it felt like all the air had been drawn out of the carriage. He couldn't breathe.

He looked out the window, and saw that they were among the barren fields, and nearing the forest. The path to the main road was too thin for them to pass the carriage. His pursuers must be right near the edge of the forest. He wanted to ask Alec what they were doing, but thought better of shouting and announcing his presence.

He ducked down under the window, on the floor of the carriage. *If they catch me, it's over.*

The carriage kept rolling, not slowing, as far as he could tell. *Just an empty carriage, its passenger left in town.* He hoped that's what they would think, that they wouldn't look too close, that they wouldn't notice the trunk on the back.

Crouched down, and bent over, he felt the blood more thickly in the back of his head. It ached. He shut his eyes tight, which helped a little, but not enough.

The carriage seemed to slow a bit, but it still moved, still rocked and thumped across the worn road. He heard horses going by, the horses his pursuers rode. *I should have listened to Alec. I should never have stopped for that girl.*

Don't look inside. He implored every deity he could think of to let him pass safely.

Soon, the sounds of the other horses had passed, and the carriage sped up a little. He dared not raise his head yet, in case they decided to look back.

It seemed forever, and he heard nothing to indicate they followed. *Please, let the Tracker continue to follow the older trail.*

Petyr heard a shout from behind the carriage, and then he heard Alec yell, "Hold fast Petyr!"

Then, "Hya," a crack of the reigns. The carriage jolted ahead. It took several attempts to get back onto the seat as the carriage tossed him around. Only moments passed before they entered the forest. The branches, which had so unnerved him the first time through, slapped at the sides of the carriage as they raced by.

He wished for a window in the back of the carriage so he could see how close his pursuers, his executioners, trailed behind. They were not in a carriage. They would catch up, he was sure. The only question was when and where.

The closeness of the forest on this road should prevent them from catching him here, but on the main road through the forest?

He heard a crack, a loud bang. The carriage tilted and began to roll onto its side. The windows broke out, and he found himself tumbling amid broken glass and broken branches that had fallen inside the compartment.

The horses continued to drag the carriage even after it was on its side. Petyr lay against the wall. The movement of the carriage scraped dirt and moss into the cabin, throwing much of it into his face.

He heard another crunch as the carriage came to an abrupt stop. The sudden stop threw him into the front end of the cabin. He jammed his wrists in his effort to protect himself.

He tried to get up, but his vision swam. He couldn't focus on anything.

"Alec!"

He waited a moment, closed his eyes. He thought he heard horses, voices.

"Alec!"

The smell of the forest, the dirt, was in his nostrils. Cloying, rotting.

Thumps, someone climbing onto the carriage, and then the door above him opened.

He looked up. "Alec?"

"Not this time, Petyr." A halo of light streamed down among the trees to surround the shaggy, blurred face he saw there. He couldn't focus on it, but he recognized the voice.

"Dyllan?"

"Why'd you make me do this, Petyr? Why'd you make me chase you down?"

CHAPTER 9

Petyr had thought Dunsriver was too small a town to have had any sort of jail. He'd discovered he was wrong. Buried under the town hall, the town had several cells. He imagined they were mostly used for holding unruly drunken loggers until they slept off their inebriation.

His cell was damp. Water seeped in through cracks in the outer stone walls. The rest of the cell was built from iron bars, which left it open to the rest of the cellar. The cells appeared to be an afterthought. Light streamed through the slit of a window on the far wall and showed him that the rest of the cellar was devoted to the storage of various items and food.

The cot he lay on had a thin mattress, through which he could feel every rib of the cot's frame. The lone blanket they'd given him would not stretch the length of the cot. Prisoners certainly didn't appear to be held here long term.

He rolled over, pulled the blanket up around his shoulders and neck, and curled into a ball in an effort to keep warm. Beyond the ache of his head, the rest of his body was sore from the tumbling he'd taken when the carriage crashed. The uncomfortable cot accentuated every ache. After a few minutes, he had to search for a new position to alleviate new pains the cot gave him.

It didn't help that he couldn't stop worrying about Alec. Dyllan had told him Alec was missing, though Dyllan had said, "Your driver...". Petyr didn't know what to think. Alec had either crawled off to die after being thrown from the carriage, or had managed to escape, somehow. As far as Petyr could learn, Dyllan didn't know who Alec was. Petyr hoped that was the case.

Don't come back Alec. I don't want to see you hanged for aiding me.

Petyr wished Alec would hear his thoughts, that he would stay away.

But he knew that wasn't likely. If Alec was alive, he'd be around, looking for an opportunity to break him free, again.

It was different, this time. Two Questioners, two Protectors, a Tracker. The Tracker posed the greatest threat. If he wanted to have any chance to escape, Petyr would have to kill the Tracker, otherwise they'd find him again, quickly.

Petyr had seen him while they walked him back to the town, an older man, balding, but with a thick mustache and road weary skin. The Tracker had come close to him only once, long enough to place his hand on Petyr's forehead. Long enough to establish a direct link to Petyr. After that, he kept a good distance from Petyr, never said a word, and never gave Petyr a chance to find out more about him.

Petyr, even in his cell, thought he could feel the link, feel the Tracker's eyes on him. There would be no more slipping past the Tracker or out-maneuvering him. Until the Tracker was dead or had another target, the Tracker could point straight to him, no matter where he went.

The door to the cellar opened, and Petyr sat up. A shadow descended through the opening, then solidified into a man carrying an oil lamp. The light of the lamp revealed a face wearing a thick beard, and matching, barely kept hair, belonging to a man Petyr recognized—a man he had no wish to see.

"Petyr, wake up!" Dyllan said. His voice boomed through the previously quiet cellar.

"I'm awake."

"Good. I need to speak with you." He shut the cellar door behind him.

"So this is something you don't want your Questioner to hear? He'll find out, you know."

Dyllan walked across the cellar and stopped outside Petyr's cell. "He already knows what I'm going to tell you, though he doesn't know that I'm telling you."

"You walk a fine line."

Dyllan raised the lamp a bit. "Come to the door, let me see you. We were friends once."

Once, back when I trusted you.

"We were, once." Petyr pushed himself up from the cot and hobbled to the door of the cell. He didn't want to give Dyllan the satisfaction of seeing him broken.

I'm a fool. Hobbling might give him more evidence than doing nothing.

It had been a long time since he stood this close to Dyllan. His old Protector stood at least a head taller, and his shoulders were immense. A Protector's Protector.

"It wasn't my decision, Petyr. I didn't want to follow you."

"I'm not guilty of the things they charged me with."

"I'd like to believe you, Petyr, but it's not my place to judge. You didn't involve me, and the evidence…"

"Is all lies," Petyr finished. "None of it was my doing. I wasn't involved with any of those cases."

Dyllan stood silent for a moment. His eyes blinked a few times. "That's not what I'm here to talk about."

"Then why are you down here?"

"Alura. She's alive."

Petyr's muscles went limp, and he fell against the bars, sliding down them to the floor.

"Don't lie to me," he said. But he knew Dyllan's pronouncement for truth.

"I'm not lying, Petyr. She survived the fall."

Alura, alive. It changed everything. "The child?"

"It lives, too. A daughter."

"A daughter?" *A miracle!*

Dyllan knelt down so he was face to face with Petyr. "They told me to tell you that if you came back willingly and gave no trouble, your wife and child would receive support after your execution."

A partial truth. It strengthened him a bit. Gave him something to fight against, a reason to fight. "Dyllan, you should know better than to lie to me."

"Why do you say I lie?"

"I may no longer have the title of Lord Questioner, but they can't take away my abilities. You are slipping into half truths. You're trying to keep something from me."

"No, Petyr. I'm not keeping anything from you."

Petyr reached through the bars and tried to grab at Dyllan, but Dyllan backed away. He was no match for the speed of a Protector. "Answer me, Dyllan!"

"I don't have to answer to you. You are not a Lord Questioner anymore."

The window in his mind that sometimes allowed him to see answers without asking questions opened, and he saw what Dyllan was trying to hide.

"You have them. They're at your estate, and... You wouldn't dare."

"Wouldn't dare what? How do you know that?"

"She's my wife! You cannot do this!"

"There, you are wrong, old friend. You forfeited her when you committed your treason. She was given to me to hold as a reward should I manage to bring you back. I didn't want to tell you this. I didn't want to make this any more painful for you, but you couldn't leave well enough alone."

"You were my Protector!" His hands grasped the bars, and he held himself close.

"Only until you threw everything away. What did you think you were doing?"

Following the truth! He couldn't say it out loud. *How could I have so mistaken what you would become?*

The ache in his heart threatened to overcome the ache in his head.

"Well," Dyllan said, "keep your own counsel, then. I'll treat them well." He turned to walk away.

Petyr thought, once, that he and Dyllan were as close as a Questioner and his Protector could be. *How could I have been so wrong?*

He let himself sag to the floor completely, allowing the dampness to soak through his clothes. He didn't care. He'd made so many mistakes.

⚔ ⚔ ⚔

By the time Roderick came to visit, Petyr had climbed back up on the cot. His clothes were wet through, and he was colder than before. The blanket helped only a little, but he barely noticed between the the pain in his body and his newly rent heart, a gash he'd previously thought healed.

When Roderick asked, "Petyr, are you well?" Petyr didn't even respond. "Petyr?"

Petyr rolled over. Roderick was carrying a plate with something on it. "Why are you here?"

"I brought some food."

Petyr sniffed and caught the aromas of fish and bread. His stomach rumbled at the smell.

"Thanks."

Roderick slid the plate through a small gap near the bottom of the cell.

"Is what they say true?"

Petyr sat up. His muscles ached even more than they had earlier. "What do they say?"

"That you are a traitor to the empire, and that you accused High Lords of treasonous acts that you, yourself, perpetrated."

Petyr picked up the plate and held it to his nose. The bread was fresh, and the fish, trout from the river, he thought, was still warm. He turned back to his cot and sat on it, then took a bite of the bread. From the first taste, the bread seemed to leak some energy back into him.

"I did accuse more than one High Lord of treasonous acts."

Roderick's shoulders slumped a bit. "Then you are..."

"I am not a traitor. They were involved in subverting the Emperor's wishes and sewing discord so that the Emperor might be overthrown. I only accused them of the truth."

"In public?"

"No," Petyr said. "You're better off not knowing."

Roderick sighed. "Without Eduard and Willam, this will be hard."

Petyr remembered then what he'd forgotten since he'd been captured. Dunsriver had lost an Elder, and one of its daughters. Roderick had lost his son to that beast. The whole reason he'd risked himself in the first place.

"What will be hard?" he asked.

"Getting you out of here."

"No. Don't even think it. You can't risk yourself like that. Not for me."

"I'll risk whatever I want. I lost my son to that demon, today. I need you." Roderick's voice broke. "You're the only one who seems to have any idea how to track this thing down. You're the only one of them that seems to give a damn."

Petyr stood up and went to the cell door. "You didn't even want me here."

"I don't like the Empire. Not out here. We go years without Empire interference, and then the Empire decides to take notice and come in and take our money, disrupt our lives, and they give us nothing.

"You're the first to ever try to give us anything while asking for nothing. I apologize for my earlier—misjudgment."

I can't let him do this. "I was leaving," Petyr pleaded.

"You were leaving because you knew they had found you. I talked to Sim. He told me before he left."

"He left?"

"Crazy fool said he was going hunting."

Petyr sighed. At least Carree would be safe. "It's probably a smart thing to do."

"With that demon out there? It's the craziest damn thing the fool has ever done."

"Roderick, has that demon ever appeared within a week of taking someone?"

"No. It's never taken one until…"

"Until after you found the last one. It won't be back for a while."

Roderick turned and looked up at the door. Petyr wondered what could be going on his head. He seemed stable, for the moment. If the death of his son hadn't really hit him yet, who knew what would happen when it did.

"Petyr, I have to go. They're probably wondering what's taking me so long. Be ready."

"You can't do this."

Roderick smiled for the first time Petyr could remember seeing. It wasn't a smile of joy. "You can't tell me what I can or can't do in my town."

Roderick left and closed the door to the cellar behind him, leaving Petyr alone with his bread and his fish. Petyr sat down on the cot and started eating. If Roderick was intent on getting him free, Petyr would be ready. *I just have to figure out what to do about Dyllan.*

⚔ ⚔ ⚔

The cellar grew dark as the sun set. Shadows replaced the light that had previously streamed through the open window. Then blackness.

No one had come to see him since Roderick left. No supper.

No water. Petyr almost felt forgotten, which suited him fine. He needed time to think.

As the afternoon had passed and turned to evening, he'd become less and less sure that breaking out would solve any problems. Roderick would have to subdue the Lords in a way that wouldn't bring even more Lords down upon them. And he needed the Protectors. They could help. A pair of Protectors could possibly be a match for that thing.

They'd at least last long enough for help to come.

If Carree were here... Petyr banished the thought. He didn't want her here. Didn't want her to expose herself and her ability. They'd take her, too.

But if she were here, she could make them... He tried to stamp that thought out, too. She wasn't here, and he didn't know how much control she had. It wasn't right to put her in any more danger than he already had.

The thought wouldn't go away. She could make them help. She'd put herself at risk if she did, but it could work.

No, I have to try to convince them myself.

"But I can't do anything left alone like this."

The broken silence returned to sweep his words out of the air.

He heard footsteps above his head. Dust fell through the cracks in the floor. Someone was moving about.

He tried to think of the layout of the hall, what might be above him, but drew a blank. It could be anything. He hadn't seen every room.

The doorway opened and light from a lamp entered the room. Someone was coming down the steps. Whoever walked above him was still there.

The lamp lit Dyllan's face with a yellow glow. Dyllan held something else in his hand, a plate, it seemed. At least they weren't going to let him go hungry.

"You still with us, Petyr?"

Petyr tried to keep his anger and despair out of his voice. "Yes."

A trickle of dirt fell into his cell, and the footsteps moved away. Whoever it was, they were leaving.

Dyllan approached the cell. "Good, I've got food for you. Have you thought about my offer?"

"It's not much of an offer."

"It's all you'll get. Safety for your family. Isn't that worth it to you?"

Petyr held in a sigh. It was worth it for him, and under different circumstances, such as if they'd caught up with him before he found the girl, he'd take the offer. He'd learned his lesson. Alura was worth more than life itself to him. It had taken her death to show him that.

But she wasn't dead. He had to do more to protect her than he had before.

"I have a counter offer." He said.

Dyllan laughed. "You? What could you offer?"

"It's not exactly what I have to offer, it's more what I'd like from you for my cooperation."

"Hah. From me? There's nothing you can get from me."

"It's not for me. It's this town. There's a giant out in the forest, and it's killing people. Did they tell you any of this?"

"They said something about a beast. I don't see why they just don't go out and hunt it down. It's nothing they need me for."

Petyr scoured the corners of his mind, trying to find anything that could pique Dyllan's interest. "They need you, and the other Protector that's with you. I've seen it."

"You've seen it? What's it look like?"

Petyr didn't really want to remember. "The wall out front of the town? It's as tall as that wall. Man like, but huge. A giant, like I said."

"A giant. They're myths."

"It's not a myth. I saw it. It clubbed me down, and tore two other men into pieces. They shot it and only made it angry."

The wry smile Dyllan had been wearing started to droop at the corners. "You've got to be lying to me. Nothing like that exists."

"Bring one of your Questioners down. They can tell you I'm speaking truth."

Dyllan shook his head no. "I can't bring them down. I'm under strict orders to keep them from asking you questions."

Petyr snorted at that. "To keep them from finding out the truth."

"To keep you from contaminating them with your lies. They're only along to help find you."

"When did you turn against me, Dyllan? When?"

"When you lied to me." The loathing in him was palpable. Petyr could feel it.

"I never lied to you."

"Just stop, Petyr. I don't want to hear it."

Petyr ran a hand through his hair, and pulled it away immediately when he touched the spot where his head had hit the ground and the pain that had seemed to be less shot through him again.

"Dyllan, if you don't want to believe me, go talk to Roderick. He'll tell you. His son died this morning. Have one of your Questioners ask him. I swear, if you help this town, if you let me help this town, I'll go with you when that thing is dead."

"If you are lying to me again, I swear you will wish you hadn't."

Some of the tension slipped out of Petyr. It was as much of an agreement as he was likely to get.

Dyllan turned to leave.

"Uh, Dyllan?"

"What."

"The food?"

Dyllan looked down at his hand. "Oh, right." He slipped it through the opening. "I swear..."

"Just go ask him. Go examine the bodies of the men that died."

"I'll do that." Dyllan looked at him again, and Petyr looked right back, trying to hold his eyes, trying to make him accept it. The Dyllan turned and went to leave the cellar.

As soon as they broke eye contact, Petyr stooped to get the plate. He didn't want to lose it when darkness enveloped him again. More bread. More fish. A small bowl of water.

Then the light went out and blackness enveloped him.

"What are you doing, Petyr?" Alec's voice came to him out of the dark.

"Alec?"

"You can't give in, Petyr. They'll execute you for treason. Do you know what that means?"

"What are you doing here, Alec?"

"I came to get you out."

Then Petyr put it together. Alec used his gift so seldom around Petyr, he sometimes forgot Alec was gifted. "It was you traipsing around above me. You've got to leave, Alec. They'll kill you, too."

"They can't find me. The Tracker is tuned to you. They think I'm dead, anyway, or run off."

"Look, Alec, I can't leave."

"Why not?"

"Alura is alive."

"No."

"Dyllan told me." Petyr still hardly believed it himself, but Dyllan believed it true. "If I go with them and don't cause them trouble, she'll be safe."

Alec swore under his breath. Petyr couldn't make out exactly what he said, and thought it probably better that he couldn't.

"I'm trying to get them to stay and help kill that thing."

"Why?"

"There's something that bothers me about it. It knows where things are. It knows the people here. It destroyed that house to get at its victim. There's a pattern to it, but I can't see it. There's an intelligence driving it, Alec, and I fear it means something dire, not only for this town, but maybe for the whole region."

"No, Petyr, it's just a giant beast."

"Then why is it raping them? It wants to make more."

"Petyr..."

"I need to protect Alura, Alec. I'm going with them. If she wasn't alive, things would be different."

"You can't protect her by dying, Petyr. Dyllan may believe she'll live, but you know how the High Lords work. Deception, deceit. They're lying to him. She's bait, and you know it."

"What choice do I have, Alec?"

With that, Petyr felt his way to the cot, where it sagged a bit under his weight. He set the plate of food of to his side, and put his head in his hands.

"Leave with me."

Petyr heard the cell door creak open.

"No. Save yourself, Alec. They already think you're dead. They won't chase you."

"I won't leave you to die. Besides, if they stay here, what about Carree? If they find her, it's a death sentence for her, too."

I can't win. Someone's going to get hurt. But not Alura. "Get out of here Alec. I'm staying."

"Fine. Wallow if you want." The cell door shut and locked again. Alec fell silent.

Petyr knew what Alec felt. He couldn't help it. Alec felt Petyr was betraying everything they'd fought for over the past year since Petyr had met him. Petyr couldn't blame him. But he couldn't stand to think of Alura suffering.

He leaned back against the wall, carefully keeping the bruised portion of his skull from touching it. He thought about his options late into the night until, eventually, he fell asleep without any solutions. His food went untouched.

CHAPTER 10

Petyr woke in the morning to the sound of his cell door opening. He looked up, but the grime from a night of sleeping in a cold cellar blurred his vision, and he couldn't see who'd opened it.

"Get up." Dyllan's voice.

At least he knew who. If only he knew why. But he forced himself up, then wiped at his eyes with his hands, trying to rub the sleep from them.

Petyr blinked a couple times, and his eyes cleared up. Dyllan grabbed his arm. "Let's go."

"Where are we going?"

"We're leaving, and we've got a long ride."

Petyr was confused. "What about helping this town?"

"They can help themselves. We did talk to Roderick. Seems he had some idea about breaking you out."

"I told him he shouldn't try."

Dyllan pulled him out of the cell and toward the stairs. "I know. We're leaving because we can't trust these people not to do something stupid, even after they've been advised against it."

Dyllan pushed Petyr up the stairs ahead of him. Petyr wouldn't even bother trying to run, and he knew Dyllan knew it. The

Protector was a beast of a man, and could outrun him and out-fight him. It wouldn't even be a contest.

"What did you do to Roderick?"

"Locked him in his home and set Nathyn to guard him. We told him if he tried to come out before we were gone, we'd kill him."

Petyr wasn't all that surprised. Dyllan only had the one charge. Bring Petyr back. Petyr had never thought of Dyllan as a man prone to excessive violence. But he never hesitated when he thought it necessary.

"Who is Nathyn?" Petyr asked.

"The other Protector."

They emerged from the cellar into a hallway on the main floor. Dyllan directed him down the corridor, which led to the main room.

"Promise me one thing, then, Dyllan."

Dyllan laughed. "Why would I promise you anything?"

"Because we were friends once."

"Fine. What?"

"Send some Protectors back to this town to kill that thing. There's more at stake than a few murdered villagers."

Dyllan looked sideways at him. "Why do you even care?"

"You haven't seen what that thing does to the bodies. It's evil, Dyllan, and whether you believe I'm a traitor or not, believe me about this. Whatever that creature is, it should not be allowed to live."

Dyllan pulled on his arm and stopped his walk. "You're serious about this?"

"I'd ask you to have one of your Questioners come and ask me. You'd understand, then. But you won't do that."

"I can't do that, Petyr. I'm under orders."

"You know those orders are keeping you in the dark, too. You could know the truth."

"I know the truth. You betrayed our partnership. You betrayed your wife. You betrayed the Empire." Dyllan stopped and appeared to contemplate something. "Fine, I'll have Protectors sent."

He gave Petyr a shove. "Get moving, we've got a long way to go."

Petyr walked to the door, and prepared himself for whatever came next. He'd get on a horse, he assumed, and ride to his death. *If Alura lives because of it, I can accept that.*

⚔ ⚔ ⚔

The horse they put him on was tethered to Dyllan's. Dyllan may have trusted that he couldn't get away on foot. That trust, apparently, didn't extend to his being mounted.

Dyllan rode at the front of the group, with Petyr following behind him. The other Protector, another brute of a man, trailed Petyr. The Tracker and the two Questioners rode last.

The two Questioners were both young, probably just out of the Academy. Young enough to not question their leadership, or their orders.

The first one still carried some of his baby fat, or maybe he was just generally pudgy. Petyr couldn't really tell.

The second one was thin, light boned, and somewhat effeminate. The only thing that caused Petyr to think of him as a man was the somewhat dirty looking smudge of a mustache he wore.

Behind them, a small group of people watched as they left the town and made their way between the fields. Petyr didn't recognize anyone in the group. He'd thought at least Roderick would see him off. Or Carree.

"Do you want to sit the horse backward?" Dyllan asked him.

Petyr turned around. "What? No."

"Then quit looking back. There's no one there for you."

He's right, too. Why did I hope to see Carree? She's out hunting with her father. He resigned himself to a long trip. A thousand miles or more to Genova, through the early part of winter, over a mountain range.

Winter? It was already near, he knew. The pass through the mountains might already be filling with snow. A week to the pass, another week on the other side, and who knew how long to cross the pass. Two weeks at a minimum until he faced them again. Probably longer.

The immense blackroot trees of the forest loomed in front of them. Something felt odd. He looked around and didn't immediately see anything. Nothing in the trees, no one in the fields. It just felt wrong.

Nothing.

He looked again and realized what was nagging at him. There weren't any loggers working the forest edge.

He chewed on what it could mean as they rode among the shadows of the huge trees. He was on edge, but not sure why. He almost expected an ambush, but that would be foolish. The Protectors, at least one of them, would likely get away and bring back an army. It would result in a carnage the townsfolk couldn't imagine.

As they came to the wreckage of the carriage, he put down his musings as wishful thinking, the hopes of a man who knows his dying day. He had seen no sign of any large group of men.

He eyed the wreckage from the back of his horse. It had mostly been cleared out of the way. He searched for his trunk, but found no evidence of it. It was missing. All his work, his notes, his proof. *I guess it doesn't matter anymore.*

They left the wreckage behind. Thoughts about traversing the pass again occupied his mind. He had to say something.

"Dyllan."

"What?" The Protector looked back over his shoulder.

"Are you really going to take us over the pass at this time of year?"

"Why not?" The look on his face seemed puzzled.

"You know the pass is possibly snowbound even now. We could spend weeks trying to get through, or die in the process."

"Really?"

Petyr realized then that Dyllan might not know. Dyllan had grown up on the southern coast. He and Petyr had shared long hours over drinks discussing where they'd come from.

"This isn't another attempt to put me off leaving, is it?"

"Of course it is, but I'm serious. Have you ever seen a man freeze to death?"

Dyllan shook his head.

"It's an unpleasant way to die, and if you get us stuck in those mountains in the middle of a storm, it'll kill us all."

"There's a town at the base of pass. They'd have to know if it's safe. If it's not, we'll stay there."

Petyr realized he'd lose this fight. Dyllan wasn't about to give him anything he wanted, and he obviously felt staying in Dunsriver was a danger.

Dyllan's horse started its tumble to the ground almost before Petyr heard the crack of gunpowder. He realized immediately that it would pull his own horse down as well, tethered so close as they were. He barely swung his leg over before his horse followed the other to the ground. Petyr landed on top of it and then quickly moved clear to avoid getting caught in its struggles.

More shots echoed through the forest, and he looked behind to see the horses fall out from under the two Questioners. Their riders reacted slowly, or not at all. The other Protector's horse still stood, but Petyr couldn't see the Protector. Petyr assumed he had leapt into the forest at the first shot, going after the shooter.

A hand grabbed him from behind and started pulling him into the trees. He tried to fight it, but his aching muscles protested. He was still too weak to accomplish much against his attacker.

"Petyr, stop struggling," Alec's voice said from behind him.

Petyr stopped resisting immediately, and went with wherever Alec was taking him. "What's going on?"

"A rescue."

"They shouldn't do this, Alec."

Alec was pulling him deeper into the forest. Petyr looked around. He didn't see anyone, but he heard shots among the trees. The screams of the horses, and of men, filled the air.

"I know they shouldn't," Alec said. "They know they shouldn't. I told them."

"Then why?"

"You'll have to ask Roderick, if he survives. Now be quiet. We don't want that lumbering carcass of a Protector finding you."

"The Tracker, he'll find me anywhere."

"Only if he lives. Now quiet."

Petyr decided his questions could wait. Prudence dictated following Alec's advice. Petyr had anticipated exactly this type of situation when he'd befriended the Ghost soon after his escape from Genova. It was fortunate the arrangement had benefited Alec, too.

Petyr hadn't anticipated the friendship that sprung up between them. He hadn't anticipated the Ghost would come back for him at risk of his life.

Alec appeared to be leading Petyr somewhere specific. Alec kept his head down, subtly shifting from side to side while searching for something.

The gunshots fell silent after a few more moments. Only the sounds of dying animals and wounded men continued to assault Petyr's ears.

Petyr pulled up on Alec. His aching body felt like it had only a few more steps in it before he just collapsed. "Slow down, Alec. I can't keep up."

"It's not much farther," Alec said without stopping.

Just about the time Petyr thought his legs would give out completely, Alec halted in the middle of a small clearing. Petyr didn't know what he'd expected, but he'd expected something. The clearing seemed empty.

"Why are we here, Alec?"

"Look around, Petyr. Look closer."

"I don't..." Petyr started to say while he spun in place, and then he saw what Alec was talking about. A skeleton, about four feet tall, hung from iron spikes pounded through its chest into a tree. A third spike protruded from its mouth. Just like the body he had found. *But the height... A child? Why didn't they tell me about this? How could I not find this out?*

"What is this?" He looked closer, and realized the skeleton was old. It had spent years, perhaps decades, hanging from this tree. After a moment of staring at the skull, he realized it was oddly shaped. A little too thin, the eye sockets placed a little too wide. *Not a child. Something else.*

"I was hoping you could tell me," Alec said.

"It's not human, but it's not a giant, either. It makes no sense. How did you find this?"

"I found it after I escaped from the carriage wreck. Sorry about that."

Petyr waved at him to go on.

"I was running through the forest, and just stumbled into this clearing. I fell to my knees to catch my breath, and it was staring me in the face."

Petyr moved in a little closer to examine it. It had pointed, sharp teeth, and the bone was still white. He couldn't tell much else about it, except the spikes seemed near rusted away. He wondered if the preservation spell was still active. If it was, maybe it hadn't died decades ago. Maybe it had hung here, undisturbed for centuries. The tree it was on was certainly large enough. *I wonder if the spell or whatever it is even protects the tree. I wish I could ask it questions.*

"I have to get Ilsan out here to examine it. It'll probably crumble to dust if we take it off the tree."

"So, what do you think it means?"

"I think it means that something has been killing things like this for far longer than the town has been here."

Turning away from the tiny skeleton, he saw an expectant look cross Alec's face.

"We're not leaving."

"Why not, Petyr?"

"First, we don't know if the Tracker is alive. If he is, he has to be taken care of, one way or another. Second, those people risked their lives to help me. I owe them whatever I can give them."

"What about me, Petyr? I don't want to stay here and get eaten by that thing, nor do I have any interest in visiting an Empire gallows. If they ever catch me, Petyr, I'll go quicker than you."

Petyr thought for a moment, and realized Alec had a point. Rogue Ghosts, just like rogue Coercers met their deaths if they were found. The usual ruling, a danger to the Empire. He'd been in too much pain to realize why Alec had disappeared when the carriage wrecked.

"You're right, Alec. I owe you. You risked your neck for me, and you deserve my thanks, and a whole lot more.

"I'm not going to make you stay with me. I can't do that. It's not your duty to help these people."

Alec smirked. "It's not yours, either, Petyr. Not anymore."

"It is my duty. My expulsion was a travesty, and I will see those bastards hang if at all possible. And though I no longer have the title, I still feel I have the duty. Especially after they risked their town for me today."

Alec looked like he would say something, but Petyr cut him off. "I would like nothing better than to leave with you, go find my wife and daughter and sneak them away from Dyllan's estate. My heart yearns for it.

"But what kind of man would I be if I ignored the problem here?"

"Alive."

"Alive in the flesh. My spirit, I fear, would wither away, just like the flesh of that creature," Petyr said, pointing at the skeleton on the tree.

Its empty eye sockets stared at them, questioning.

CHAPTER 11

Petyr followed Alec through the forest back in the direction of the Ambush. Alec often left him for minutes at a time to scout ahead. When Petyr asked why, Alec said, "It was a good plan. It should have worked. I just don't want to be surprised if it didn't."

So their trip back took nearly three quarters of an hour, as Petyr judged it. Four to five times as long as their flight from the ambush. On more than one occasion, Petyr found himself glad of the slow pace as the pain in his head swelled to the point it blurred his vision.

When they made it back, Petyr found himself a bit surprised anyone was still there. Roderick saw them immediately, and jogged over to them, sidestepping one of the downed horses.

"There you are." Roderick said. "I thought you'd got lost."

"No," Alec said. "I just wanted to be sure that the festivities were well over before we returned."

Roderick reached out, took Petyr's hand, and shook it. "Glad to see you're well."

"Thanks," Petyr said, not really sure if he was well at all. "Why did you do it?"

"Do what?" Roderick asked, as if he didn't know quite well what Petyr was asking.

"Risk the whole town to rescue me." Petyr pulled his hand free.

"The whole town is already at risk, Petyr. Your friends, when I went to talk to them, they figured out I was planning to help you escape from my cellar. I think he wanted to execute me on the spot."

"I'm surprised he didn't."

Roderick laughed. "I had several of my woodsmen with me at the time. I suspect he thought he might not make it out of the town if he did that. You'll have to ask him, though."

"He lives?"

"The one that was leading you, Lord Dyllan, I think. His leg is broken, but I've heard Protectors heal quickly."

Petyr knew they did. The leg would heal in a week, perhaps less. *I hope my head heals in a week.* "So he locked you in your home, instead."

"And planted the other Protector there to watch me."

"So how did you set this all up?"

"Your driver, Alec, seems to have some tricks you neglected to tell me about. You could have told me he was a Ghost."

Petyr looked around quickly. Nobody was near them to listen. The motion made his vision swim. "He's not as useful if people know what he can do. I trust you'll keep that information to yourself."

"Right, sorry."

"Well, then how'd you do?"

"Pretty well. We weren't intending to kill any of them, but the chubby Questioner fell off his horse awkwardly and broke his neck. The other Questioner and the Tracker are alive. Lord Dyllan, I already told you about."

"The other Protector?"

"He's dead. But he took four of my men with him, and injured another three. I won't weep for him."

Petyr breathed a sigh of relief. *I'm safe for now.* "I need to talk to the Questioner."

"It might be tough."

"Why?"

"He's unconscious. Ilsan says he'll live, but he has no idea when he'll wake up."

Petyr wanted to swear like one of the woodsmen, but he held his tongue. Another spike of fire erupted in the back of his head, and he shut his eyes to try to quell the pain.

"You look upset."

The pain subsided a bit, and he opened his eyes again. "I am. I've been trying for more than a year to find a Questioner that I could talk to, one where I wouldn't immediately find myself heading for a noose."

Roderick looked confused. "That should be easy, shouldn't it? There's a Questioner in every town."

"And they all have a Protector with them. Any time I get close enough where they can find out who I am, I've had to run. It also seems that Questioners have been instructed to avoid Questioning me at all costs."

"That seems odd."

"Under normal circumstances, I'd say it is. However these aren't normal circumstances. I have..." Petyr remembered his trunk was missing. "I *had* information that would put several of the High Lords into the position I'm currently in. Running for their lives to escape the executioner. They don't want another Questioner to hear what I have to say. They've accused me of being a traitor, and if a Questioner asked me about these things, they'd know the truth."

"Didn't you tell anybody else?"

"That's why I'm no longer in Genova, and why these Lords were set on bringing me back. I told the wrong person. And for your own interest, I would suggest you not tell anyone I told you any of this."

Roderick stepped up and put his arm around Petyr's shoulder, pulling him tight. "Petyr, I suspect what you've told me is enough to send me to the executioner should I run afoul of another Questioner. But I'm already bound for it if we don't kill the rest of these Lords and bury them in the forest. I'm glad Sim let you stay. You certainly aren't what I thought you were."

"Why didn't you kill them?"

Roderick laughed. "I thought if we didn't kill them, when it came time to pay the harper, they might go easier on me."

"Well, don't kill them yet. If I can talk to the Questioner, especially with Dyllan in the room, we might be able to bring them around."

"Might? Wouldn't it be clear?"

"Dyllan was my Protector, yet he chooses to believe I betrayed him."

A cart arrived from the town, carrying three men wearing long aprons. They jumped down and started butchering the dead horses.

"Practical," said Petyr, shrugging himself out of Roderick's embrace.

"Winter's coming on. Some of our animals will get to live a little longer. We can't leave them here, in any case."

"I thought you said no one comes here."

"You came, and then these came. Who else might be following you?"

Petyr looked over the carnage. The butchers were making quick work of the horses. The smell of the horses blood was cloying among the dampness of the forest. In a couple hours, no one would know anything happened here.

This forest seemed to like to keep its secrets.

"I hope," he said, "no one else."

At that moment, the pain spiked in the back of his head again, and caused him to stagger a bit. The world started to weave, as if slowly dancing. Alec stepped up to catch him and keep him from going to his knees.

"I think you need a rest, Petyr."

"I think I..." The world went dark.

⚔ ⚔ ⚔

When Petyr woke, he saw rafters above his head, bathed in the soft glow of an oil lamp. He was back in Ilsan's rooms. He knew that much. He tilted his head to look around a bit.

A rickety looking chair sat empty in the corner. The oil lamp sat on a small side table. A book rested on the table next to the lamp. Someone, Ilsan perhaps, had been here recently.

He turned his head back so he could study the rafters some more. The intense pain in the back of his head was gone. A dull ache had replaced it, but it was an ache he could live with.

Footsteps sounded outside of the room, then the door opened. Petyr looked over to find Ilsan letting himself in.

"Ah, Petyr. Good to see you're awake."

"How long…"

Ilsan came over to the bed. "Shh. Don't push yourself. You've been out for a couple days. I think I remember suggesting that you not leave. You should have listened to me."

"What…"

Ilsan pulled a tool from his pocket. It reminded Petyr of a looking glass. The doctor put his fingers to Petyr's eye and spread it open, gently, and looked at it with the glass. "You nearly died, Petyr. Roderick and your friend brought you here, and at first, I thought you dead." Ilsan switched to peering into the other eye. "But you had a heart beat, slow as anything. They told me you just passed out, perhaps from the sight of them butchering the horses.

"No."

"Oh, I know that. I brought you in, and your heartbeat got weaker and weaker. So I reexamined your head. Would you believe I found something, about the size of a pin, embedded in your skull?"

"What?"

Ilsan grasped Petyr's head and tried to turn it away from him. "Let me see the back of your head." Petyr let him turn it. "I should have shaved your head the first time, and I would have found it. A sliver of something hard, almost like metal, but it's not metal."

"Do you still have it?"

"Of course I still have it," he said. He let Petyr turn back to face him. "It's healing well, now."

Petyr reached a hand to his head and felt at it. No hair, only skin. Ilsan had done a proper job of it and shaved everything.

"Do you want to see it?"

"Yes."

"Wait here," Ilsan laughed.

Not a problem. Petyr didn't feel like going anywhere. He already had an idea of what Ilsan had pulled from his head. He contemplated the grain in the beams that crossed the ceiling. Anything more seemed too strenuous. He felt weak.

Petyr was just beginning to wonder if Ilsan had forgotten him when Ilsan reappeared at the door carrying a tray. Petyr saw bread on it, and a hot steaming cup.

Petyr tried to sit up, but couldn't. The smell of the bread caused his stomach to grumble.

"No, no. Wait and I'll help you," Ilsan said.

Petyr waited while Ilsan cleared the book from the table, and set the tray down. The book, he put on the chair. Then he came over and helped Petyr sit up, then leaned him against the wall. He handed Petyr the tray.

On it, Petyr saw the bread and the cup, which held tea, and something else. A small, curved sliver, probably an inch long, colored blue with a finish like a pearl. Petyr picked it up and examined it, spinning it around in his fingers. One end held a point as fine as any needle, the other end, a bit dull, like it had broken off of something. On a hunch, he tried to bend it with his fingers, but couldn't make it bend.

"Do you know what it is," Ilsan asked.

"I've never seen anything like it, but I have a good idea. That creature, the giant, struck me, knocking me off the platform. It would not surprise me if this were part of a fingernail."

"Something that hard breaking off from contact with your skull? I'm not sure I believe it."

"I don't know what else it could be."

His stomach rumbled again, and he set the sliver down. He

pulled a hunk off of the bread and started to eat it. Ilsan went back to his chair, moved the book back to the table, and sat down to watch Petyr eat.

After several bites of bread, Petyr drank some of the tea to wash it down.

He watched Ilsan while he ate and drank, studying the man's sapphire colored eyes. They were the only real bit of color in his ghostly form, and they seemed to see everything.

After a bit, it struck him as surprising that Ilsan was sitting with him. Had been sitting with him, and him alone.

"Ilsan, tell me about your other patients."

"Other patients? Oh, the Lords."

Petyr nodded and stuck another bit of bread into his mouth.

"I set the Protector's leg, and then they took him to the holding cells. He'll be back to normal in a couple more days. I wish all my patients had that particular gift."

"What about the Questioner?"

"He's still alive."

"That doesn't sound promising."

"He won't wake. Between you and him, I'm really tired of dealing with head injuries."

"I need him awake, Ilsan." *If he doesn't wake, I'll never get Dyllan to believe me.*

"I'll do what I can, but there doesn't seem to be much to do. I force water down him, but beyond that, it's up to the Mother whether he comes out of it. Why do you need him awake?"

Then, Petyr remembered what he'd told Roderick. *I shouldn't have told him that. What was I thinking?*

"What's wrong, Petyr? You look distressed."

"I would love to tell you, Ilsan, but telling you would put your life in danger, and I've already done that to Roderick." *If any Questioner asks him anything about me, he won't be able to keep it silent.*

"Done what?"

"Told him things he's better off not knowing. Things that could get him executed for knowing them."

Ilsan looked a little distressed himself. "Well, then I don't want to know them, but I'll do my best to keep that Questioner alive."

"If he wakes, let me know, will you?"

"Of course. I should go check on him. Finish your meal, then lay down and get some more rest. Listen to me this time."

"Could you send Roderick to me, and Alec?"

"They're not here, but I'll send for them."

"Thank you," Petyr said while lifting another piece of the bread to his mouth.

Ilsan left the room and shut the door behind him. His book still lay on the table, inviting Petyr to step over and pick it up. But Petyr didn't. He followed Ilsan's advice and finished the bread and the tea, then lay down to rest while he thought about everything that happened, and what he had to do.

He had no idea how to fight that giant. He had to hope the Questioner would wake and would listen to him. He had to hope that the Questioner would confirm to Dyllan that Petyr told the truth, and he had to think of a way to keep all three of the Lords from running to report the ambush in the forest to the closest garrison once they were free. Last, he needed to figure out how to get home to Alura and his daughter.

The ache that overcame him at that thought did not stem from his head, but from his heart, and for the first time since hearing they lived, he shed the tears that he'd stored up for a year.

CHAPTER 12

When he woke again, Petyr couldn't remember his dreams. If he'd had any, they were gone. The ache in his head had faded a bit, and he felt pretty good for the first time since he'd taken the swipe from the giant. He refused to call it a demon. Calling it a demon implied that it couldn't be killed, and he didn't want to believe that. There had to be some way to stop it.

The light in his room was low. The oil lamp burned, but someone, most likely Ilsan, had brought the flame down. The book and the food tray were gone, but he spied the sliver next to the lamp. Petyr didn't know if it was important, but he felt he needed that sliver. It might lead to some sort of answer. He'd need some small box or pouch to put it in.

The door to the room opened slowly, and Petyr saw Carree poke her head in to look. With the knowledge that Alura still lived, Carree's visage had lost the allure it previously held. She was still lovely, but he saw her now for the young woman she was, still learning about the world outside her father's home. At least, she would learn if she were allowed out.

She had put no compulsion on him, he realized. It had been his own needs that had done it to him. She could compel him if she wished. He knew that. But she didn't. She did have a measure of control over herself and her ability.

A smile crossed her face as she saw he was awake. "Hello, Petyr."

"Hello Carree. Your hunting trip is over?"

She stepped fully into the room.

"Yes, it's over. I hate hunting."

"I'm sorry."

She came over to his bed, and he sat up. "You should be sorry. My father told me you suggested it."

"I was just trying to keep you safe."

"How did you know?"

"How did I know what?"

She put her hands on her hips, reminiscent, he thought, of her mother. "Now Petyr, don't play coy with me. You knew about my ability. How did you know?"

"I'm a Questioner," he said. He hoped that would end it.

"Questioners can't learn truth without asking questions."

Petyr hesitated. If he told her, would it do any harm? He didn't know. But he wanted to tell her.

"I know your secret. If I tell you my secret, will you keep it to yourself, always?"

"I will." She looked eager, as if she couldn't wait to have a secret to keep.

Petyr heard the truth in her promise. She would keep it.

"I don't always need to ask the question aloud."

She looked stunned. "You can read minds?"

"No. I can sort of ask a question in my head. If the person I'm thinking of has strong feelings about whatever I ask, I can feel them, make sense of them. If they have no strong feelings or opinion, I'll have to ask more directly."

He saw fear tugging at the corners of her eyes. "I never used my ability on you," she said.

"I know. Who trained you?"

"My father hired a woman when I was younger. She played the part of a maid for several years. She trained me."

Petyr rapidly pondered the implications. He wondered how

many others there were that escaped the Empire's grasp. He'd always been told the Empire found them all. He'd believed it. The people telling him had believed it.

And now, out here near the Fringe, he knew of two who had escaped the Empire's grasp. Coercers frightened people. Carree frightened him, to a degree. If she held any large amount of power, she could make a person do just about anything. Tales Petyr heard while growing up talked about battles between Coercers, before the Empire arose, with hundreds of people compelled to fight and die.

"Do you know where she is?" he asked.

"She passed away of a fever a couple years ago."

"You're training is incomplete, isn't it."

She nodded and lowered her eyes. "She said, at the end, that I mostly need practice, but..."

"You can't practice here. You can't really practice anywhere. If you make a mistake, you'll end up with a death sentence here just as quick as you would in Genova."

"What? I thought, in Genova, they would take me in and complete my training."

"Why would you think that?"

"Father told me that's where most Coercers are trained, but he would never let me go there."

"The reason he would never let you go there, and the reason you can't until you're fully trained and can hide what you are completely, is that they wouldn't train you. They would execute you."

The blood drained from Carree's face. Petyr wanted to reach out and hug her, comfort her, but there was little comfort to give. She needed to know.

"Carree, they only train Coercers from birth. They need them completely loyal to the Empire. It's the reason your father left and came out here. He didn't want to lose you to the Empire."

"So he doomed me to a life of what? Running? Hiding? How is that better?" Large tears began to form in her eyes, and were pushed out when she squeezed her eyes shut.

"You're safe here," he said, wanting to offer her something even though he didn't really believe it.

"Am I? Really? Then tell me why I went hunting with my father while you tried to escape?" She whirled and stamped out of the room, slamming the door shut behind her.

He heard Carree yelling at someone in the hallway, but the walls and the door were thick enough to muffle the words into indistinct syllables.

But when the door opened again, and Sim came through it as angry as he'd been in the carriage days earlier, Petyr had an idea what was said.

Whatever anger Sim had, when he spoke, he used a tightly controlled voice. "What gives you the right to tell her those things?"

"They're true, and you know it." Petyr didn't bother to feign ignorance. "She's old enough to be on her own, and you're risking her life not telling her the truth."

"She didn't need to know the truth if she stayed here."

Petyr almost couldn't believe his ears. "Sim, if I hadn't told her, she would leave, and she would find out the truth the moment she stepped into Genova." Petyr tried to keep his voice down, but this was the second time that Sim withheld the truth from someone in his family, and his anger at that overrode everything.

"She wouldn't leave," Sim said.

Petyr's headache started to grow in strength. "You're blind to what your daughter is doing. She's been trying to convince me since the day I arrived to take her along when I leave. She desperately wanted to go to Genova to complete her training."

Sim shook his head, apparently trying to deny what Petyr told him.

"You are going to lose your daughter, Sim, if you persist in this folly of protecting her from what she is. It makes me wonder. What sorts of things did you hold back from your son? What sorts of fabrications did you tell him that led him to his fate?"

Sim's eyes flashed with renewed anger. "I didn't!"

"You can't lie to me, Sim. Don't even try. I've seen, more closely than you know, the damage that is caused by false words."

Sim stood, his body rigid with anger, and said nothing. All Petyr wanted to do now was lay down and go back to sleep, but he couldn't. Not while Sim stood there, weighing, Petyr assumed, the consequences of strangling him.

He wished Dyllan were still his Protector. These situations were the very reason the Empire paired a Questioner with a Protector. People didn't like having their lies exposed.

Ilsan came into the room, which worked just as well. Irritation played across his face. "Sim, get out of here. I will not have you upsetting my patients."

Sim stared at the doctor, then turned to Petyr. "You and I will have words about this later. You are not welcome in my home any longer."

"Get out!" The doctor pointed at the door.

Sim backed out of the room, glaring at Petyr the whole way.

Things in this place only get worse. Maybe I should have just passed that girl by and gone on to Rocktree.

"Fine," said Ilsan. "Lay back down and rest. I can see you're not fully recovered yet, and I'm not letting you out of here until I'm sure you won't end up back here."

Petyr complied. The ache in his head beat worse against his skull with the blood pulsing from the argument.

"I don't know what you said to Sim, but I've never seen him that angry."

Petyr closed his eyes. "People don't like having their lies exposed."

Ilsan chuckled. "No, they don't."

⚔ ⚔ ⚔

Petyr didn't feel like he'd slept very long before Alec interrupted his rest by knocking on the door and letting himself into the room. Roderick followed Alec in.

"Glad to see you're awake. Nice haircut," said Alec.

Petyr groaned. "I was sleeping." He ignored the dig about the hair.

"You sent for us."

Petyr sat up. The headache seemed only a minor annoyance.

"I did send for you. Have you taken Roderick to see your discovery?"

"He did," said Roderick. "It's disturbing. Some four foot high little gnome, tortured in the same way our girls have been. What do you think it means?"

"All I know is that it means the giant predates the town. That gnome, or whatever it is, has been in that clearing for a long time."

"But why did it never bother us before? Dunsriver has been here for decades."

"I don't know. Maybe it was asleep and something woke it up. Maybe it left for a while and only recently came back."

Alec took the seat in the corner of the room and sat down. "You know what's strange about it?"

"Everything is strange about it," said Petyr.

"No tracks. That thing didn't leave any tracks, at least, not beyond the fields."

"How could a thing that size not leave any tracks?"

"Well, it did leave tracks, in the town and the fields. But as soon as they reached the forest, the tracks disappeared, as if the thing just vanished."

"That doesn't even make sense."

"I was with him," Roderick said. "There are large tracks, right up to the edge of the forest, then nothing. It's been that way every time."

Petyr put his hands up to run them through his hair, but felt only skin. The lack of hair unsettled him. It didn't help him think. Carree hadn't even mentioned it.

"Did you bring the body of that gnome back?"

Alec shuddered. "No, we left it."

"Good, I want to have Ilsan examine it, but I want him to see the clearing. He might see something we've missed."

"Good luck getting him out there," said Roderick. "He's a good doctor, but…"

Petyr cut him off. "I think he'll go to see this."

"See what?" Ilsan peeked his head into the room.

"A four foot skeleton in the forest."

He stepped all the way into the room. "Why didn't you bring it here? I don't like going out. You know that."

"It's staked to a tree."

"Just like the girls?"

Petyr nodded.

"It's good you didn't move it. I suspect it would crumble to dust before you got it out of the forest."

"Then you'll go?"

"I'll go."

Roderick looked from Ilsan to Petyr. "How did you get him to do that? I can't get him out of this place to go a block down the street for a drink."

Ilsan laughed. "You've never offered me a four foot skeleton."

Roderick laughed, too, though it sounded strained. Petyr realized Roderick wasn't over the loss of his son or the girl that was out there, somewhere, in the forest with that thing.

"Roderick, there is something else I need to ask of you."

"Oh?"

"I need a place to stay. Sim expressed to me that I'm no longer welcome in his home."

Roderick's brow grew furrows. "Why would he say that?"

"I suspect he thinks I intruded into family matters I had no right to get involved in. I really can't say."

"You're talking about Bran."

Petyr held his tongue. It was about Bran, and Carree, and everything Sim had lied to them about. But saying anything more would put Carree at risk.

Roderick seemed to take his silence as confirmation. "Bran was a good kid, a skilled woodworker. It's a shame what happened to him, but that family has never gotten over it. And before three days ago, I didn't understand it." He didn't say any more, and sank, it seemed, into some internal contemplation.

Ilsan broke the silence. "You two can stay here. I've more than enough space and no secrets I fear you learning."

"Thank you."

"No need to thank me, Petyr. You bring interesting problems into my abode, which is something I rarely get here. Now, when do I get to see this skeleton?"

"We can go now," Alec said from the chair.

Petyr thought about staying behind, but quickly discarded the idea. He felt he had to see the skeleton again, to see the odd, alien face, to be there when Ilsan examined it. "I'm coming," he said. Then his stomach made sucking noises loud enough he thought the rest of them heard it. "After I get some food. I feel like I haven't eaten in days."

Ilsan quickly went from eager to businesslike. "After food, and an examination. I'm not letting you go out there without proving you're recovered."

"Fine." *At least he didn't say I couldn't go, yet.*

CHAPTER 13

Two hours passed before they finally made their way to see the skeleton. Ilsan cooked up soup and bread for Petyr. Then he spent a good half hour or more poking and prodding, making Petyr stand up, sit down, jump, and run in place. The headache still remained, but it seemed to have become more of a background ache than anything. Petyr almost didn't notice it.

Eventually, Ilsan declared him fit to go with them, but cautioned him against anything too strenuous.

Ilsan had also spent time checking in on the Questioner in his care, but had nothing new to report. The Questioner slept, unconscious still. Petyr despaired that he would ever wake up.

"It's in the hands of the Mother at this point," Ilsan had said.

Petyr resigned himself to the frustration. His salvation was as close as the next room, but as far as the Eastern sea, for all the good an unconscious Questioner would do him.

By the time they left, a light mist blanketed the town. Petyr knew they'd be wet through before they returned, but he felt time was running out. They had to do something.

Alec led the group across the field. Roderick walked next to him. Roderick seemed to have taken an interest in Alec after discovering what he was. He'd said nothing more about it, but he talked to Alec about topics from hunting, to tracking, to the politics of the outside world. Petyr had never really heard Alec discuss his positions on politics beyond his general distaste for the Empire.

Petyr and Ilsan followed behind. Ilsan had bundled up in a cloak and gloves that, combined, covered nearly every inch of his skin.

"Is all that necessary with the cloud cover?" Petyr had asked him.

"Yes. I can feel my skin burning even then."

As they crossed the Barren fields, Petyr felt like he was in an odd dream, or a bubble of sorts. He could see maybe a hundred feet around him. The mist obscured everything else, even the forest.

Soon, he heard voices, shouts. The loggers were working the edge of the forest again. The logging continued, despite the events of the last few days, and apparently, despite the mist.

As they approached the edge of the forest, the loggers came into view. A large tree lay on the ground, and they swarmed over it, clearing the branches from its length. A couple of the loggers saw them and stopped momentarily, curiosity on their faces. Roderick waved at them, and they went back to their work.

"They seem surprised to see you here, Roderick."

"Oh, I don't think it's me they're surprised to see. I think the three of you are the curiosity."

The trees loomed over them, but the mist obscured the tops. A wall of giants.

Alec led the rest of them, unflinchingly, into their midst. Among the trees, the light dimmed. The mist hung in the forest like a blanket, smothering everything.

"I think we need to hurry," said Petyr. It had to be past noon. "It's only going to get darker."

Alec picked up the pace. He worked his way through holes in the underbrush and found animal trails with an ease Petyr wished *he* possessed.

Petyr found it tough to keep up with him. Alec wasn't running exactly, but the forest didn't seem to slow him much. Every branch in the forest seemed to reach out and grab at Petyr, however. He imagined the forest was trying to keep him from going back to the clearing.

Petyr glanced back at Ilsan, thinking he might be struggling even more. Ilsan's sapphire eyes, however, stayed right on Petyr, and he appeared to have little trouble with the forest.

Eventually, after Petyr felt beaten and scratched all over, they emerged into the clearing. The skeleton still hung where they left it. The mist seemed a little lighter. He hoped it was starting to dissipate.

"Well, that skeleton is interesting," Ilsan said, and moved quickly over to it. "I've never seen anything like it."

"What do you think of it?" Petyr asked.

"It's not human, for sure. Other than the obvious height difference, which we could imagine it being a child, it has only four toes on each foot, and the eyes are offset to the side.

"The manner of death appears to be the same, though. Give me some quiet, would you?"

"Of course."

Roderick was looking at the skeleton. He seemed bemused by it.

Petyr had seen it before, and it held little interest for him, other than what Ilsan might uncover, so he started looking around the edge of the clearing. Alec joined him.

"What are you doing, Petyr?" he said softly.

"There's got to be something else here in this place, something to help figure out what's really going on."

"What's there to figure out? That thing is taking girls and dismembering them in the forest."

"I feel like there's more. This clearing, the skeleton. It happened before to whatever that thing is. Why did the people here not know about it until a few months ago? Was it laying dormant? Sleeping? Was it somewhere else and came back?"

"What does it matter? All we have to do is kill it."

Petyr stopped searching the ground and stared Alec in the eye. "Did you see what happened when Eduard and Willam shot at it? The shots were like bee stings to that thing. Painful, but hardly fatal.

"There are other questions, too. Why does it only come with the fog? Why is it only taking young women? Why does it seem to know where they are hiding? That last time, Roderick said it went right for the girl, through their home. It has a purpose."

"So it has a purpose. What does it matter if it does?"

"Alec, what if there are more than one? It's raping these girls. What's it trying to accomplish doing that?"

Alec's eyes grew wide. "You think it's trying to reproduce?"

"I think it's a possibility."

Petyr went back to searching the clearing. He didn't know what he was looking for, but there had to be something to give him some clue, something he could follow to someone he could question. Alec left his side and went to stand near Roderick, speaking quietly to him.

The loam on the floor of the clearing was thick. Anything left over from when the skeleton met its demise long ago was likely buried underneath. He hoped something might stick up from it, like a marker, or a bone from a washed out grave.

Near the edge of the clearing, right up against the gnarled roots of a tree, he thought he saw something and bent down to look at it. It turned out to be just a broken branch, the white of its wood exposed. The break was fresh.

As he examined it, he gradually began to feel that someone watched him. He looked at the others, but they were still engaged with the skeleton.

He looked over his shoulder, across the clearing, and thought, for a second, that he saw a flash. A pair of blinking eyes in the gloom of the forest. He got up, ignoring the broken branch, and ran to the other side of the clearing, but the eyes he thought he saw winked out and never reappeared.

What are you?

All he got back were alien thoughts. A feeling of curiosity with an undercurrent of fear, and a bit of sadness.

Where are you?

Nothing. It was gone.

The alien thoughts reminded him of something, but whatever it was escaped him.

He heard Alec step up behind him. "What's going on, Petyr?"

Petyr didn't look at Alec. He kept searching the forest depths for whatever he'd contacted. "Something was out there, watching us."

"Did you see it?"

"Only its eyes. It's gone now."

"Where was it?"

"Over there, somewhere," he said, pointing to where he'd thought it was.

Alec stepped out in front of him, moving slowly through the forest, examining the ground. Petyr trailed after him.

"Do you think it was dangerous?" Alec asked.

"I didn't get that feeling. It seemed afraid of us." *Or was it afraid of something else?*

Alec paused a couple times, then continued on. Petyr didn't think they'd find anything. The underbrush was just too thick, the bed of fallen needles, too spongy.

"Let's go back, Alec. There's nothing out here anymore."

Alec put his hand up to stop him. "Wait. Look here."

"What, where?"

Alec pointed to a spot on the ground where there was a puddle of water, where the dead needles were curiously absent. The lack of needles was the least of the curious things about the puddle.

On its edge, clearly visible and slowly filling with water, a footprint.

"Four toes," Alec said.

Four small ones. "Whatever that is hanging on the tree, there are still some of them alive. Could you follow it?"

Alec stared out into the forest. "Only if it wanted me to."

"What do you mean?"

"This footprint was deliberate. It wanted you to know."

"Why?"

"You're the Questioner. Why don't you ask it?"

"I tried." Petyr thought back to that attempt. The utterly strange response had reminded him of something, but he still couldn't place it. "I couldn't get an answer I understood."

Alec stood up. "We better start heading back, or we'll be out here in the dark."

"Right," Petyr said, then followed Alec back to the clearing. Petyr rolled over the incident in his head and couldn't make sense of it. *Why did it want me to know it was there? Was it trying to tell me something?*

They met the others in the clearing.

"Petyr," said Ilsan. "The specimen is completely intriguing. I wish I could bring it back and study it at length."

"Why can't you?"

"I fear it will crumble to dust as soon as those spikes are removed. It seems that whatever preserves the bodies is tied to those spikes. It's the only thing that make sense."

Petyr nodded. "Were you able to tell if it was raped?"

Ilsan glanced at it again, then turned back. "If it was raped, it wasn't raped by the creature that is taking the girls. The pelvis would have broken, and it's clearly not broken."

"So it's not the same creature."

"Who knows? This one died long ago. Decades, if not longer. The creature could have grown, or it could be different, or this one wasn't raped. There's no way to know."

"We've got a long way to go, and it's going to be dark soon," said Alec.

Ilsan looked at the skeleton one more time. "Right, right. I can come back."

Once again, Alec led them through the forest. It always amazed Petyr. Alec seemed to know where he was at all times. He didn't believe the trait came from being a Ghost. He'd have to ask Alec some time where the ability came from. Petyr didn't know much of Alec's past. One of the stipulations Alec had set when agreeing to help. Where did you to go?" Roderick asked.

"I thought I saw something in the forest, but it turned out to be a rabbit." Petyr felt reluctant to tell Roderick of what they found. *Why did I just lie to him? What's the harm in him knowing?*

He saw Alec turn his head to give him a curious glance, but Alec said nothing. Relief washed through Petyr. But he had to figure out what was going on. That creature had wanted him to see, to know. Why was he reluctant to tell Roderick?

He pondered it the entire time they worked through the forest, and still hadn't come to any conclusions as they emerged from the silent monoliths.

As they crossed the fields, Petyr realized the mists had parted while the group was ensconced in the forest. A layer of clouds still obscured the stars, but he could see the town in the distance.

Something tickled at the back of Petyr's head, like the eyes were watching him again. He looked back over his shoulder, and for a second, he thought he saw those bright eyes staring back from the dark of the forest.

A bright blue flash washed out whatever he'd seen in the forest, lighting up the clouds above.

"What was that?" It reminded him of lightning, but it had the wrong color.

"The Fringe," said Roderick.

"The Fringe?"

"It flashes like that, on occasion. We don't know why."

When the light faded, the eyes he thought he'd seen were gone. The color of the light had reminded him of something. For the second time, he thought he had a clue to something, but he couldn't place it. He worried that the damage to his head went deeper than a headache.

Another flash washed everything in that blue color.

"How long will it flash like that?"

"Most likely the rest of the night."

Petyr turned and followed them back to town. The Fringe flashed irregularly behind them, lighting everything up in that bright blue color. It was beautiful and fascinating and terrifying all at once. His blood raced with every flash. His mind raced in between.

I have so many questions for which I'm not getting answers. The idea that he couldn't get the answers bothered him almost as much as the flashing light behind him.

Then, like one of the flashes, a thought struck him. I have to visit the Fringe. I need to start finding truths.

CHAPTER 14

Petyr checked on the comatose Questioner the first thing after waking. Ilsan told him the same thing he'd said before. "There's no telling when he'll come to, if he ever does."

Petyr huffed, angry at no one in particular. The Questioner had to wake up. *I can't make that happen, so what do I do now?*

The blue flashes. They continued for several hours after he had returned to the town.

"Ilsan, do you have any idea how far it is to the Fringe?"

He laughed. "I've never been there, myself."

"I want to go see it today."

"Why would you want to do that? Strange things happen right near it, I've heard."

Petyr rubbed his head. It still felt strange to touch skin instead of hair. "After those flashes last night, I realized that I need to see it up close. I don't know why, really, but I feel like I need to go. Like I might find answers to some of my questions."

Ilsan nodded. "Then you must go."

He'd need a guide. The only person he knew that had been there was Sim. *I doubt he'll be excited to take me. Roderick might know someone else.*

He checked in on Alec and found him sleeping.

"Alec, wake up."

Without moving, Alec said, "Why?"

"We're going to visit the Fringe today."

"Whatever for?" He opened an eye.

"I don't know. Those flashes last night, they reminded me of something..."

"Lightning?"

"No, not lightning. Something else. The Fringe affects this whole town in some fashion. I need to see it to try and understand it."

Alec pushed himself upright. "Fine."

"Get something to eat. I have to talk to Roderick first and see if he knows someone who will guide us."

Alec nodded. "I'll be ready."

Petyr turned and stepped out into the hallway, heading for the front door on his way to the town hall.

As the tower of the town hall came into view, he realized he'd find Dyllan in the cellar. Petyr changed his plan. He'd see Roderick, but only after he looked in on Dyllan.

He had to find out Dyllan's state of mind, had to try to convince him of the truth. He needed Dyllan. If he ever had a chance at returning to his former life, he needed a Protector, and Dyllan was his only choice at the moment. Petyr just had to somehow convince Dyllan that he hadn't betrayed him, that he hadn't lied to him.

I didn't lie to him. I just didn't tell him. The argument felt hollow.

The entrance to the cellar of the Town Hall was guarded by a man with a gun. By the looks of him, he was a logger. He was nearly as large as Dyllan, though surely lacked Dyllan's gifts. He sat away from the door, facing it. He'd likely get one shot off before anyone coming out could stop him.

"Lord Questioner," the man said, shifting a little in his seat. "You seem better."

"I am, thanks. Do I know you?"

"I don't know if you saw me or not. I was one of the shooters at your rescue."

Petyr shook his head. He couldn't place him. "I need to speak with Dyllan."

"The Protector?"

Petyr nodded.

"Go on down. I warn you, though. He's got a foul temper."

Petyr chuckled. "I know." He remembered seeing the results of that temper more than once. He'd never been the recipient of that temper, but he was prepared for it. "Is there a lamp I can use?"

"There are two others down there guarding him. The mayor, he said to take no chances at letting him escape."

Probably not a bad idea. The bars down there were not set in stone at the top, and were instead drilled into a thick wooden beam. A good rush from Dyllan could possibly break them free.

Petyr opened the door and descended the steps into the cellar.

A pair of lamps lit the room. They rested on small tables next to a pair of men, both of similar build and stature to the man upstairs. They both glanced up quickly at Petyr, but just as quickly, returned to watching their prisoner.

Dyllan was in the same cell Petyr had recently occupied. He lay on the cot, seemingly docile. The Tracker was in the next cell, sitting on his own cot. He was looking straight at Petyr, even as Petyr came into view. The Tracker had known he was coming. *I'll have to do something about him.*

"What do you want Petyr?" Dyllan asked without moving.

The Tracker had told him.

"I came to see how you were doing."

"Horseshit." Dyllan sat up, favoring his leg in the move. It still wasn't completely healed. "You came here to gloat."

"You know me better than that." Petyr stepped up to the bars, but remained far enough away that Dyllan couldn't reach him. Dyllan stayed on the cot.

"You're right. You just prefer to betray people, and now, you've done it again."

"What did I do?"

"You lied to me again. You told me you'd come along quietly."

"The ambush was none of my doing."

Dyllan made a noise that sounded like a snarl. "Another lie. When are you going to stop?"

"Dyllan, you were my Protector for years. Why do you persist in believing that I'm lying to you? When did I ever lie to you?"

"It's the only answer that makes sense. Why would the High Questioner accuse you of treason and sedition? You skulked around, went places without me, and didn't tell me what you were up to. What else am I supposed to believe?"

"Me," Petyr said. "You're supposed to believe me. I was investigating them. Several of the High Lords were plotting against the Emperor, somehow. I had enough evidence they were plotting something. I told the High Questioner what I found. I didn't believe he was involved. I was wrong. I never thought about questioning him first." *And that was about the least intelligent move I've ever made.*

"But, all the Questioners?"

"Nobody ever Questioned me. He didn't let them. Why do you think you were told to keep your Questioners from Questioning me?"

Dyllan stood awkwardly and hobbled to the cell door. "Come here."

Petyr was reluctant. He didn't think Dyllan would hurt him. They're history went back too far, but he needed reassurance. "You won't harm me?"

Dyllan put his hands down to his side. "I promise."

Petyr heard the truth in Dyllan's statement and stepped up to the bars so that Dyllan's face was only inches from his. He heard the men behind him move so they could have Dyllan in their view.

"Look, Petyr," Dyllan whispered. "You should have told me what you were doing. I might have helped, it might have been easier to understand. But instead, you ran when they came after you. What was I supposed to think?"

"You should have trusted me."

"You broke that trust."

"I knew what I was doing was dangerous. I didn't want you to get caught up in it."

"That worked out well, didn't it. Here's my offer. If you bring the other Questioner down here, and you tell him what you're telling me, and he confirms it as the truth, I won't chase you any more."

Dyllan surprised him. Petyr hadn't thought Dylan would propose bringing the Questioner down. Still, it wasn't enough.

"I need your help," Petyr said.

Petyr could see the hurt in Dyllan's eyes. In trying to protect him, he'd hurt him worse than he could have imagined.

"I can't promise you that," Dyllan said.

$$\text{人} \quad \text{人} \quad \text{人}$$

By mid-day, Petyr and Alec stood facing the wall of trees that grew between them and the Fringe. Petyr was counting on Alec's ability to know where he was to get them to the Fringe. He hadn't found anyone willing to guide him. The best he'd managed were instructions from Roderick that it lay northwest of the road that passed by Dunsriver. Sim just slammed the door in Petyr's face.

He had wanted to bring the horses, but had been discouraged by Roderick. A somewhat thick underbrush clogged the space between the trees. He could see paths through it, but none were large enough to travel while riding. They'd be leading the horses all the way to the Fringe.

Petyr glanced over at Alec, who stood straight despite the heavy pack burdening his thin frame. Petyr's own pack, filled with a donated change of clothes, some food, a tarp, and a bedroll, caused him to hunch over a bit to keep him from falling backward. By the end of the day, he suspected he wouldn't be able to stand.

"You ready for this?" Petyr asked.

"Does it matter?"

Petyr shook his head. "I suppose not."

Alec stepped forward and into a breach in the underbrush

without another word. *Why are you still standing here? Visiting the Fringe was your idea.*

He adjusted the pack on his shoulders, trying to keep it from chafing. Then he took a breath and followed Alec along the path that would lead him to the Fringe.

He quickly caught up to Alec. Alec had already pulled out a hatchet they'd been advised to bring and was using it to clear some thick vines out of the way.

"Tell me, Petyr," he said between swings, "just why are we going to the Fringe? Why aren't we leaving?" A last whack, and they broke through to a thin trail that seemed to lead in the right direction, at least for a while.

"We already had the conversation about leaving," Petyr said.

"I want to hear it from you again. The situation has changed since the last time we discussed it. We could be days gone before they could follow us. They don't have any Questioners to speak of."

"They have a Tracker."

Alec looked over his shoulder, and Petyr saw a dark look cross his face. "The Tracker could be taken care of, and you know it."

"I do know it, and I don't want to solve the problem that way." Petyr knew little of Alec's past. They hadn't talked about it much. A rogue Ghost wouldn't survive without some sort of ruthlessness in his nature, and Alec had lived with a death sentence over his head his entire life. Petyr had only lived with it for a year. "I don't want to kill anyone, Alec."

"What is your plan, then? Tie him up and hope he stays tied?"

"I need that Questioner to wake up. If I can get him to question me in front of Dyllan and the Tracker, they'll see I'm telling the truth."

Alec stopped his trudge through the forest and turned to face Petyr. "And that will get you what, exactly?"

"Dyllan was my Protector. He's got Alura and my daughter. I *need* him to believe me. I need his help."

Alec snorted. "We don't need his help. We're better off without him."

"Alec, my wife and my child are alive, and he knows where. I need him in order to get them back."

"Get them back? How do you expect to get them back? If you go anywhere near Genova, you'll find yourself hung within an hour."

Petyr didn't have anything to say to that. Going back entailed a huge risk, a risk anyone going with him would share. He stared past Alec into the forest, hoping something would occur to him.

"Tell me something, Petyr. Why do you even think the Questioner would tell them the truth?"

Petyr felt like a naive little boy being lectured by his father. Of course, there was nothing to prevent the Questioner from lying.

"Not all Questioners are like you, Petyr. They lie and keep secrets like the rest of us. Look at what the Tribune did to you. Questioners are held up by the Emperor as paragons of virtue. You're the only one I've met who has ever lived up to that standard."

Petyr didn't know what to say to that. He still remembered his lie to Roderick, and Alec had caught him at it. It had been a little thing, but it proved Alec's point as much as anything. "I'm no paragon of anything, Alec."

"Are you referring to that little evasion of Roderick back in the clearing?"

"Evasion? I lied." *For the first time since I took the Questioner's Oath.* "I don't even know why I lied."

Alec nodded. "You lied because to do otherwise would be breaking a confidence. That creature wanted you to know it was there. It went to all that trouble to hide itself, but left that one print just for you to find. Ultimately, you were only withholding knowledge until you have all of the facts. In our situation, it is only prudence."

"Withholding information lost me my wife, my child, and my Protector." Petyr pushed past Alec and strode down the trail. More of the forest reached out to grasp at him without Alec in front, but he didn't care. Memories of his meeting with the Tribune, the vision of the Tribune's eyes growing colder and colder as Petyr spoke, drove him onward along the animal trail.

He heard Alec hurrying to catch up with him. "Petyr, you know that's not true. Confiding in the wrong person is what cost you those things."

"You can't have it both ways, Alec. I can't be a paragon of virtue and be evasive at the same time."

"Petyr, stop."

The command in Alec's voice stunned Petyr, and Petyr did stop. He didn't turn around, though.

"You are a fugitive, Petyr. You must use care in choosing whom you trust. You don't have the luxury of telling the truth all the time, or it will kill you. I can't believe you haven't learned that after all this time."

Petyr listened, but kept his mouth shut. He knew Alec spoke the truth. Could feel it. Could hear it. *I can't accept it, though. How can what he says be true, yet conflict with everything I believe?*

"If you insist on rescuing your wife and your daughter, make a plan. Be thorough. Don't rush back and grab them. Where would you take them? How would they handle surviving like that?"

Petyr tried to shake his head, but it felt like it hardly moved. "I don't know," he whispered.

"Mother, I can't believe I'm saying this. Petyr, I'll help you get her back. Just have a plan, first. Know how you'll get them, and where you'll take them, and what you'll do to stall any pursuit."

Petyr nodded, still refusing to look at Alec.

Alec stepped around him, put cold hands to either side of Petyr's face, and forced Petyr to look at him. "If you ignore what I'm telling you, they'll die, too." After a moment, he dropped his hands, and strode off along the trail.

Petyr stood, frozen, watching the distance between him and Alec expand. *How long will it be before I see her again if I listen to Alec? But, he's right. They'll die for real this time if I don't come up with a plan.*

He had no idea what that plan would look like, though.

He heard Alec's voice call out, just as Alec was about to disappear around a bend in the trail. "Are you coming, Petyr?"

She's safe for now. I have time. Keep telling yourself that. You have time.

He hurried after Alec.

⚔ ⚔ ⚔

It seemed to Petyr several hours passed while they worked their way through the depths of the forest. During that time, Alec said nothing to Petyr, and Petyr kept his thoughts to himself.

He used the time to ponder a number of plans. He didn't want to admit it, but Alec had been right. Petyr's original idea for going back to Alura had several flaws, not the least of which was the complete lack of an idea of what to do after he found her. His entire thought process had ended at the idea of reuniting with her.

He tried thinking back to what his plans were prior to finding out she lived, prior to stopping at Dunsriver, and he came to the conclusion he didn't really have any plan of action, which was why he'd become sidetracked at the sight of the tortured woman. He'd only had a vague notion of using the notes and evidence he'd collected in his trunk to illuminate the truth, to light the dark paths those above him trod.

He couldn't go back to that, the running and hiding with little purpose. Alec was right. He couldn't just run to Alura and hope for the best.

Petyr despaired over the loss of the trunk. Whatever chances he had of righting the wrong done to him was lost with the chest. *There's little chance of gathering that kind of evidence again.*

Every plan he devised ultimately broke upon the lack of the trunk and its contents. He couldn't think past proving himself innocent.

Lost in thought as he was, he didn't notice when Alec stopped ahead of him. He walked right into Alec, nearly knocking them both to the ground.

"Petyr!"

"Sorry, I was trying to follow your advice."

Alec turned and looked at Petyr, his face scrunching up. "What?"

"A plan. I was trying to make a plan."

"Ah," said Alec. "Worry about that later. Look ahead of us, through the trees."

Petyr looked where Alec directed, and for a moment, didn't see anything special. "I don't see..." But then he did see, a sliver between a pair of distant trees. Something blue beyond them, and his heart seemed to double beat for a moment as he recognized it. It was the same blue as the mist.

Fear lanced through him. "The mist, it's spreading again, out here?"

"I don't think so."

Petyr looked again through those trees, but couldn't discern any changes. He could only see the sliver peeking through. He tamped the fear down. "Let's move closer. I can't tell anything about it from here."

Alec crept forward. Petyr kept as close to him as possible, even putting a hand on the back of Alec's pack. He kept his eyes on the sliver of blue as they moved through the trees.

As they drew closer, more and more of the blue mist showed through the gaps in the forest. The ground beneath their feet grew rockier, and the underbrush thinned out.

When they came to within about twenty feet of the mist, there were few trees between it and them. The mist swirled, in place. Petyr felt reasonably sure it was not spreading. It looked much like a giant, blue wall, extending in either direction as far as they could see. Petyr thought, for all that he knew it shouldn't be possible, like it was aware of him.

"I don't like this, Petyr," said Alec.

Petyr ignored him, and moved in closer. Something about it felt familiar. He pressed up close to it, almost within arms reach, and watched the patterns swirl in it. He couldn't see through it, though. It watched him.

"Petyr!"

Alec's voice. Distant. *What is this? Why does it move, yet look solid, and remain in place like a wall?* It was the same color as the mist that swept over the town and brought the giant. He reached out, his fingers just shy of touching it. Something about it seemed familiar, even more familiar than the memory of the fog.

He leaned forward, just a little, and let his fingers brush its surface.

The world reeled as something entered his mind, a malevolent force, intent on a goal he didn't know. He tried to pull away, but he couldn't. The mist seemed to solidify, trapping his fingers. The force, the being, rummaged through his mind, bringing thoughts and memories he could barely recall into stark relief.

"Petyr! Come away!"

He should know that voice, but the reason why escaped him. He couldn't pull away if he wanted to.

It searched through memories of his training, sifting them, looking for something. It found the memory of his first encounter with the treasonous behavior of the Lords that eventually cost him Alura. It followed that thread through to his meeting with the Tribune, then to his escape from the Hall of Questioner's and his return to his home and the tragedy that had occurred there. It lingered over Alura's defense of him, and her fall to the floor. And then, it skipped quickly over everything after, until his arrival at Dunsriver, and his first talk with Sim where he learned about Bran, and saw the brandy cabinet, and the carving on its face, and the veil strung between the trees.

And then the contact broke, and he was pulled away from it and tumbled to the ground in a heap mingled with Alec.

Alec was talking to him, but Petyr couldn't focus on anything Alec said.

Petyr remembered the malevolence he'd felt when he touched the veil on that cabinet. That same malevolence had touched him just now.

"Alec," he said. "We've found the Fringe."

CHAPTER 15

"The Fringe?"

Petyr struggled to push himself up from the pile Alec and their packs had created, but found his equilibrium off, and fell back to the ground. His elbow landed on something soft, and forced an "oof" to escape from Alec's lips.

"Sorry," he said.

Alec pushed him off, and Petyr rolled onto his side.

"What do you mean? How can this mist be the Fringe?"

"It is, I know it. It's alive somehow. It..."

Alec's hand came down from above, and Petyr reached out. Alec pulled him to his feet.

"Alec," Petyr said, "it searched my memories, somehow."

"Searched them?" Alec's eyes narrowed.

"I'm not sure how to describe it exactly, but it brought all of my memories to the surface. It ran through my life. I relived it, in a way."

"You just stood with your hand extended touching it."

"How long?"

"A minute, at most. You wouldn't respond to anything I said."

Petyr looked up at the Fringe. The patterns in the swirls almost made sense to him now. In a way, he felt connected to it. "It seemed a lifetime," he said under his breath.

Petyr felt Alec pull at him. "Let's get away from it. I don't like being this close. It feels…"

"Malevolent. That's what you're thinking. It's not directed at us, though."

"What do you mean?"

"I'm not sure. Just a feeling I guess. It… I don't think you could have pulled me free if it didn't want you to." As Petyr thought about it, it felt more like a certainty.

"That doesn't make any sense, Petyr. It's just a mist."

"But it's not. It has a consciousness, a purpose."

"Well, I'm getting away from its purpose. I have no desire to sleep so close to it."

Petyr watched him turn and walk away, then turned back to the wall for a moment. *What is your purpose?*

Whatever malevolence he'd felt from it was gone, replaced with ambivalence. After a moment, he looked around and realized that evening was upon him. The daylight had begun to fade.

Off to his right, he heard the snap of a branch, and he looked quickly toward it.

Among the trees, he saw a moving shadow stop and grow still. He watched it, and thought about moving closer to investigate, but with the darkening forest, he decided it might not be the best idea. *It's probably just a deer or something. Nothing to worry about.*

And indeed, he realized it didn't worry him. He turned away from it and started down the trail after Alec.

"Petyr, wait," a voice called out from behind him. A female voice he recognized.

He spun around. "Carree?"

She stepped forward out of the shadows of the trees. "Listen, I…"

"What are you doing out here?"

"I followed you," she said while picking her way toward him. She wore a pack like his, only smaller. She'd prepared for the trip.

"Why?"

She stopped a few feet in front of him and looked up at the Fringe. "It's beautiful, isn't it? I can see why Bran went in."

"Why are you here, Carree?"

"I wanted to see it. My father never brought me here."

"You shouldn't be here."

Her head turned back to him, and he caught a flash of her eyes. The Fringe seemed to be reflected in the whites. "I can be wherever I want."

"Your father..."

"My father will not do anything about it. What's he going to do, lock me in my home?"

"You shouldn't Coerce him, Carree."

She laughed. "I don't even have to do that, Petyr. I'll threaten to tell Mother about his lies. I'll tell her the truth about Bran. My father holds no power over me any more."

Petyr didn't have any response for that.

"I want to apologize, Petyr."

The sky had darkened more, but the area around them remained lit, though tinted with an eerie blue reflection of the Fringe.

"Why?"

"You told me the truth. I shouldn't have run out on you, I was just so upset."

The glow unnerved him. Something else picked at his mind, but he couldn't place it. He no longer felt comfortable so close to the Fringe. "I accept. Let's find Alec and get food and sleep."

"Petyr, I want to go with you when you leave." She said it in a rush.

"No," he said. His thoughts leaned another direction. *She could be useful.*

"Please, Petyr?" She stepped even closer to him, and looked up, the pupils of her eyes dilated and pleading.

"You don't know what I face, Carree. It wouldn't be safe for you."

A hint of defiance ran through her. "I have an idea of what you face. I heard your argument with Alec. I could help."

She could help, but I don't want to put her at risk. He didn't have an answer. His opposing desires warred within him with near equal force, preventing any sort of resolution. He looked up to the sky and saw it had turned black. The light from the Fringe washed out the stars.

"Can we discuss it later? I really think we need to make camp."

Carree smiled at his offer to postpone it as if she thought it was a concession. Then she moved off through the forest down the path that would lead to Alec, leaving him there alone in the light from the Fringe.

I can't bring her to Genova, but then, I'm not going there yet. He strode off after her. It seemed the war in him had already been won without a declaration. Maybe something would happen before he left that would change his mind. He didn't have to tell her his decision right away.

With his mind settled, he picked up his pace to hurry after her. Despite knowing that the Fringe wasn't going to harm him directly, he had no desire to be left alone anywhere near it.

⚶ ⚶ ⚶

"What is she doing here?" Alec asked when Carree and Petyr stumbled across the camp Alec had started to set up on his own. A low fire already burned in a small pit, despite the generally damp conditions of the forest.

"She followed us," said Petyr. "I'm surprised you didn't know."

"I'm a Ghost, Petyr, not a Tracker."

"You could have fooled me," Petyr said, shrugging out of his pack. It landed with a thump on the forest floor.

Carree set her own pack next to his. "I can hide in the forest as well as anyone," she said.

Alec laughed. "Not as well as I can. Petyr's right, though. I should have noticed you. If it weren't for his stubborn refusal to listen to good sense when he hears it..."

"He loves his wife, Alec. I think it's romantic that he's willing to risk his life to get her."

Petyr started delving into his pack, searching out the food.

"Romantic? It's idiotic," said Alec. "She's better off where she is right now."

"Don't you read stories, Alec? Haven't you ever been in love? She's probably laying in bed right now, wondering where Petyr is, wondering if he is still alive."

Petyr found the food he'd brought. Bread and smoked venison. He wished he'd brought wine or some of Sim's brandy to help him ignore the argument.

"Stories are for children. Romance, when you are a fugitive, will get you killed. You need to learn that, Carree."

Carree stamped her foot. "Romance is the only thing that will keep you alive. What else is there to live for?"

"Tomorrow is the only thing that people like us can hope for."

Petyr looked up at Alec. The flickering firelight made it difficult to discern Alec's expression, but it was easy to see his attention was still directed at Carree. "Do you really believe that, Alec?" Petyr asked.

Alec's gaze flicked to Petyr. "Yes, I do," he said, then went to his pack and started digging through it.

"Well," Carree said, "I don't." Petyr thought she was trembling. She then bent to her own pack and started rooting through it.

Petyr bent over to her and whispered, "If it helps, I don't believe it either."

She looked up from her pack, but not at Petyr. Her eyes went back to Alec. "Why is he like that?" She held her voice low, but Petyr thought Alec could hear it anyway. If Alec heard it, he ignored them, instead picking at the bread he'd found in his own pack.

"Like what?"

"So—cold."

"He's lived for most of his life hiding from the Empire's servants. If the wrong person found out about him, it could mean a quick death at the end of an executioner's rope."

"That's horrible."

"If you leave this town, if I let you come with me, your life will follow a similar path."

Alec looked up from his bread. "You can't seriously be thinking about bringing her with us."

"You said yourself I need a better plan. Until I'm done making that plan, I'm not going to eliminate any possible help." He still didn't want to bring her along. *I'm not sure I can stop her.*

"She'll be a liability, and there's no reason for her to leave. Dunsriver doesn't want Empire interference. There isn't a safer place to hide."

Carree almost growled at Alec. "You think this place is safe for me? With that demon or whatever it is taking women my age and killing them in such a disgusting fashion? It's just a matter of time before it comes after me!"

Alec sat back, almost leaning away from her. Petyr flicked his gaze back and forth between them. With his own troubles, it was easy to forget why he had even stopped in Dunsriver.

"Carree," Petyr said, "If we can stop this thing, you would not need to leave."

"By the Mother, Petyr," said Alec, "what makes you think we can stop this thing? It'll kill us just as sure as it killed Eduard and Willam. Guns don't even bother it."

What is the difference between us, Alec? Why are you so eager to leave? "I've told you already, you can leave any time you want. I have to figure this out. It's who I am."

Petyr withstood a stare from Alec for several moments, before Alec broke off and pulled out his bed roll, unrolled it, and lay down as if to sleep. "It's not who you are, anymore," he said, and then turned his back to them.

Petyr and Carree stayed silent as Alec shut them out. Then, as if some unspoken agreement passed between them, they pulled out their own bed rolls and laid down to sleep. Petyr stared into the flames of the fire. *You're wrong Alec. It is who I am. It is the Empire's servants who are not who they should be.*

"Seeker," the voice whispered in the back of his mind.

Petyr tried to open his eyes, but they felt heavy, filled with sand. They wouldn't open.

"Not out there, Seeker. In here."

"In where?"

"Open your mind. Follow path."

Open my mind? Follow path? What does that mean?

"Use your talent, Seeker."

You can hear my thoughts?

"As you hear mine. The path is clear. Follow."

Petyr cast around in his mind, searching for the path, but found only darkness.

"Open your mind, Petyr. Follow my thoughts to path."

Talent? Open my mind? Follow his thoughts? An idea occurred to him, and he tried it without pondering. He used that special ability he had, applied it to the disembodied voice.

The darkness drew aside, revealing a path, lined with trees, lit with a deep blue glow he thought seemed familiar. Someone stood at the other end of the path, but he could not make them out.

"Follow path, Seeker."

Petyr found he was standing, and he took a step toward the path.

Why do you call me Seeker? Petyr kept using his thoughts instead of his voice. It somehow seemed more appropriate.

A few more steps brought him to the edge of the path.

"It is what you are."

I am a Questioner.

"Are you sure he's right one?" Another voice, deeper and cracked.

"I'm sure. He has talent. I felt it."

What? What do you mean? What is going on?

"Step onto path, Seeker," said the original voice. "There is something you must see."

Petyr moved a reluctant foot onto the path, then the other. He looked up and saw the figure at the other end beckon to him. Petyr walked the path, paying attention to the trees. They hung over it, protective and watchful.

I'm on the path. Why do you call me Seeker?

"Use talent. You will know answer."

Petyr opened his mind to the owner of the voice again, and nearly fell to his knees. He probably would have if he were awake.

I was never a Questioner.

"You are so much more, Seeker."

And Petyr knew that now. *But...*

"You know answers, Seeker. Follow path."

He looked up, and found the figure at the end of the path had changed. At first, he thought it stood in front of a tree, but as he approached it, he realized he was wrong. A young woman hung from the tree, naked, like the others, blonde hair cascading around empty eye sockets. Only, on this one, her stomach looked bloated. He stood there for a moment, pondering, and then the stomach moved.

Oh, Mother.

"Find her, Seeker. Destroy thing in her belly."

Where is she?

"Use your talent."

Petyr's eyes popped open, and he found himself on his bedroll. Only dim red coals remained from the fire. The forest was dark, but for slivers of moonlight that slipped through the canopy. Alec and Carree slept.

"Wake up," he said.

He got up from his bedroll, then went to Carree and shook her. "Wake up!"

She moaned a little, but from Alec, he heard, "What's wrong, Petyr?"

Petyr stopped for a moment, indecisive. How could he explain to Alec. Now that he was awake, he only half believed his vision.

He wanted to call it a dream, but he had knowledge in him now that he hadn't had before, and it felt true.

"Just trust me. Pack up, we need to go somewhere."

Alec started to stand, and grumbled, "I don't think we even got an hours sleep."

Petyr knelt down to Carree and shook her some more. "Carree," he said. "Wake up. We've got to go."

She rolled over, and her eyes opened. "Why?"

"There's something—I'm not even sure if it's real, but I have to find out."

She sat up. "You had a vision."

Petyr nodded.

"You woke us up for a vision?" Alec asked.

Carree put her hand on Petyr's. "People often have visions and strange dreams when they sleep this close to the Fringe, Petyr. They don't generally turn out to mean anything."

"Or maybe they always mean something, yet people don't understand them."

Carree nodded, and stood. "Where are we going?"

"I'm not quite sure. It's close, I think."

Petyr went to work packing his bedroll.

For all his griping, Alec wore his pack already and was kicking dirt over the smoldering remains of the fire as Petyr tied his pack shut and lifted it onto his shoulders. Carree was also ready to follow him. A slice of moonlight fell across her face. She was looking at him expectantly.

"Where to, Petyr?" asked Alec.

So, how does this work? He hoped he'd get an answer from the voice in his vision, but heard nothing back.

"Petyr?" Alec's voice.

"Quiet," he said.

He looked around him, thinking the path might reveal itself as it had in the vision, but nothing jumped out.

Petyr started down the path toward the Fringe, thinking that might reveal something, but after a couple steps, it didn't feel right, and he stopped. He spun around again.

"Petyr?" This time, Carree.

He ignored her.

You idiot. The vision wasn't showing you the path.

He closed his eyes and opened his mind, like he had in the vision, only this time, he opened it thinking about the young woman. He wanted to find her. He turned slowly, keeping his eyes closed and his mind open, urging his talent to show him the path.

He felt something pull at him, a certainty. His desire, to find the victim of that giant, tugged him in the direction he faced, and he stopped turning and opened his eyes.

The vision was instruction, training. He knew it. His talent, as the voices in the vision called it, allowed him to work as a Questioner. It appeared he could do much more with it than he'd ever imagined.

"This way," he said, and started working through the trees in the direction of the pulling sensation.

The path he followed did not take them along an animal trail, or any other sort of trail. He quickly found the underbrush daunting, and asked Alec for the hatchet. If he knew the forest better, he could likely find a trail to take them nearer to his goal, but in the dim moonlit forest, the only direction he felt he could trust was the feeling that drew him forward.

They called me a Seeker. What is a Seeker? He felt certain he could find out if he wanted. He could learn anything, he suspected. His talent, his ability, could lead him to the answers.

Could it lead me to a way to destroy the giant? He suspected it could, if he knew how to direct it. But he kept his focus on finding the woman. He felt an urgency to find her. He hoped what he'd seen, the thing in her belly, was as metaphorical as the path had been.

His arm grew tired as he hacked his way through the forest, but the need to find her kept him going.

"Petyr, do you really know where you're going?" asked Alec.

Petyr didn't answer him. His goal drew near. Its pull grew stronger with every step. He hacked at bushes and low branches that sprung up out of the dark to clutch at him.

With a last crash through some vines, Petyr emerged into a clearing. Moonlight fell down into it from straight above. The clearing reminded him of the other clearing, where they'd found the strange little being.

He felt Alec and Carree emerge into the clearing. Carree gasped. "Uma!" she said.

Petyr had been seeing the clearing without seeing the clearing. Across from him, the young woman he'd seen in his vision hung from a tree, just like the first girl he'd found, just like the little being. Only, as in the vision, her belly swelled with some foreign life.

Petyr stepped closer. He held the hatchet. He knew what he had to do. Whatever grew in her wasn't human. As he grew closer, he stared at the belly, watched the the skin extend around some appendage as it moved within her.

Then he looked at the face, the empty eye sockets, the spike through the mouth.

"What are you going to do, Petyr?" Carree asked from behind him.

Something seemed odd about the face. Different than the others.

"I'm going to do what has to be done. I'm going to kill that thing that grows in her."

"But Petyr..."

The mouth moved, closed on the spike. Petyr jumped back. The woman, Uma, still lived. He didn't know how.

"What is it Petyr?" Alec asked.

"She still lives."

Carree gasped, and Alec moved closer to Uma.

A gurgling growl escaped Uma's lips, but the spike prevented her from forming words.

Petyr held the hatchet, but he couldn't make himself move forward. *I know I need to destroy the thing in her, but...*

His mind balked at the thought of killing Uma. He felt sure the thing growing in her would kill her, but contemplating killing her himself locked him up.

Carree moved close to Uma, reached out and caressed Uma's head. "Uma, I'm here."

Uma seemed to try to move her head, the muscles in her neck stood out with the strain. More noises escaped her throat.

"Petyr," Alec whispered in his ear.

"What?" Petyr couldn't take his eyes from Uma and Carree.

"You have to end it."

"I know," he said. The thing in Uma's belly pushed on her belly, extruding it around several bumps. Fingers?

"Why do you wait?"

"I can't do it. I know I have to kill that thing inside her, but I can't kill her."

"Petyr, look at her. She's already dead, or should be."

"It doesn't matter."

The movement in Uma's belly grew more agitated, pushing further. Blood started to spill down the insides of her legs. A moaning, agonizing sound passed her lips.

"Petyr," Carree said, turning her face to him. Her eyes spilled tears down her cheeks. "Spare her!"

Petyr didn't know if she Coerced him or if her voice just broke through whatever barrier that kept him from ending Uma's life, but either way, her cry penetrated and forced him into movement. He stepped forward, lifting the hatchet, readying it to sever her neck. His mind felt numb.

Carree stepped out of the way. Uma's body started shaking, the movement in her belly grew violent. Whatever it was, it knew what Petyr was about to do.

Petyr pulled his arm back to swing.

Just before he released the swing, blood gushed from Uma's mouth, around the spike, and down her chest. The fingers pushing out from her belly finally broke through, and a pair of bluish blood-stained hands ripped the flesh apart.

Blood spattered Petyr's face, his clothes. Peripherally, Petyr noticed Carree had fallen to the ground, and continued scrambling backward as best she could. He had no idea what Alec was doing.

A head emerged from the cavity. The face, he'd seen in dreams more than once since he'd first seen the giant. It had the same eyes, the same nose, only proportionately smaller. It looked at him, knowing. Petyr thought, somehow, it recognized him. He tried to use his talent, tried to open his mind, but as with the giant, he got rage, anger, and utterly alien thoughts. It hungered.

"Petyr!" Alec's voice behind him.

Petyr adjusted the hatchet, and swung down into that face, smashing the blade just above its nose. He felt something crack within it. It cried a piercing scream. He pulled back and swung again, hit the same place through luck, and the hatchet broke through the bone, sliced through an eye, and into the pulp of the brain. It went limp. Petyr pulled the hatchet free and swung again, and again. For his frustration. For his anger. He couldn't stop. For every dreadful thing that creature had done to these girls.

"Petyr! It's dead!" Alec's voice.

It's dead. The words echoed around in his head for a moment as he pulled the hatchet free. He looked at the dead creature. Its head was smashed to a meaty, bony mess.

Bile and acid flowed in his stomach. The smell of blood filled his nose. He dropped the hatchet, turned, and stumbled a few steps away before vomiting into the brush.

CHAPTER 16

None of them wanted to spend the night in the forest. After Petyr's stomach settled down, they didn't take very long in deciding to head back to the town. It took longer to decide between leaving Uma's body and taking it with them. Ultimately, they decided Ilsan would want to examine it.

With a lot of effort, they managed to remove the spikes and get her body off the tree. Petyr threw the spikes to the edge of the clearing in disgust. None of them wanted to remove the thing in her stomach. Petyr knew Ilsan would want to see it, too. They wrapped her up in a tarp, and lashed it tight around her with some rope meant for stringing the tarp up to trees. Petyr and Alec took turns pulling it through the forest. While one pulled, the other broke a trail. Carree helped break the trail, too, but she stayed far away from the tarp and its contents.

Just before dawn, through either providence or luck, Petyr never could decide, they broke out of the forest and onto the road just as a merchant in a cart approached from the direction of Dunsriver. Carree knew the man, called him Horace. A quick negotiation with the merchant resulted in a ride for them back to Dunsriver.

"You're father's in a stew looking for you," the merchant said to Carree, after they had loaded their bundles and Uma's tarp wrapped body onto the already laden cart.

"It's a good thing you found me, then, isn't it." She turned away from him and didn't look at him the rest of the trip.

"Uma's parents will be glad you found her," Horace said to Petyr.

Petyr's eyes felt like closing. He didn't really want to respond to the merchant's statement. *I don't think they'll be very glad.*

When Petyr didn't respond, the Merchant looked at him, then turned back to the road, and said nothing else for the remainder of the trip, which pleased Petyr. He pulled a blanket to his neck, closed his eyes and tried to rest, but he couldn't stop thinking about the vision that led him to find Uma.

They'd called him a "Seeker". He'd hoped to find a cart to help them carry their burden. Did he make that happen? Or did he somehow lead them to it? Or was it just luck? How did his ability really work? What could he do with it? He'd always known he could do things the other Questioners could not. But now, he wondered at his limits. He wondered why he knew of no others like him.

They emerged from the forest onto the barren farmland just as the sun broke the horizon, spilling orange light onto the earth.

When they reached the wall, Roderick and Sim stood there waiting. Apparently, someone had noticed Horace returning a bit too early.

Sim rushed to the cart, almost before it came to a stop. Petyr sat up and received a look he didn't quite understand from Sim.

"Horace," Sim said, "you found her."

"I don't know about that. They were already on their way back. I just gave 'em a ride."

"And you, Carree, what did you think you were doing, and what is that all over you?

Petyr expected her to yell at her father, or not say anything, but instead, she jumped down from the cart and hugged her father. He hugged her back, surprise on his face. He looked to

Petyr for the first time, and apparently noticed Petyr covered in blood, too. Petyr had wiped at his face, but could do little about his clothes.

Roderick noticed at about the same time. "What happened to you?"

Petyr nearly answered, but looked around and saw a small crowd gathering. He thought it prudent that they not talk about it where everyone could hear. The memories of it were bad enough. He didn't want ugly rumors spreading through town, not until Roderick could hear the story and digest it.

"Can we just go to Ilsan's and talk about it there? We need to get cleaned up and rest."

Roderick looked around, and he apparently silently agreed with Petyr's assessment. "Of course."

Sim had started to turn away, but Petyr called out to him. "Sim, you should come, too."

Sim turned to him, anger apparent on his face. "I need to take my daughter home."

"You're an Elder, are you not? You need to see what we found." He wanted to mention that Carree had followed them on her own, but decided not to bring that up. Whatever problems Sim's family had, they were Sim's and Carree's to hide or expose.

"What did you find?"

Petyr glanced back at the wrapped figure of Uma where it lay in the cart. He could see some blood on the tarp. Fortunately, Sim followed his glance and figured out what the tarp hid, or at least part of it. Petyr saw some whisperers in the growing crowd.

"Fine, I'll meet you at Ilsan's right after I take my daughter home."

"Would it be acceptable to have Alec take her home?"

Sim stared at him for a moment, then to Alec. Alec had somehow escaped most of the blood that had erupted and coated Petyr. "It's that urgent?"

Petyr nodded. Petyr knew Alec likely didn't want to escort her home, but Alec didn't need to be around to explain anything, and he wouldn't scare Sim's wife when he showed up. He could also explain to her what happened in a way that Sim would not be able to.

"You take care of her, sir," Sim said to Alec.

"Of course," said Alec as he jumped down from the cart. Petyr caught a look of annoyance from him as Alec reached into the cart to grab Carree's pack, then he turned and took Carree's arm and began walking her home.

Petyr moved to make room for Sim to climb up onto the bench next to him, but after Sim appeared to take the measure of Petyr, he declined. "I'll walk."

Petyr looked down at himself, and understood Sim's reluctance. Petyr moved back to where he'd sat before, and Horace said, "Thank you." Petyr wondered if Horace would have offered them the ride if he'd been able to see Petyr clearly in the dark.

Horace got the cart moving. Roderick and Sim trailed behind, talking quietly to each other. Others also followed for a distance, until Roderick turned around and admonished them to return to their work. "I'll tell you what you need to know when I know it."

When they arrived at Ilsan's, the doctor opened the door on the first knock, almost as if he knew they were coming. The four of them maneuvered the tarp covered body into an examination room and placed it on the table.

"Before we unwrap the body, I need to warn you. This is not like the other bodies."

"What do you mean?" Roderick asked.

"It's just—I think you should imagine the worst possible outcome you can think of. What happened to her is worse."

Roderick's face paled.

Petyr undid the bindings around the tarp, then started folding it back. He began with her head, and heard Roderick whisper, "Uma." He exposed more and more of her, and then one side of the tarp fell out of his hand, pulled away, and fell to the floor, exposing the thing that had erupted from her stomach.

Gasps echoed from the walls. Sim turned away and retched.

Ilsan moved in closer. "What is that?"

Petyr pulled the other edge of the tarp from the body, exposing the rest of the creature. "I think it's the offspring of the giant that took her."

"Its head is all smashed."

"I had to kill it. All I had was a hatchet."

"You didn't have to be so thorough."

Petyr couldn't think of anything to answer that. Whatever had come over him, it had taken control. He hadn't been able to stop himself.

Ilsan poked at it with one of his tools, then lifted one of its arms to examine it. "The claws are sharp already. Amazing this grew in her in only a few days."

Petyr didn't find it amazing. He found it confusing, and terrifying. *How did this thing grow inside her so fast if those spikes keep the bodies of the girls preserved? Shouldn't the spikes have kept it from growing, too?* Whatever the answer, the spikes hadn't prevented its growth.

"Ilsan," said Roderick. His voice seemed to crack a bit. "Get that thing out of her and cover her up. I have to tell her father."

Ilsan looked up from his examination, his pale face momentarily confused. Then the confusion cleared. "Oh, right."

"And Petyr, go clean up. I need to talk to you, and I'd rather not do it while you smell like death."

Petyr heard a knock at Ilsan's front door, and then heard it open, and then voices. A man, a woman, crying. "Ilsan! Where is she?"

"Damn," said Roderick. "Someone already told them."

Roderick tried to shut the door to the room, but a man quite a bit larger than Roderick pushed his way through, followed by his wife.

Her face was red, flushed from crying. "Uma!" Then, as she saw the thing protruding from her daughter's stomach, she stopped and pointed, "What is that? Brue! What is that?"

Brue came to a stop at the sight of his daughter. He said nothing.

"Brue!" Brue's wife turned and buried her head in Brue's chest.

Sim and Roderick grabbed the two of them and started pushing them back out into the hall. "Come on, Bruent, you don't need to see this," said Roderick as he pushed at them.

At first, they made slow progress, and then Brue seemed to come to his senses a little bit and started helping to pull his wife from the room. When they were in the hall, Roderick pulled the door shut, leaving Petyr alone with Ilsan.

Petyr wished he hadn't seen that. He knew the emotions they felt. He'd had them himself, when he thought Alura dead.

"It's a shame they saw that," Ilsan said. "Would have been better had they believed she hadn't suffered much."

Ilsan surprised Petyr a little. Petyr had thought Ilsan cared little about other's feelings.

"Tell me something, Petyr. When you found her, she still lived, didn't she."

Petyr nodded, trying not to remember.

"This thing clawed its way out."

Petyr nodded again. Then shook his head back and forth trying to clear the memory. "Ilsan, I need to clean up and rest. Just—figure out how we can kill that thing's maker."

"You know, Petyr, whatever it is, it's no beast."

"I know. It has a plan, and it has a magic like we've never seen. It can keep these girls alive far past the point they should have died. I need to know why."

"I'll see what I can learn."

"Thank you."

⚔ ⚔ ⚔

After a thorough scrubbing in the bath, Petyr climbed into bed and slept for several hours. He woke up, thankful for not remembering his dreams, if indeed he'd had any.

Most of the clothes he'd worn were likely ruined. He wished he had his trunk so that he could wear his own clothes and not have to borrow from Ilsan.

He stepped out of his room and went down the hall to Ilsan's library where he found the doctor sitting in his chair, reading and sipping brandy.

He must have heard Petyr enter, for he said without looking up, "Ah, Petyr."

Petyr sat in a chair opposite the fire that burned in the fireplace. The warmth was inviting. "How did you know?"

"There are only two other people living in my home at the moment, and you make far more noise than Alec."

"Only two? What happened to the..."

"Oh, sorry. The Questioner. He woke hours ago, and they moved him to the holding cells."

Petyr jumped up, irritated he hadn't been told earlier. "You didn't tell me?"

"You were sleeping. I figured you'd want to be rested before dealing with him. Sit back down. You don't need to go rushing over there right away."

But I do. Petyr sat, however. "Why am I sitting?"

"First, you're probably hungry. I have some cakes and water here for you."

Petyr looked and found that the table bore a plate of cakes and a mug of water. His stomach grumbled, so he reached over and picked out a cake to eat. "Why else?" he asked between bites.

"I think we are very lucky you found Uma when you did. That creature in her, it grew at an unnatural rate. How long was it in her? A few days at most? How quickly would it have grown outside?"

Petyr nodded. "I wondered those things myself."

"Can you imagine having two of those things wandering around? I can only surmise why we aren't already overrun with them. Even a man's seed doesn't always take in a woman. Perhaps it is even more difficult for this creature to impregnate them."

Ilsan leaned over close to him, almost as if he wanted to speak in confidence, though no one but the two of them were in the room. "I think the spikes keep the women alive until the creature inside matures—or dies."

"Then why would it preserve the bodies after death?"

"A side effect of the magic. Who knows? But Uma should not have been alive when you reached her. The creature was eating her from the inside."

Petyr's stomach grew ill and he wished he hadn't started eating. He set the cake back on the plate.

Ilsan looked at him, then a sheepish grin crossed his face. "Sorry."

"You know, this is interesting, but I'm not sure how it's useful."

Ilsan sat back and frowned, then stared into the fire. "I don't know how it's useful, either. I studied that thing, Petyr. All it's parts are essentially in the same place as ours. Fundamentally, I would say it should be human, but it's not. Your work on its skull, unfortunately made it impossible to determine if a weakness exists there."

Petyr nodded. He'd expected this sort of report.

They sat in silence for awhile. Petyr watched the flames flicker, but thought of little. Then he let his eyes travel the books packed on the shelves. "Brion's Anatomy". "Romances Of Rein Shorewood". "A History Of The Genovan Empire".

"You seem to have books on every topic, Ilsan," said Petyr. "I haven't seen so many since visiting the library at the Academy."

"I've collected books wherever and whenever I've been able to. They are the only path I have to the outside world."

"Have you read them all?"

Ilsan looked around the room. "Some more than once."

"Tell me," said Petyr. "Have you ever heard of a Seeker?"

Ilsan turned and looked at Petyr with the same sort of eye Ilsan used when examining the bodies. "Not in my books. Why do you ask?"

"After we made camp last night, I had a dream that led me to find Uma."

Ilsan's eyebrows raised a bit. "Strange things are known to happen in the vicinity of the Fringe."

Petyr nodded. "So I've been told. During this dream, I heard a disembodied voice. It called me a Seeker."

Ilsan sat back in his chair, but still regarded Petyr with that same eye. It made Petyr uncomfortable, and he fidgeted in his chair.

"It explained to me how to use my 'talent' to find Uma."

"So that's how you found her. I asked Alec, and he wasn't very specific."

Petyr closed his eyes, re-imagining their dash through the forest. "I concentrated on her, and I had this certainty as to her direction. It led me right to her."

Ilsan said nothing, and the room again grew quiet, but for the crackling of the fire.

It's time I go talk to that Questioner. He started to stand.

"Petyr, wait. I was just trying to see if I could recall anything helpful. I don't know of any references to a Seeker in my collection. However, I read an ancient book once, the title of which I can't recall. It was a book about the talents. There are, or were, many more talents than we recognize today."

Petyr was surprised at this. They had never mentioned it at the Academy. "How many more talents?"

"I didn't count them. I had access to the book for only a short time. I read what I could about the current talents."

Petyr's excitement ebbed. He'd have to go looking for the book and read it for himself.

"When I read about Questioner's, though, it said something you might find useful."

"What?"

"A Questioner is a lower form of Seeker."

Which would make sense, then, since Petyr had been trained as a Questioner. He could perform as a Questioner. But he could do more. If he only knew what.

"I wish you had followed that thread."

"I find myself wishing the same thing, now."

"Where is the book?"

Ilsan looked away from Petyr, returning his gaze to the fire. "My homeland."

A thousand miles. More. "I guess that helps a bit. It concerns me, though. If there were Seekers before, what happened to them?"

"What happens to any talented group that threatens a government?"

Petyr knew all too well. The answer was an extension of what happens to any one person the government believes threatening.

He stood up. Thinking about the possibilities wouldn't solve his immediate problem. Seeker or no, at the moment, if the Empire caught him, he'd find himself just as dead.

"Thanks for the cakes. I'm going to go visit our Questioner guest." *I can only hope he isn't involved with the conspiracy against me.*

CHAPTER 17

Petyr opened the door, expecting to step outside, but found Sim standing in the rain, blocking the doorway. Sim looked cold and wet through, and Petyr wondered how long Sim stood at the door before Petyr opened it. Petyr saw conflict in Sim's face.

"Sim," said Petyr.

"I need to talk to you."

Petyr made room for Sim to step in. "Come in out of the rain."

"No, I…" Sim stopped and looked back toward the street, as if he would run.

Petyr waited. He thought about trying to use his talent to figure out what Sim had to tell him, but decided against it. From long experience, he'd learned allowing someone to work through their reluctance to talk often yielded better results.

Sim turned back to him. "Look, I need to thank you for bringing my daughter back."

"That's not what's eating you, is it?" Petyr stepped out into the rain and shut the door behind him. "Come with me. I think you need to hear something."

"Where are we going?"

Petyr started walking, and Sim fell in behind him.

"To talk to the other Questioner," Petyr said without looking back.

"Why?"

"So certain people, and it seems you as well, can learn the truth."

Sim didn't ask another question, but Petyr could hear Sim's feet squelching through the mud.

Petyr hoped the truth would help Sim understand what his daughter faced. Maybe it could help Sim tell his wife the truth.

⚔ ⚔ ⚔

Petyr stood just outside the door that led to the cellar and the cages where they'd held him. He took a deep breath, then opened it and started down. Sim followed him.

He had no idea how this would go, if he could even get the Questioner to talk to him, or if Dyllan would hold to the bargain.

Lamplight touched the walls, revealing the three men in the cells. The Tracker, the Protector, and the Questioner. As Petyr descended, he caught the eyes of the Tracker following him.

It made Petyr uneasy to think that, wherever Petyr went, the Tracker could follow him. He didn't want to admit Alec spoke the truth. He didn't want to carry the burden of the Tracker's death. But he could think of no other way, unless the Tracker heard the Questioner confirm Petyr's truths.

"Petyr," Dyllan called out to him. "Who's that with you?"

"One of the elders."

"You should make him go."

Petyr thought about it. *Does Sim really need to hear this? Or am I only having him listen for my own purposes?* Petyr couldn't decide, so he turned to Sim to ask him.

"What do you want to do, Sim? I'm going to tell them the truth about why they were sent after me. If you listen, you risk your life."

"Isn't my life already at risk? Mine and everyone in Dunsriver? If the Empire discovers Dunsriver's uprising against these Lords, not one of us will live. I should just take Carree and my wife and go."

Petyr nodded. "That's the safe choice."

Silence stretched out between them. Petyr looked at Dyllan for a moment, and remembered their last conversation, the pain Petyr had caused by leaving his friend out. "But I think I've learned something about hiding the truth recently," Petyr said. "I've hurt people by keeping the truth from them in an effort to keep them safe."

Sim frowned. "Don't you lecture me about my choices."

"No, no," Petyr said. "What you chose to do is up to you. But I'm here, these Lords are here, because I hid the truth from the people that cared about me. In a moment, one of them will hear that truth confirmed, I hope. I have no control over whether it will heal the breach I created.

"But I might be able to help you if you listen."

"What do you mean?"

"You know Carree won't stay here."

Sim only stared at him, so Petyr continued. "She asked if I would take her with me."

"You didn't tell her you would!"

"I haven't told her I wouldn't, either. I fear she would..." Petyr stopped. He couldn't reveal her secret here.

"What?"

"I fear she would just follow, no matter what I say. If you know the truth, it might make your decision easier."

Dyllan laughed. "Just send him away, Petyr. These people don't care about the Empire until the tax collector shows up. You'll just end up getting him hanged next to you."

Petyr wanted to throw something at Dyllan. "That's where I went wrong, Dyllan. I should have told everyone I met this past year what I learned, instead of keeping it to myself. By keeping my secrets, I only made it easier for them to erase me and hide their conspiracy."

"Sim," Petyr said, "I don't care what you do. I think you should hear this, but if you're concerned..."

"Concerned about what? My family? Dunsriver? Everything

I've worked for the last seventeen years is already in danger." In the dim lamplight, Petyr thought he could see Sim's left eye twitching. "I have only one goal left, at this point. I will do whatever I must to protect my wife and my daughter. If you think listening to what you have to say will help me do that, I will hear you out."

Petyr wished he had an answer for Sim. A glance at Dyllan, who stood watching them, told him nothing. The Tracker wasn't much of a problem while locked in the cage, but the Questioner, if he listened too closely, if he understood the subtext... *But he's not me. He can't discover truths without asking.*

He grabbed Sim's sleeve and pulled him as far away from the cells as he could get, and then whispered to him. "What I am going to tell them could very well get you killed, but I think you need to know. It will help you decide what to do with Carree and her talent."

"But..."

"No, listen. You won't be safe anywhere. Dunsriver is about as isolated a town as exists within the borders of the Empire. You can't go dragging her off somewhere else. Someone will discover her talent before you can find another place. It didn't take long for me to recognize it."

"You want her to go with you."

Petyr couldn't deny it. "I could use someone with her talent if I'm to clear my name and get my wife back."

"So this is just about you?"

"No, it's not just about me." Petyr cast about for what to say that would convey what he needed without putting Sim and his family in more danger than they were already in. "I don't know why you lied to your wife. I don't know why you risked everything to run from Carree's talent. I do know why I am doing what I'm doing, and the only reasons I can tell you without putting you at greater risk are clearing my name and finding my wife.

"I don't think you're taking a much greater risk listening to me talk to the Questioner. If I'm lying, then you've heard nothing but lies. If I'm telling the truth, those three won't tell anyone what you know for fear of risking their own lives."

Petyr could come up with nothing else to help Sim in his decision. Petyr felt strongly that Sim should hear what he had to say, but Dyllan was right. Danger lay in the knowing. Of course, if Petyr couldn't convince Dyllan and the Tracker of his innocence, then the town was likely doomed, or the three Lords were.

It dawned on him, as he waited for Sim to decide, the town had doomed itself. Even if they let Dyllan and the others free, and somehow convinced them to lie about the deaths of the others, a Questioning would reveal their duplicity.

He'd thought, somehow, he could find a way out of it, but now, he couldn't deny it any longer.

"I'll listen."

Petyr was still wrestling with his epiphany, and didn't quite catch what Sim said. "What?"

"I'll listen. I can't make any sort of decision without knowing what your purpose really is. I know you're right, we won't survive here, and I won't be able to hide her if we leave. I don't like it. I don't like it at all, but I suspect her best chance is to leave with you. But I can't know that if I don't listen to what you have to say."

Petyr didn't want to say anything now. *They doomed themselves trying to save themselves, because of me. Because they somehow thought I might be able to save them.*

He felt himself swirling down a whirlpool of despair. He needed Alec here. He needed Alura. *She'd know what to do.*

"Petyr?"

What should I do? Who can help me save this town?

Something tugged at his mind, a sense of purpose invaded it. He knew where he had to go.

What in the Mother's name? He knew the feeling. It was the same feeling as the one that pulled him through the forest to find Uma on the tree. He knew there was an answer, and he knew he could find it. *Is this what being a Seeker is? I just have to think of what I want, and I can find it?*

"Petyr!"

He blinked his eyes a couple times. Sim was staring at him. "Sorry, I just..." *How do I explain?* "I just thought of something that I need to look into... You said you'd listen?"

Sim nodded.

"Then there's no reason to delay any longer."

Petyr stepped back over in front of the cells, positioning himself between Dyllan and the Questioner. Sim stood at his shoulder.

The Questioner lay on his cot. In the dim light, he looked young to Petyr, maybe not even a year out of the academy. *Of course he'd be young. They wouldn't want someone who might not follow Dyllan's orders.*

"Lord Questioner," Petyr said.

The Questioner looked up, and Petyr saw he was indeed just out of the Academy. Straight, dirty-blonde hair hung below his ears. The dirty smudge of a mustache had spread across his face. "What do you want?"

"I want you to question me."

The kid blinked and sat up. "I was ordered not to question you."

"Dyllan?" Petyr asked.

Dyllan stepped to the bars and met Petyr's eyes. "You're really going to go through with this? He's a kid."

"Order him to question me. He's a Questioner, let him do his job. It won't matter if you're right, anyway. If you're right, I'm telling lies. And you proposed this."

"Petyr..."

"No, you put us in this situation by refusing my offer. I agreed to go back with you if you would just help these people, but you refused. I was doing my duty to the Empire, Dyllan, and I'm truly sorry if, in trying to protect you from the consequences, I brought ruin to our friendship.

"Don't you want to know who the real liars are, Dyllan? Don't you want to know if your mission to bring me back is in fact an act of treason?"

They stared at each other for several moments. No one spoke.

"Order him to question me, Dyllan. Find out the truth."

They stood silently for a few moments more, before Dyllan looked over at the young Questioner. "Question him."

Shock found its way to the young man's face. "What?"

"You heard me. Question him. Ask him about the offenses he's charged with."

"But I was ordered by the Tribune…"

"Elsalan, when you took your oaths, who did you swear duty to?"

"The Empire and the Emperor," Elsalan said slowly.

"Did you swear duty to the Tribune?"

Elsalan shook his head.

"If Petyr is telling the truth, and we have been told to hunt him based on a lie, then don't you think it's our duty to discover that?"

Petyr relaxed a little bit. He hadn't been sure Dyllan would give the order.

Elsalan stood slowly. He looked a bit wobbly in the legs, but he made his way to the bars without any mishaps. "Come here," he said.

Petyr moved so that he and the Questioner faced each other. Petyr looked right into Elsalan's eyes.

Elsalan inhaled, preparing himself, and then asked, "Why did you commit treason?"

Petyr sighed. "I didn't commit treason."

The kid's eyes opened wide and he turned to Dylan. "He's telling the truth!"

Petyr thought back to the time after he had just graduated from the academy. He couldn't remember making these kinds of mistakes. "Look, uh, Elsalan. You asked the wrong question."

"What do you mean?"

"Any number of people could answer that question, believing they're telling the truth, and still be wrong. Your questions need to lead to the heart of the matter, the specific accusations against me."

"I don't know what they are."

"Dyllan?"

"We were only told you'd committed treason, that your crimes were numerous, and that you were to be brought back for trial."

Petyr wanted to bang his head against the bars. *I wonder if this kid is even strong enough to hear truth without asking questions.*

"Fine, then. Ask me if I found evidence of treason on the part of any of the High Lords."

The kid looked to Dyllan and Dyllan nodded for him to proceed.

Elsalan's voice shook while he asked, "Petyr, did you find evidence of treason on the part of the High Lords?"

"About a year before the events that precipitated my flight, I had chance to find myself down the street from the High Protector. I saw him slip into an alcove, where he stayed for a few moments before emerging and looking around rather carefully to see that he wasn't observed. I felt fortunate that he did not see me amongst the crowd.

"Moments later a man known to me to be a rogue Blocker also slipped from the alcove. I followed him as close as I dared, but lost him a while later."

"Why didn't you come get me?" Dyllan asked. "You should have brought him in."

"It wouldn't have mattered if I'd come get you, as he would have been gone by the time we came back. I was also curious as to the proximity of the High Protector to this man. Something about it struck me false, but I couldn't go accusing the High Protector over a feeling.

"So I proceeded to gather what evidence I could against him. I followed him when my duties allowed. I saw more clandestine meetings with rogue talents. I discovered other High Lords were involved when I followed one of the rogue talents to the High Coercer."

Elsalan put his hands to the bars to hold himself up, and Petyr saw his face go pale. "Is something wrong Elsalan? Do you need to sit down?"

"No." He turned to Dyllan. "He's telling the truth."

"He still hasn't given us any evidence of treason."

"You're right," Petyr continued. "To that point, I had nothing but clandestine meetings that I could never get close enough to overhear.

"Eventually, I did manage to overhear a conversation between the Lord Protector and a rogue Ghost. The Lord Protector offered him amnesty if he would join their cause."

All three of the men standing near Petyr gasped. "How could he do that?" asked Dyllan. "Why would he do that?"

Petyr looked at the Questioner. "Do you need to ask the question?"

Elsalan shook his head.

"I didn't know at the time. But it was enough that I felt I needed some help. I took what I had gathered and brought it to the Tribune. I could not imagine the High Questioner would be involved in whatever was going on. He'd trained me. I'd learned everything I knew about being a Questioner from him.

"I presented my evidence to him, and he told me, 'I need some time to think about this, my son. Leave it here for me to examine. If what you have discovered is true, it is a scandal that must be handled delicately.'

"He commended me for being circumspect, and sent me on my way.

"Later that night, the arrest warrant was announced. They came for me in my home, and I fled." Petyr didn't want to relive the scene on the stairs.

"Every word he says is true," said the Questioner.

Dyllan went back to his cot and sat down. "It doesn't prove anything."

"It does, Dyllan," Petyr said. "The three of them, at least, are doing something they don't want known. They're involved in some kind of plot or illegal activity. You know the penalty for harboring a rogue. A year in prison, and death for the rogue. Why are they secretly offering them amnesty?"

Dyllan sighed. "Fine. You've proved yourself. As far as I'm

concerned, you are not a traitor. But you haven't proved that they are. I agree with you on one point. I can't see why they would clandestinely offer amnesty to rogues."

"So you'll help me?"

"Dammit Petyr, give me some time to figure this out. You know you've likely damned everyone in this room to the gibbet with that story."

"Not if we fight it."

"Just give me time."

Petyr sighed, then looked to the Tracker who had said nothing the entire time. "What about you, Tracker?"

"My name is Jeb. I'm not sure I can thank you for making me hear that."

"You know why I had to."

Jeb nodded. "I do. I don't like it. And I'm not much sure I like you for it. Dyllan's right, though. I need time to think."

Petyr nodded. He didn't even ask Elsalan. He didn't think the kid would be much help, and he wouldn't get much done on his own.

He turned to Sim. He couldn't read Sim's face in the dim light.

But he didn't have to. "To think I thought my daughter would be safer with you. You know what the High Lords are planning, don't you?"

"I have a guess."

"I spent a lot of years in Genova as a merchant. Merchants get to know a place and its politics. High Lords wouldn't ally themselves with rogue talents for money. They could only be after the throne."

"That's what I fear."

Sim turned without another word and ascended the stairs.

Petyr took one more look at the three prisoners, then followed Sim out of the cellar.

CHAPTER 18

When Petyr entered the doctor's abode, he found Ilsan sitting with Alec drinking tea. The fire, as always, burned warmly, producing a feeling of calm that sifted through Petyr from the moment he entered.

In that warmth and calm, the urge he felt in the cellar when talking with Sim, the insistence that he follow, returned. *Why did this manifest now? Shouldn't I have recognized this trait before?*

"So you went to see your Protector without me?" Alec asked without even turning around.

"I didn't think bringing you anywhere near the Questioner would produce the results we wanted."

Alec lifted his cup to his lips and sipped. "Wise. Did you get the result you wanted?"

"I don't believe I'll know for a while. They will ultimately have to help, I think. They can't return home, whether they understand it or not."

"Why is that?" Ilsan asked.

Petyr stepped forward and knelt near the fire so he could look at Ilsan. "I proved to them I am innocent of the charges against me. Unfortunately, my accusers are powerful people within the Empire. Anyone who knows what I discovered for truth is in danger of the same sentence.

"I've decided I need to tell more people what I know. I need to spread it, but I'm not sure how I want to go about it. I don't want to put people at risk who have little chance of having an effect."

"You should let me choose if I risk my neck, Petyr," Ilsan said.

Alec nodded in agreement and took another sip of his tea.

Telling Ilsan didn't sit well with Petyr. "Not yet, Ilsan. I like you too much."

"Is it your place to decide, Petyr?" Petyr detected a hint of anger in Ilsan's voice. "How do you know I can't help?"

"You don't have a talent. You don't leave your home because of your..."

"My what? My condition?" Ilsan's hand shook. "I don't leave because I choose not to. And lack of a talent doesn't mean I am worthless. If you are intent on telling others, start with me. *Trust* me, Petyr. I did not become a doctor through luck. It takes skill and knowledge. My studies ranged far beyond the body and its illnesses and frailties."

"But I don't want to be responsible for your death."

"Petyr," Alec said. "What has keeping your secrets to yourself accomplished? Those Lords have chased you across the empire, given your wife and daughter to a man they sent to bring you back for your execution."

Alec was right. *Didn't I just resolve to tell more people? Why am I so reluctant?*

The room grew silent, the crackling of the fire the only noise, as Ilsan and Alec waited to see what Petyr would do.

In the silence, the compulsion to follow his talent's lead grew. *What question did I ask that led to this compulsion?* He tried to think back, to his talk with Sim. And then it came to him. "Who can help me?"

"What?" Alec asked.

Petyr realized he'd said it aloud. "While I talked with Sim, I asked myself a question, and I instantly had an urge to go to a place, and I knew the answer to the question lay at the end of the path. I stuffed it down while talking with Dyllan and the Questioner, but the compulsion returned when I arrived here, and it's growing stronger, I think."

He felt it in him, urging him to go, now. Tugging at him. He stood. "I have to go."

"It's the Seeker in you," Ilsan said. "You should follow it."

"Ilsan, you and Alec are right. It's your decision if you want to know my secret. I've told you the risk. When I return, if you still feel the need to hear my story, I'll tell you. Maybe you would know something that can help. I guess I just worry that what happened the last time I confided in someone I trusted will happen again."

A puzzled look crossed Ilsan's face for a moment, before a look of understanding replaced it. "It is hard to trust after a betrayal."

Alec stood up. "I'm coming with you."

Petyr looked over the Ghost. They'd been at odds over staying here the whole time, but despite being given the option of leaving more than once, Alec hadn't left. *I wish I understood him.* "Good. I'll feel better having you along."

⚐ ⚐ ⚐

Petyr and Alec packed much like they did for their earlier trip to the Fringe, except this time, Alec insisted that they find a gun to take with them. Petyr didn't argue the point despite his feeling that whatever, or whoever, they were looking for should help them. He couldn't see that it would hurt to have more protection than a hatchet.

They stopped by Roderick's home to borrow a gun.

Roderick left them at the door and came back quickly with a flintlock, powder, bullets and everything else they'd need.

"Why do you need it," Roderick asked as he handed it to Alec.

Petyr didn't want to lie to him, but he couldn't tell him the truth, exactly, either. He didn't understand it enough himself. "I'm hoping to find some answers," he said at last.

"Are you going back to that thing in the forest?"

"We'll probably start there."

Alec pulled the rope out of his pack and handed it to Petyr. "I need to make room for this stuff."

Petyr stuffed the rope into his pack.

"Can I ask you a question?" Roderick asked, looking a little nervous.

"What is it?"

"About the prisoners. They were after you. What do you think we should do with them? We can't afford to let them leave."

Petyr sighed. "No, you can't. You can't kill them, either. Eventually, the Empire will send a Questioner looking for them. Too many of your citizens know what happened."

Roderick nodded, and seemed to shrink a little. "Then what do we do?"

"I don't know, yet. I'm hoping a solution will present itself. The Questioner confirmed my innocence to the others."

"That's good, isn't it?"

"Not for them, not really. They can't just return to Genova anymore. I'm hoping they will help, but when I left them, they hadn't come to terms with the idea that they'd been lied to."

"Are you ever going to tell me why?"

"If I can figure out how to keep the Empire from sending a Questioner here, then yes, I'll tell you."

Roderick nodded, then looked up at the sky. Petyr looked up, too.

"You'd better get moving," Roderick said. "It looks to rain soon. I don't think you want to be caught out in a storm. Maybe you should wait until it passes."

Petyr shook his head. The compulsion he felt carried with it a sense of urgency. He couldn't wait much longer. "I need answers now, before that thing comes to take another."

With that, they said their farewells.

Petyr led Alec to the gate in the wall, and when they were through it, he turned away from the river and followed the wall.

"Where are we going, Petyr?"

"Downriver. I'm just following a sense."

"Are you going to tell me what this is about? Is this just like how you found the Uma girl?"

"Yes." Petyr looked around. Men stood atop the wall every ten yards or so, watching for the giant. Not that they'd do any good if it came. Eduard and Willam proved that.

"But not now," he continued. "There are too many ears near, and I don't really understand it myself. Wait until we get into the forest."

The two of them walked across the barren fields to the forest line where the woodsmen were busy felling trees. They had to wait for a bit as the foreman held them back while his men finished dropping a huge tree to the ground. The thud when it hit shook the ground. The wind from the branches raced past them.

When it was down, Petyr and Alec continued into the forest.

Once they were among the trees, the sense of urgency he felt grew greater. He knew where he was going; it didn't feel terribly far. He thought if he had more experience, he might be able to guess at the distance.

"So, are you going to tell me what this is about?" Alec asked. "How were you able to find that girl?"

"I don't know. I had a dream. There was a voice, it showed me where she was. It urged me to use my talent."

"How would a question help?"

"Not a question. He said I was a Seeker."

"I've never heard of such a thing."

Petyr came upon a fallen tree, and started climbing over it. He waited to answer until after his feet were on the ground again. "I hadn't heard of a Seeker either. When we returned, I asked Ilsan about it, thinking he had something about them in one of his books."

"Did he?" asked Alec as he jumped down from the tree.

"No. But he'd heard of Seekers. He said he'd read of them once, long ago."

"Wait a minute. If you're a Seeker, how can you act as a Questioner?"

"I'm not sure, but Ilsan said he'd read a Questioner is a lower form of a Seeker."

"A lower form? What does that mean?"

"It appears to mean that I can do the things a Questioner can do, as well as some other things."

"Like finding people. Like a combination of a Tracker and a Questioner."

Petyr stopped walking for a moment and turned to face Alec. "I hadn't thought of it like that, but I don't think it's quite the same. Trackers need to know who they're following. They use objects their target owned or touched to help them link with their target. I don't think I have to do that."

Alec squinted his eyes a little. "So what do you do? Just think of the person you want to find and you can find them?"

"I don't know how it works. I don't know what the limitations are, yet."

Alec smiled. "You realize you've just become a very dangerous man. You probably shouldn't be telling me these things."

"You're right, I probably shouldn't. But you've had so many chances to leave."

"I've thought about it."

"You haven't left, though. I used to think Dyllan was a good friend. I had no idea what a real friend was like. I need help, Alec, learning my limits, learning the dangers."

"You need help, for sure. I'm a rogue, Petyr. You can't trust me."

"Why do you stay? Even when you disagree with my path, why do you stay?"

Alec looked off into the forest.

He doesn't want to answer. I wonder if he even knows. "Alec, in the time we've been together, you've never once tried to play me false, rogue or not."

"You're a Questioner. Why would I lie to you?"

"You wouldn't believe how often people try to lie to a Questioner. Even with the threat of exposure, they lie to try to protect themselves, they lie to protect others."

"I don't have anything to protect. Shouldn't we be going somewhere?"

Petyr felt the compulsion. They should be moving. But he needed to know the answer. He could question him but Petyr had learned long ago not to do that with friends. They resented it. "We should, but I really want to know. Why do you stay?"

"Why don't you question me?"

"I don't question friends."

"That's a dangerous habit, you know. Especially considering what happened the last time you failed to question someone you thought a friend."

Petyr looked away into the depths of the forest. *I know.* "If you don't want to tell me why you stay, I understand. You don't have to. But know this. I appreciate that you do stay. I can't imagine I'd be anywhere other than hanging from a gibbet if you hadn't stayed."

Petyr started working his way through the forest again. After a moment, he heard Alec following him.

"Petyr, there are reasons I came with you in the first place. We have similar goals. I have many reasons for staying..."

Petyr stopped again and turned around.

"And one of those reasons is that you don't question me. You could find out everything I've done, every illegal act and treachery."

"I don't need to. I know the most important one."

"What do you want, Petyr? I don't understand why you even bother to threaten me with that."

Petyr felt a drop of water hit his cheek. "I don't know, Alec. Even though I've decided to spread my knowledge of the Lords' deceit, I'm unsure if I can do it and live. I need help. I could use yours, but spreading the tale will inevitably bring attention on us.

"I guess I want to know how far you'll go with me, and it's hard to know without knowing why you're staying."

Alec looked up to the forest canopy. "It's starting to rain."

"Alec..."

"Stop. I understand, Petyr. I do. But I can't tell you why I stay. Isn't it enough to know that my cart is hitched to your horse until you reach your destination?"

"Whatever the destination?"

The rain started working its way through the forest canopy in earnest.

"Wherever you lead," Alec said. "Though, right now, I wish you'd lead us wherever we're going before we get too wet."

⁂

Two hours later, cold and wet with the light fading, Petyr felt he was finally nearing his goal, whatever, or whoever, it would turn out to be. He was ready for the trek to end. He wanted a fire and some tea. Ilsan's sitting room sounded like a good place to be right now. His new-found ability urged him onward, however.

"Petyr, don't you think we should stop and find a place to take cover for the night?"

Petyr pushed past some large ferns. Alec's suggestion made sense, but the feeling that had brought him this far made him think he could almost reach out and touch his goal. "No, we're close. I feel like we're almost right on top of..."

The ground gave way beneath him. Amidst an avalanche of dead leaves and other forest detritus, he fell, sliding down a steep slope until he came to rest in a pool of water. He checked himself and didn't find anything broken. His ankle hurt a bit, and he would wear some abrasions on his hands for awhile.

Looking up, he saw a halo of gray light above him, broken by Alec's head.

"Petyr?" Alec called down.

"I'm all right, Alec. Just a bit bruised."

Petyr assessed the slope he'd slid down for the first time. It was too steep to climb, even if it wasn't mostly mud. Alec hung over the lip twenty feet above him.

"It'd be easy to climb out of this sinkhole," Petyr said, "if you were carrying the rope."

He heard Alec curse above him. "Petyr, it's not a sinkhole."

A trap. "Who would dig a trap twenty feet deep?"

"I don't think it's a trap, Petyr."

"Then what is it?"

Petyr heard some rustling off to his left, and then a voice. "It is entrance."

Petyr felt around in the water for the hatchet he'd carried, while trying to peer into the gloom. He thought he saw something sway a little bit, something much shorter than him.

"Who are you?"

"Please, you do not need weapon. I am friend." The voice sounded familiar to Petyr, but he couldn't place it.

"Friend? I don't know you."

"I help you find girl."

Petyr tried to peer through the shadows, but he still couldn't get a good look at it. He didn't know why, but he no longer felt afraid of it. "You helped me find a girl."

"In dream, I help you."

"My dreams? You were the one that told me I'm a Seeker?"

"I am Dreamstrider. I know."

Petyr didn't understand. "Your name is Dreamstrider?"

"No. I am Dreamstrider like you are Seeker, like your friend is Ghost. Use your talent. See."

Petyr didn't have to use his talent. He already knew. He only had to pay attention. The urge to find his target was gone, and he knew the Dreamstrider spoke truth.

But what do I do now?

"Have friend come down. I offer shelter for night."

Petyr stood up. His ankle was sore, but held, and he limped out of the way, toward the Dreamstrider. Petyr called up to Alec. "Slide down, Alec."

"What?"

"He's offering shelter."

"How will we get back out?"

"Is easier way out," the Dreamstrider said.

Petyr relayed the message, and heard Alec grumbling. Alec didn't waste any time, though, and slid down the slope, more gracefully than Petyr had, Petyr felt sure.

"Dreamstrider, what is your name?" Petyr asked.

"Ullikillanee," the Dreamstrider said, "but if you prefer, may say Ulli. Please follow."

Ulli turned and started moving down a tunnel that Petyr hadn't seen until then. Petyr turned to follow, but Alec held him up by pulling at his pack.

"Do you really think it's safe?"

"I don't know if it's safe," Petyr said, "but Ulli is who I was looking for."

Alec released Petyr's pack and Petyr started trying to catch up to the diminutive creature. He had to stoop to fit through the tunnel, and it quickly grew dark enough that he could see little. He kept bumping into the walls of the tunnel as he made his way down it.

"I wish I had a lamp," he said.

"Ah, Ulli forgets. One moment."

Seconds later, a cool glow filled the corridor, emanating from something in Ulli's hand. For the first time, Petyr could see the creature, and he couldn't help thinking it looked very similar to the creature they'd found nailed to the tree, and had an odd resemblance to the giant.

"Better?" Ulli asked.

Petyr nodded. "Much better, thanks."

Ulli started down the corridor again.

"Uh, Petyr," Alec whispered, "doesn't he look like..."

"Yes, he does."

"Follow, follow," said Ulli.

Petyr started following him. After a moment, he heard Alec

stumbling along behind him. Wherever this creature was leading them, Petyr knew he had to find out why it looked so much like the giant that had nearly killed him.

CHAPTER 19

Petyr and Alec followed Ulli along a winding path underneath the forest. Water trickled down the walls in places to meet up with the small stream that ran down the center of the tunnel. Petyr kept to the side of the tunnel, where he could, in an attempt to keep his shoes from taking on more water than they already had.

The tunnel took on more slope as they went. Petyr heard the sound of water falling.

"Is there a waterfall ahead?" he asked.

"Yes. Quite a long drop. Do not worry. We turn off before," Ulli said without turning around.

"I should like to see it."

"Is not much to see. Water falls so far, light can not see end."

They continued on for a while, the sound of the falls growing louder. Though the stream of water running down the center of their tunnel had grown, Petyr couldn't imagine it was large enough to create the sound he was hearing.

Ulli lead them around a bend in the tunnel to find it opened up onto a much larger tunnel. Ulli's light did not extend to the far side of the new tunnel, but it extended far enough for Petyr to see why the falls sounded so much louder. A river flowed through the larger tunnel, and their small stream ran into it.

As they stepped out into the larger tunnel, they emerged onto a landing that was only a few feet across. Petyr found he was able to straighten up. His back muscles had cramped from the stooping. He tried to quickly massage the pain from them, but Ulli didn't leave him much time.

Ulli turned down a path that seemed to have been cut into the stone above the river. "Follow, follow."

The path was cut for someone of Ulli's size, which made it a bit treacherous for Petyr and Alec to tread. *I'm glad we're not going to see the falls, if this is the path I'd have to take.*

Petyr worked carefully down the path which was slick with moisture. He didn't feel any spray from the river, but the air felt thick and damp. Petyr wanted to look back to see how Alec fared, but didn't dare take his eyes off the dimly lit path.

About the time Petyr felt like his calves would cramp from the effort of keeping his feet, Ulli ducked around a corner and disappeared from view. Ulli's light showed what looked like another tunnel. Petyr turned down it, then stopped.

The tunnel he'd thought he'd entered was an entry way. There was room enough for the three of them, and several more, if necessary. The walls extended up beyond the reach of Ulli's light. The parts Petyr could see were carved in friezes depicting a sequence of events that Petyr didn't quite understand. The figures in them seemed to be running from something, then erecting a wall. On another side of the cavern, he saw the image of someone hanging from a tree. All of the figures appeared to be like Ulli.

He looked down to see that Ulli had opened a door.

"What is this, Ulli?"

Ulli looked up and around, taking in the carvings. "History." Petyr thought he saw sadness reflected in Ulli's black eyes, illuminated by the thin light Ulli still carried in his hand. For the first time, Petyr realized Ulli was old.

"Your history?"

"Inside. I will tell, inside."

Ulli went through the door, taking his light with him. In the fading light, Petyr looked to Alec, who shrugged. Petyr followed Ulli through, bending over to fit through the door.

Ulli led them down a short hallway. The hallway opened into a gigantic cavern. A gentle yellow light, emanating from the roof of the cavern, bathed it in the warmth of an early spring day. The walls of the cavern were carved with pathways leading to smaller entrances that looked like they might be dwellings. The floor of the cavern was covered in plant life. Petyr thought it might be a garden.

"How is this possible?" Alec asked as he squeezed past Petyr into the cavern.

"Magic of my people makes it so," said Ulli. "Follow."

Ulli led them across the floor of the cavern along a path through the garden. The closer look this afforded Petyr led him to find the garden full of edible plants, berries, and fruits. Every so often, the path crossed over small culverts filled with water. Petyr suspected they were used to keep the garden fed.

Petyr glanced up to the top of the cavern, looking for a light source. He couldn't discern a single point, and it did not hurt his eyes to look. The cavern roof seemed a hundred feet or more above him. He hadn't thought they'd descended so far.

"Petyr, have you noticed?" Alec asked in a low voice.

"Noticed what?"

"This place seems built to house hundreds, but it's quiet as a tomb."

Petyr hadn't noticed, not until Alec said something. He'd been too awed by the impossibilities around him. He looked around, searched the cavern for signs of life other than their own, and found nothing.

"What do you think happened?" Alec continued.

"I don't know," Petyr said. "But Ulli plans to tell us something."

"Yes," Ulli said. "Ulli will tell, once we sit and share food. Follow."

So Ulli has good ears, despite his age.

Petyr turned to watch Ulli from behind. The little humanoid wore some type of cloth that covered him, much like a robe, but stopped short of his knees. His feet were bare. Ulli's arms were somewhat longer than they would have been were Ulli human. White tufts of hair ran along the sides of his head and met at the back, running down his neck and beneath his clothing. His ears, while normal seeming at the top, had lobes that hung down to points that dangled just above Ulli's shoulders. Petyr had the most trouble with Ulli's bluish skin. He couldn't keep the vision of the giant, its leap onto the platform and its huge arm swinging down at him, out of his head.

Eventually, Ulli led them out of the garden and to an alcove carved into the cavern wall. It was much like the others lining the cavern walls, only the entrance was wider and taller.

"I apologize for bringing you here," said Ulli. "My home would not fit you."

"Where is 'here?'" Alec asked.

"A—gathering place. Inside," he said, urging Petyr and Alec through.

Petyr stepped through and found he could stand up straight, though it was a close thing. The walls of the room were delicately carved with more of the same style of work that adorned the entryway to the cavern. Only, these carvings were more detailed and appeared to tell a larger story.

His gaze panned around the room, until he came to one that showed a wall in a forest. Only, it wasn't a wall. It was something alive. It reminded him of something he'd seen, first on the doors of the brandy cabinet, and then again in person and close up.

The carving seemed to come alive, just like the carving on the cabinet. In fact, the scene looked so much like the carving on the cabinet, Petyr thought they could have been carved by the same hand.

"The Fringe," he whispered.

"Our Protector," said Ulli.

"I've seen this carving before," Petyr said, "only, I didn't see it here."

He could feel the pull of the Fringe, even through the stone, just like he'd felt it through the cabinet.

"My shame."

Petyr pulled his gaze from the carving and focused on Ulli. The little creature's eyes glistened with water. "Your shame?"

"You are not first human to see this. Another visited us. I brought him here. He could not take eyes from from wall. If I not bring him here, our Protector would still protect."

"Do you know his name?" Petyr felt sure he knew already. The carvings were too similar.

"He said his name Bran."

Bran. It didn't feel better to have his suspicion confirmed. Bran must have been entranced by the image, like Petyr had been when he'd first seen it carved in the cabinet doors, and copied it.

"Wait a minute," Alec said. "What do you mean by 'our Protector would still protect?'"

Ulli sighed, and fidgeted a bit before answering. "Our Protector, what you call 'Fringe', lives. It decides who may pass. It protects from Quenikuhg. Bran compromised our Protector, allowing Quenikuhg to extend reach through it."

Petyr felt lost. "Who is Quenikuhg?"

Ulli rolled his eyes. "Follow. I show you." He walked to the other side of the room, where the pictorial story started.

"A thousand years past, when your Empire could reach no further than infant, the Keekele, my people, tended this land. Here, and beyond our Protector.

"We have been a race of secret seekers."

Ulli moved to the next panel, a scene depicting one of Ulli's people working over the body of another. "Soon after we discovered your people," Ulli continued, "and your drive to expand your demesne, we realized our time neared its end. We might survive as a people, but we would change.

"A young, intelligent youth, refused to accept this. He delved far and deep into researches better left alone. His goal, to change us to defend against your people

"What he found, what he became, changed him, and he grew to scourge us."

Petyr thought he had an idea where Ulli was going with his story.

"What did he find?" asked Alec.

"An entity. Something ancient, older even than Keekele. It usurped his body, used it for unspeakable things. It tried... No." He looked at Petyr for a moment. "You are Seeker. I shall not hide truth. It created more of itself in desecrated bodies of our daughters."

"Like the giant," Petyr said.

"Yes, only it is not giant. It is Quenikuhg."

Ulli moved on to the next scene, which appeared to Petyr to depict some sort of battle. He looked to the next few scenes, and they showed many similar scenes.

"We fought Quenikuhg as we could, losing our youth, and our daughters. More in each battle. Quenikuhg made more and more of itself. Its army grew as ours declined."

He walked past the other scenes of conflict. Over and over, it seemed the Keekele lost and retreated. It took them around the curve of the room. They stopped at a scene where three Keekele surrounded something that seemed to glow. Petyr had the impression of many others surrounding the three.

"Lekata came together..."

"Lekata?" Petyr asked, interrupting.

"Ones you call Lords. Ones with talent."

Petyr nodded.

"Lekata came together once we understood threat, used our power to create Protector. Many Keekele gave of themselves to create it."

Petyr sensed something in Ulli's voice that made Petyr believe Ulli thought it a necessary tragedy. "How did they give of themselves?"

"They became part of Protector."

"How many?" Petyr didn't want to hear the answer, didn't want to confirm his suspicion. Didn't want to confirm what he'd not quite understood when he touched the Fringe.

"Thousands."

"You killed thousands of your people to create your Protector?" Alec asked, disbelief in his voice. Petyr was surprised to hear it from him.

"No!" Ulli turned to face Alec, his eyes nearly bulging from the deep sockets. "They did not die. They still live as Protector. They surround our home, protecting world from Quenikuhg."

Petyr spent a moment digesting the idea. He knew the truth of it. What he didn't understand was why it failed. He had so many questions. *I don't even know where to begin.*

He decided to start with the problem. "If they are protecting the world from the Quenikuhg, how is it getting out?"

"It is not getting out, yet. It is only stretching Protector. Young human who I brought here entered forbidden land…"

"And broke the barrier," said Alec.

"No, no. Didn't break it. Our Protector unbreakable, but only protects against Quenikuhg and Keekele. Not human."

Petyr saw it now. "The Quenikuhg took Bran for itself, giving it the ability to stretch the Protector."

Ulli nodded. "Yes, you have right of it."

"And in trying to impregnate human women, it's trying to build up an army to help it break down the Fringe and let it free."

Ulli nodded again.

"So how do we stop it?"

Ulli looked up at Petyr expectantly. "You are Seeker. You can find way."

Petyr's heart sank into his stomach. "Are you saying you don't know how?"

"I do not know. But you can seek."

Petyr glanced around the carvings again, hoping to find some clue, but found nothing. "I tried," he said. "Seeking brought me to you."

CHAPTER 20

U lli bid Petyr and Alec wait while he went to prepare some food for them.

Petyr settled against the wall with the with the carving of the Fringe. He didn't want to look at it. Unfortunately, this left him in a position to see the rest of the story. He found himself mostly looking at the floor, which seemed well worn. If there had been any decoration, it no longer existed.

"What do you think of it all?" Alec asked.

"It's a lot to take in. What I don't understand is why this is happening now. Why did it let Bran through? Haven't there been others before him that stepped through the Fringe?

"The only thing I can come up with is that somehow, Bran was special. Dunsriver isn't the only town near the Fringe. Surely some hunter stepped through before."

"Bran not first," said Ulli as he returned to the room. "But he had talent."

Petyr looked up. Ulli carried two large bowls filled with berries and roots and various leafy vegetables. "I'm even more confused than before. I thought you said the Fringe, your Protector, couldn't keep humans from going through it."

"Protector can not keep them out. Without certain talents,

however, it will confuse them and turn them around. Sometimes, they are lost forever. Sometimes, they return."

"Is this how it works for you?"

Ulli shook his head. "If I enter, I become part of Protector. I will not return."

"And the Quenikuhg?"

"My understanding is Protector presents solid barrier to Quenikuhg and causes great pain upon touching—until human passed through."

Ulli handed one bowl to Alec, and the other to Petyr. Petyr looked in and saw the food was unprepared.

"But the Fringe doesn't kill it." Alec said.

"No. We could not discover how to kill."

Petyr picked at the food in his bowl. The berries exploded with flavor in his mouth, and he ate them all first. "If you don't know how to kill it, what are we supposed to do?"

"Use talent to find way."

"My talent brought me here, to you. I'm still not sure what it is, or how to use it."

Ulli sat in front of Petyr. "Put bowl down. Focus on me."

Petyr followed Ulli's instructions, his gaze coming to meet Ulli's yellow eyes.

"A Seeker can find answers to any question, solutions for any need."

Petyr nodded.

"You must ask of your talent right questions. Concentrate on your goal. Your talent will show you what you need."

"What are the limits?"

A quick frown crossed Ulli's lips. "I do not know."

"How do you know what a Seeker is, and what a Seeker can do, but not know the limits?"

"Keekele do not produce Seekers."

This surprised Petyr. "Never? Then how did you learn about them?"

"Seeker is human talent. Dreamstrider is Keekele talent. I learned of Seekers through dreams."

"Whose dreams? I had never heard of such a thing as Seeker until you showed me."

"Dreams of those long dead."

"How long?" Petyr was beginning to realize something about the creature in front of him, the Keekele. Ulli wasn't just old. He was ancient.

"Our lives encompass eight of your human lifetimes. I discovered Seekers, searched their dreams before they disappeared."

"What happened to them?"

"I do not know. They dwindled until none were left. It is not easy to pluck answers from dreams."

Ulli blinked slowly, then straightened up. "We have wandered far from path. Close eyes."

"Why?"

"Close."

Petyr shut his eyes. *I wish I knew why I'm doing this.*

"I may not know limits of your talent. I do know how to use them. It is why Kinefea chose for me to stay."

Petyr's eyes flipped open. "What?"

Ulli raised his voice. "Close your eyes, human. Explanations of past are unimportant, now."

Petyr couldn't resist the command, and shut his eyes. He couldn't keep his mind from working over Ulli's statement. *Chosen to stay? What does he mean? Where did the others go?* Then he remembered the second voice in his dream, the lower, gravelly one. The one that had seemed not to trust Ulli's assessment of him.

"Calm your thoughts. Clear your mind of all but sound of my voice."

Petyr tried to do as asked. He remembered back to the early days of his training as a Questioner, where they'd started him almost the same way. He tried to remember what that was like. He hadn't needed it in so long.

Once he remembered, he found it easy to follow his earlier training and banish the thoughts until he had nothing.

"Good. Think of something for which you do not know location."

Petyr cast about for something that might fit Ulli's request, and could think of nothing for a moment. Then he remembered his trunk with his notes and his clothes and every other thing he owned in the world.

"You have something," said Ulli.

"Yes," said Petyr.

"Now, like in dream, put your thought into finding what is lost. Look for path."

"I already know how to do this. I found you."

"Quiet. Focus on loss. Look for path."

Petyr tried to do what Ulli asked. He pictured the trunk in his mind, the way the bands of brass held it together, the dents he remembered, the way the latch was off just a hair and had to be pushed shut.

He looked for the path, tried to feel the pull that had brought him to Ulli. Anything. He found nothing.

He tried asking questions. *Where is my trunk? How can I find my trunk?* He waited for some response, some feeling, some direction. When he asked for help before, the knowledge of where to go came almost instantly. This time, nothing.

"I see it in my mind, but there is no path," he said after he'd exhausted all of the ideas he could think of. "There's no pull, no sense of direction. Nothing."

Ulli grunted. "If we dreamed, I could see what you see."

Petyr thought back to his earlier questions that led him to Ulli. *What exactly did I ask? How did I phrase the question?*

A moment later, he remembered. *I asked, 'Who can help me save this town?'*

He felt the tug again pulling him toward Ulli.

Who. Who? Maybe it only works for finding people.

Who knows where my trunk is?

Nothing changed. Petyr opened his eyes, frustrated, and upon seeing Ulli, the compulsion fell away.

"Why do you open eyes?" Ulli asked.

"I tried everything I could think of, even asking questions like the ones that lead me to you. 'Where is it?' didn't work. After a moment, I thought maybe it only works for people, so I asked 'Who knows where it is?', but that didn't work either."

Ulli frowned. "I think second question would find success."

Petyr's stomach grumbled. He picked up the bowl and started picking through its contents again. He yawned as he brought a long, yellowish root to his mouth. "Maybe I'm tired."

"Perhaps that is it," said Ulli.

Petyr wanted to stand up and throw the bowl at the wall. He wanted to hit something. He remained sitting. "I don't understand what brought me to you. I asked who could help me save the town, and the path to you came clear immediately. But you say you don't know how to save the town. That you don't know how to kill the Quenikuhg. Why am I here?"

Ulli stood. "You should sleep. Dreams sometimes make things clearer. I will leave you here. Light will dim when you are ready for sleep."

Petyr watched Ulli exit the room, and then he watched the door for a few moments, waiting for Ulli to return. When Ulli did not return, Petyr went back to eating the food Ulli had provided.

Alec came over to him. "Do you know what I started to wonder, Petyr?"

Petyr shook his head.

"This place is so large. It obviously used to hold hundreds of his people, if not more. Where did they all go? What did Ulli mean when he said he was chosen to stay?"

Petyr pondered the question for a moment, then said, "I have no idea. I hope to find that out in the morning."

"Are we leaving in the morning?"

Petyr shook his head. "We're not leaving until I figure out what Ulli knows that can help us save Dunsriver."

⚔ ⚔ ⚔

Petyr awoke with little more idea of why he'd been lead to Ulli than when he went to sleep. Alec still slept, snoring softly, and Ulli hadn't joined him yet. He had some time to think—or go exploring.

Petyr rolled up the mat he'd slept on, which had barely broken the unforgiving stone floor. Despite the poor sleeping conditions, he felt well rested.

He poked his head out of the room and looked around the main cavern. During the night, he'd seen the light dim so that it was easy to sleep. He assumed it was the work of some Keekele magic. The Fringe, this cavern. They held some special types of powers he'd never seen in the Empire. Of course, most of those types of things were either controlled by the Empire, or outlawed.

Now, though, the light in the cavern had returned to its near daylight brightness.

Without the need to follow Ulli, he could take some time to examine the walls of the cavern. Off to his right, one of the ramps started up from the floor, rising slowly as it circumnavigated the cavern walls. He went to it and started climbing it.

It was thin. He could see two of Ulli's people passing by each other on it, but he couldn't imagine he and Alec executing the same maneuver without one or the other falling from it. It felt more like a ledge than a ramp.

He approached one of the openings he'd earlier assumed to be a door, and found it covered in glass. A window. Not an entrance. He peered through it, but the room beyond was dark and he couldn't make out much of anything.

I wonder where the door is? He searched around, and was

about to give up before finding a crack in the cavern wall and three small holes, arrayed in a vertical line.

It must be a door.

If his fingers were smaller, he might have been able to slip them in. He tried to pull at the indents, but could not fit his fingers in far enough to grip anything.

Perhaps farther up.

As he ascended the wall via the walkway, he passed more closed off, empty rooms. He tried to keep from looking down too much. One wrong step, one overbalanced lean, and he'd find himself falling to the floor of the cavern.

When he reached the top of the ramp, he found a room that did not have a door. He had to stoop to fit through the opening. Inside, he could stand a little straighter, but he knew his neck would soon ache if he spent any time here.

The room seemed dark. The light from the cavern did not light much more than the area around the door. The room didn't have its own illumination.

Once his eyes adjusted to the dim light, he could see deeper into the room and found that it extended farther than he imagined. He wished he had a lamp so that he could see into the black. Barrels and crates lined the walls of the room.

He worked himself deeper into the room, trying to see if there was a back wall. His foot caught something and, overbalanced as he was from stooping, he stumbled to the stone floor, banging his knee.

He sat on the floor and rubbed at his knee which now ached. His fall had left him facing the door, and against the light that came through, he could see the outline of the thing he had tripped over. It looked familiar to him.

It can't be.

He put his hands on it, felt the wood beneath his finger tips, felt the metal bands that held it together, searched for the latch and the lock that held it shut, and found them where he expected them.

My trunk. How did it get down here? Or up here? He tried,

but couldn't imagine Ulli dragging it up the ramp he'd recently ascended. He couldn't imagine Ulli dragging the trunk anywhere, for that matter. He had to have had help. *So many questions.*

The room lit up and Petyr heard Ulli say, "Such as, 'Why did Ulli bother to bring big box here?'"

Petyr looked up and found Ulli standing at the door. "Yes, like that, and how you seem to read my mind."

"Ulli does not read minds. It is question Ulli would ask first."

Ulli stepped into the room, bringing the light with him—a small ball of light that rested in his hand.

"Normally, it might be my first question," Petyr said while thinking back to the previous night. "But right now, I'm wondering why I couldn't find it last night."

"This is what you tried to find?"

Petyr nodded.

"How did you seek?"

Petyr thought back. "First, like with the girl. I pictured it in my mind. Tried to make a connection somehow. Looked for the path, but saw nothing."

Ulli moved in closer to Petyr and put a hand on the lid of the trunk.

"Next," Petyr continued, "I tried asking questions, like I did when I found the path to you. 'Where is my trunk?' No path, no urge presented itself. No compulsion to go in any particular direction."

Ulli, standing, was only a little taller than Petyr sitting. "You seemed to find compulsion."

"When I asked myself the question that brought me to you. 'Who can help me save this town?' I felt the compulsion then. So I tried rephrasing my question about the trunk. 'Who knows where my trunk is?'"

"And?"

"Nothing changed."

Petyr thought he saw a smile cross Ulli's lips, the first he had seen. Ulli seemed so sad most of the time.

"Why do you smile?" Petyr asked.

"You expected answer to question to differ from result received, so you did not see it."

"I don't understand."

"You said nothing changed. Nothing changed because you were already compelled to seek me."

Petyr wanted to slap himself. He'd somehow expected Seeking to be different than Questioning, to have different rules.

"As a Questioner, I was taught to be specific in my questions, and to work at avoiding expectations. Expectation can influence the Questioner's ability to determine truth.

"I'm guilty of expecting the trunk to be anywhere but here."

"Do not be so hard. You are guilty of learning."

Petyr didn't want to argue the point. His knee felt a little better. He stood up, knee complaining, and found himself looking down at Ulli. The height difference reminded him of an earlier question he'd wanted to ask. "Ulli, how did you manage to bring my trunk here?"

Whatever smile had remained on Ulli's face fled. "It is difficult…"

Petyr interrupted. "I didn't mean to upset you."

"No, no. Not your fault. My, I think you would call him husband, helped move it."

Ulli is female? Petyr couldn't quite contain his shock, couldn't keep the surprise from his face. He did manage not to speak the thought. "Your… your husband?"

"Yes. He helped me bring it. Do you remember other voice from Dreamwalk?"

"Yes."

"That was husband."

"Where is he?"

Ulli turned away from Petyr. Petyr felt an urge to put his hand on her shoulder, but he resisted it. He did not know if it would be welcome. He thought he heard a sniff, but it only happened once.

"He is with others."

Petyr thought he should somehow understand this, but he couldn't make sense of it. "Where are they?"

When she spoke again, her voice seemed to echo off the walls, hinting of a despair that ran deeper than the waterfall outside the cavern. "He joined Protector."

CHAPTER 21

P etyr couldn't quite grasp what Ulli told him. He sat down on his trunk. "Why would your husband join the Protector?"

"Protector needed strength."

It occurred to Petyr that he knew where all of Ulli's people went, but he had to ask anyway. "That's where everybody went?"

Ulli nodded.

Petyr remembered something Ulli had said the night before. "Last night, you said you were chosen. You were chosen to stay behind?"

"For you. I must teach you of Quenikuhg, then I will join my husband and my people."

Petyr understood. Until he'd heard Alura lived, he'd often contemplated what would happen after he completed his quest to avenge her death, to bring justice to those who were responsible. "I too, once, thought about dying to be with my wife."

Ulli's eyes grew wide and she waved her arms. "No. Not die. The Keekele with Protector live. Protector lives. They are together in life. I alone, suffer. I do my duty here, while they fight battle against Quenikuhg. It may be my strength, added to Protector, will keep Quenikuhg trapped."

"You don't believe it, do you. You don't believe you will be enough."

"I will do what I can."

Silence fell between them.

After a moment, Petyr stood and put his hand into his pocket, but couldn't find a thing in it. He realized he didn't have the key for the trunk with him. He would not be able to open it to get his things. He bent down to check the lock, hoping that somehow it had broken, but it remained solid as ever.

"You wish to open?"

"I don't have my key."

Ulli stepped toward him, and he moved out of the way. She reached into a pocket and pulled something from it that Petyr couldn't see. Ulli set the glowing orb on top of the trunk, and set to work on the lock. She stuck whatever she'd pulled from her pocket, Petyr guessed some little bit of metal, into the lock and started twisting it around until the lock fell open.

She picked up the orb and stood back.

Petyr bent down, removed the lock, flipped the latch up, and opened the trunk. The clothes and other items were jostled around, but all seemed to be there. *It'll be good to wear my own clothes again.*

"So how did you and your husband bring this up here? You didn't carry it up the ramp."

"No. We brought through other entrance."

"Other entrance?"

Ulli pointed to the back of the room, where light faded to black.

"Yes. A door leads to another tunnel. Tunnel comes out near glade where I first saw you."

Petyr looked and couldn't find the door immediately, but in the dim light, that didn't surprise him. While he searched, his mind worked over the last part of what Ulli said until it caught on a thought.

"You, you were the one at the clearing where the..." He stopped. He didn't know how to say it delicately.

"Where daughter was taken by Quenikuhg."

Petyr slumped down against the side of the trunk. *Are there any tragedies you haven't suffered?* He wanted to know, but wouldn't ask. It was not his place. And it had happened long ago. At times, Petyr had thought the tragedies and betrayals he'd suffered in the past year were more than he could bear. He could not imagine suffering what Ulli suffered. To lose her people, her husband, her daughter, and in such horrific fashion.

"You do not ask about her."

"It's not my place to ask."

"It is your place. You are here to learn about Quenikuhg so that you may kill it. If you do not ask, I must tell you. Do not think to spare me suffering. I have already suffered."

"You've already said you don't know how to kill it. What point is there in asking you to relive an old loss? I know the pain that comes with thinking you've lost everything. My loss was not greater than yours, but I wouldn't want to talk about it if I didn't have to."

"Petyr, my loss becomes your loss if you fail to stop Quenikuhg. If it breaks free, nothing your people can do will stop it."

"If my people can't stop it, what makes you think I can kill this thing?"

"You are Seeker. There might be others, but they do not have Ulli to teach. You can find way, but you must know enough to ask proper questions. You have learned, already, you can not ask, 'How do I kill it?'"

Petyr nodded.

"Tell me. How can you know if you ask proper question if you do not learn what you can from me?"

Petyr couldn't argue with her, especially if she was willing to tell him everything. He sighed. "Please, Ulli. Tell me about your daughter."

Ulli got a far away look in her eye, then turned and headed for the opening to the main cavern. She said over her shoulder, "Your friend is awake. I will tell while we eat." Then she went through the opening and disappeared around the corner.

Petyr groaned. He stood up, looked through the contents of the trunk, thought about grabbing a change of clothes, and decided against it. He shut the lid, then followed Ulli out of the room, dreading the descent to the cavern floor. This time, he'd have to look down.

⚔ ⚔ ⚔

Petyr found Alec awake and angry when he made it to the cavern floor.

"Why didn't you tell me where you were going?" Alec asked. "I woke up and you were missing. I couldn't find Ulli, either."

"I didn't expect to be gone very long. I just wanted to look around. You could have called out."

Alec gave Petyr a look that said everything Petyr should have known. No Ghost would call out, ever. "When are we leaving?" Alec asked.

"As soon as I know what I need to know. My talent brought me here for something. I don't know why, yet."

"What do you mean?"

"Ulli doesn't know how to kill it, but I was Seeking someone who could help me save the town. Ulli knows something that will help. I can't leave until I know it."

"What if Ulli isn't supposed to tell you anything? What if he is supposed to come with us?"

"She. Ulli is female."

Alec's brow lifted. "Well, what if *she* is supposed to come with us?"

Petyr hadn't thought of that. He'd followed Ulli's assumptions. *By the Mother, I've been making that mistake a lot, lately. Still...*

"I don't know."

Petyr saw Ulli approach from behind Alec and stop a good distance away.

"Follow," she said, then turned and started walking toward the garden.

Petyr followed her. Alec stepped up beside him.

"Maybe you're right, Alec. Maybe I'm supposed to do more, here, than ask her questions."

"At least you admit the possibility. That's a step."

"A step?"

About halfway through the garden, Ulli turned to the right down another path.

"You've tried to do everything on your own. I came along to help, and most of the time, I've played driver. You can't save the world by yourself."

The path Ulli lead them down ended on a circular platform raised over the center of a pond. Some low benches, probably the right height for the Keekele, ringed the platform. Ulli had bowls of some sort of vegetable broth prepared and waiting on the benches.

"Sit," she said. "Sit, eat. I will tell you of my daughter."

Petyr sat, grateful for the opportunity to end the conversation Alec seemed keen on having. He picked up the bowl next to him and found it hot. A delicate looking white spoon rested in the bowl. When he grasped it, he was surprised to find it was made of stone, or something much like it.

He ladled some of the broth into his mouth and found it peppery. He'd expected it to be more in line with the meal from the night before.

"This is good," he said to Ulli.

"We do not cook final meal of day, eating it as it was provided to us. Morning meal is often more exciting."

Petyr felt grateful. It still lacked meat, but it suited his palette better than raw berries and roots.

"Please," he said, after swallowing a mouthful of the broth, "tell me of your daughter."

Ulli leaned her head back and shut her eyes before she started speaking. "Among Keekele, being Dreamstrider confers much status. I was able to join my husband, who you might call king, because of my talent.

"We had daughter. She grew into all we imagined she could become. About age she started looking for husband of her own, she met young, ambitious Keekele with great number of talents.

"We felt excitement for her and encouraged their union. We could not have been happier—until day he disappeared.

"We commenced search and could not find him. We searched for month without sign. We feared humans took him. We feared many things. We feared anything but what happened."

Petyr took in a breath. In an instant, he realized what happened to the young Keekele. Ulli had lowered her head, but still kept her eyes shut.

"What did happen?" asked Alec.

"He came back one night and took our daughter. He had changed. He was bigger. Blue fire filled his eyes. He killed people in our home, went to her room. She disappeared."

She sniffed a bit. Even with hundreds of years having passed, Petyr could tell she still hurt for her daughter.

"We found her weeks later, hanging from tree, mutilated."

Petyr set his bowl down. He couldn't eat any more. "Why did you never take her body down?"

"We can't touch her. Spikes are poison."

The light in the chamber turned blue, creating a surreal landscape within the cavern.

"He comes," said Ulli. Her voice was filled with terror.

Petyr stood. "Who comes?"

"Quenikuhg."

CHAPTER 22

Petyr stood. "I need to go back," he said. "I need to help them."

He ran off through the garden, back to where he'd slept. *I need to get my pack. I can toss everything from it and grab my notes and a change of clothes from the trunk.*

He heard someone behind him, turned and saw Alec. Behind Alec, Ulli followed distantly.

Ulli. I need Ulli. I need to know the fastest way out of here.

He pulled up in the room where they'd slept, found his pack and started emptying its contents on the floor. He kept the hatchet, but left everything else.

Alec ran in. "Petyr, what are we doing?"

"Empty your pack of everything except the bullets and powder. My trunk is up at the top of the cavern. We need to take my notes and other evidence with us. Ulli says there is a way out up there."

"Why the hurry? We can't stop it."

Petyr cast about in his head. *Why do I need to hurry back? Alec is right. I can't stop it.* It was almost a compulsion, though. "I don't know. I need to try to help."

"This is crazy, Petyr. You almost got killed last time. What makes you think it would be any different?"

Petyr stood and turned to leave the room. Ulli stood in the

doorway. "Alec, please just accept that I have to do this. I have to try to help. They risked their town to save me. I have to at least try."

"It'll be over before we get back."

Petyr ignored that. "Ulli, you said there was a way out from the room where you have my trunk?"

"There is."

"Will you lead me?"

Ulli blinked her oversized eyes a couple times, then said, "I will."

Petyr looked over his shoulder. "Are you coming?"

Alec groaned and stood up, his pack empty, the gun in one hand.

Ulli lead them out of the room and up the ramp. Petyr was so preoccupied with thinking about how he might stop the Quenikuhg when he returned to Dunsriver, neither the thin walkway or the long drop bothered him at all. But by the time they reached the top, he still hadn't come up with any ideas. He didn't worry about it. *I've got time to figure this out.*

Once they entered the room, he opened the trunk and started pulling the ledgers and notebooks out of it. Alec took them and stuffed their packs. They put as many of his clothes as would fit into the packs until they couldn't hold any more. There were still things left in the trunk that Petyr would have liked to take with him—hats, shoes and other bulky items—but they weren't important enough to bother with.

"We're ready, Ulli. Lead us," Petyr said.

Ulli lead them to the back of the room. The door had that same series of indents into which he would not have been able to fit his fingers. Ulli put her fingers in and pushed. The door slid open easily. It looked to Petyr that it could have been as light as wood from the ease of its movement, but a touch as he passed convinced him it was rock, like the walls around them.

Ulli held her light out in front of her, allowing Petyr to see down the length of the passageway, at least until the light gave way to dark.

The passage was dry, unlike the one that had brought them to

Ulli's cavern. It also seemed a little taller. Petyr thought he would be able to avoid too many bumps to his head, though he would still have to stoop a bit.

Ulli looked over her shoulder, than started running down the passage. She was quicker than Petyr had thought she'd be. Petyr and Alec kept up with her despite the need to stoop.

Petyr was surprised when Ulli came to a stop. He couldn't see an entrance, or any way out. The passageway appeared to have ended.

"How do we get out?" asked Alec.

Ulli shoved her fingers into some indents that Petyr had missed, and a piece of the wall opened away from her as she pushed. "It leads to a hole among the roots of a tree."

Alec stepped through into the passage beyond.

Petyr stood and watched Ulli for a moment. Then he closed his eyes and questioned again. *Who can help me save the town?*

The path appeared, the compulsion came back, leading him to Ulli. He opened his eyes again.

"Ulli, come with us."

Ulli shook her head. "I can not go to human town."

"I need you. The path still leads to you."

"Then perhaps you ask wrong question. I have lived nearly eight hundred years. I have searched five hundred of those years for a way to correct our sin. I do not have answer."

"Please, Ulli? Perhaps you have an answer, but don't know it."

She seemed to think a moment before answering. "I do not have answer." Petyr's hopes fell. "But I will wait here for you. Now go. If you do not hurry, Quenikuhg will be gone."

Petyr went through the door, then turned back and said, "Thank you," before continuing on. Something in his heart tugged at leaving her.

⚔ ⚔ ⚔

Alec had already squeezed through the opening by the time Petyr found his way to it. It lay just around a bend in a natural cave system. He could see the roots of the tree. A bit of light slipped down between them.

He looked back at where the door had been, and it looked like an unworked stone wall. He hoped Ulli would come out if he needed her.

Never mind that. Time to get back to the town and see if there's anything you can do.

Petyr had to remove his pack to squeeze through the opening. He had no idea how Ulli and her husband managed to squeeze the trunk through. With the talents and other magic they seemed to have, it probably wouldn't have been difficult.

Once he pulled the pack out, he looked up and found the forest thick with the blue mist. *We're too late.*

"No, we're not too late," he said.

"What?" asked Alec.

"Run! We still have a chance!" Petyr started racing through the forest, running as fast as the heavy pack would let him.

Behind him, he heard Alec asking "A chance at what?"

He didn't have the breath to answer.

He passed through the glade where they'd found the skeleton of Ulli's daughter without pausing. The skeleton still hung from its tree, spikes protruding, a ghost from another age.

He dodged in and out of the trees following the path they'd used just the other day. He wasn't sure if it was his imagination, but it seemed the mist was growing thicker.

His lungs started to ache. He didn't know how long he could keep it up, but he'd do what he could. He tried not to imagine what the Quenikuhg might be doing at the moment, but the thoughts crept into his head anyway. If they couldn't stop it, some young woman would be taken away, brutalized, her life destroyed. And if that thing somehow brought another of itself into this world on this side of the Fringe, Petyr doubted his ability to find it.

Find it. Where is the Quenikuhg?

He waited a moment for a path to show itself, but nothing happened.

A tree blocked the path and he clambered over it as quick as he could. A look back as he rolled over the top showed him that Alec was close behind him. He turned and kept running.

Why didn't that work? Is it because I'm running? That shouldn't matter, should it? Because my eyes weren't closed? They weren't closed when I was talking to Sim.

He broke past the last of the trees into the open field. There was no one around. He couldn't see too far in either direction because of the mist. *There should be someone here. Unless they ran back to the town.* The mist lay thick enough over the field that he could not see the town, either.

Petyr's legs began to ache, slowing him. His breath had begun to hurt his throat. His position as a Questioner had never required him to maintain his shape. He wasn't completely unused to physical exertion, especially not after the last year, but he hadn't run this far, this fast, with extra weight on him since he was a boy.

He willed himself to go on, to keep his legs moving. That he couldn't seek the Quenikuhg worried him.

He saw the wall in the distance, and made for the gate. He still couldn't see much of anything beyond that, though.

It has to be there. How do I stop it? The answer eluded him.

He kept running.

As he approached the wall, he thought he heard men yelling.

He ran through the gate, and into the back of a man, knocking them both to the ground.

"Hey," the man said.

Petyr started pushing himself up, then felt a hand pulling at him from behind. When he was up, he found it was Alec that helped him up. He looked down and found he recognized the man. Rolend, the Master of Farms. Petyr helped him up. He heard more yelling followed by a low rumbling growl and the sound of timber splintering.

"Where is it?" Petyr asked.

Rolend seemed a little stunned. He just pointed toward the town center.

More yelling echoed through the streets.

"We can follow the shouts," Alec said.

They ran off, leaving Rolend behind.

As they approached the center, they found a trail of hurt men and broken buildings, and followed it. Something was different this time around, as Petyr didn't remember the Quenikuhg creating so much destruction.

"I wonder," Alec panted as if reading Petyr's mind, "if it knows we killed its offspring."

A moment of terror threatened to rise up and cause him to run the other direction, but he buried it, deep. "Do you think it knows who did it?" Petyr asked between breaths.

"I hope not."

As they neared the central square, the sounds of fighting grew louder. Petyr slowed. He didn't want to run right into the middle of a fight. He pulled the hatchet from its loop on his pack and hefted it, wishing it were quite a bit larger and heavier.

As they turned the last corner, they emerged into chaos.

Flames leapt from the town center building. Smoke clogged the air. The Quenikuhg, towering over the men who stood their ground at its feet, swung one arm at them like it was swatting at rats. Its other arm held something, someone. For a moment, he thought he recognized her, but he denied it. *It can't be her.*

But then he heard her voice call out as she saw him, somehow. "Petyr!"

"Carree!"

He ran for the Quenikuhg, waving his hatchet, but he was too late. The giant creature broke free of the men that had momentarily corralled it and loped off through the town, running past Petyr without a care for him.

Carree!

Petyr started to run after her, but a hand grabbed him from behind. "You can't stop it!" Alec yelled at him.

Petyr pulled at him, but he couldn't break Alec's grip.

"You can't do it, not by yourself."

Petyr looked around, then looked behind him. The Town Center building. "Dyllan!"

He broke Alec's grip then, and ran for the building. He shed his pack on its steps, then dashed through the doors. The smoke was thick, and burned his already raw lungs, but he kept as low as he could and breathed as little as possible.

He went straight for the cellar. The door was not guarded. *The guard must have fled during the fighting, or gone out to help.*

Petyr yanked it open, and smoke boiled up out of doorway. For a moment, he despaired that they were all dead, before he heard a soft cry from below. He pulled his shirt over his mouth and nose and descended the stairs.

"Dyllan!" he yelled.

"Petyr?" Dyllan's voice. Petyr felt some pressure come off his shoulders. *At least he's alive.*

When he reached the bottom of the stairs, he saw the stores on the far side of the room were the source of the fire. They had already burned a hole in the floor above them. The rest of the floor would soon be engulfed. The guards were missing.

He found Dyllan and the others lying face down on the floor.

"Dyllan, where are the guards?"

"They ran up the stairs when that thing attacked the building."

"Their keys. Did they leave them here?"

"I don't think so."

Petyr glanced up at the bars where they were embedded in the wood. "Can't you break the bars out?"

"With the floor weakened by the fire, I'm afraid I'd drop the whole thing on top of us."

"It's going to drop on top of us if we don't get you out."

Petyr thought he saw an odd look on Dyllan's face, but didn't stop to ponder it. He had to find a way to get them out. The flames were eating away at the floor above them. It wouldn't be too long before his prophecy came true. He searched around for something to use in picking the locks. They couldn't be that hard. But he couldn't find anything.

"Petyr, get out. Save yourself, at least."

"No. I need you. That thing took Carree. I have to save her."

"Who's Carree?"

"Mother burn it all! Why can't I find something to pick these damned locks!"

They were running out of time. *If I can't find something, I'll have to leave.*

A hand pulled at his shoulder. "Petyr!"

Alec. Petyr turned. "What are you doing here?"

"I think you need these," he said, then coughed from the smoke. He held up a set of keys.

"Come on."

Alec went to work on the cages, opening each of them. Petyr started coughing again from the smoke. After the first cage was open, he went in to try to pull the Tracker out. The Tracker didn't move. Petyr felt at his throat, but could feel no heartbeat. He was dead.

Dyllan's cage opened next, and Dyllan came out. Then the Questioner's cage. Alec waved at Dyllan. "He's alive, but barely breathing."

Dyllan went over, put the Questioner over his shoulder and then pushed Petyr up the stairs.

Petyr held his breath and ran past a wall of flame that was near to blocking his path. The heat from it singed the whiskers on his face. He stumbled out of the building and fell to the steps where he coughed and coughed, trying to get the smoke out.

Hands pulled at him, dragging him away from the building, and he let them. He couldn't have stopped them if he wanted.

Moments later, Dyllan and Alec tumbled to the ground next to him.

After they'd mostly stopped coughing, Dyllan asked, "Petyr, who is Carree?"

"Someone I made a promise to."

A few moments later, someone started ministering to him. He looked up to find Ilsan.

"Ilsan, where's Roderick?"

Ilsan shuddered. "Dead."

"What about Sim?" *I hope he's not dead, too.*

"I'm not sure. I think he's chasing after that thing."

"Send someone after him, quickly. I need to talk to him."

"Why?"

Petyr coughed again. His lungs ached, thick from smoke. His legs felt like they were dead. "I need to ask him a couple questions about Bran, his son."

Ilsan got up and yelled at someone to bring back Sim, then sat back down next to Petyr.

"What do you need to ask him?"

"I need to know if Bran was a Blocker."

CHAPTER 23

"A Blocker?" asked Ilsan. "Why would you need to know, and what does Bran have to do with this, anyway?"

Petyr sat still for a few long moments, watching the burning building. The men and women who weren't injured or dead were forming a bucket line, mostly in an effort to keep other buildings from suffering the same fate.

"We should wait for Sim," Petyr said.

The unconscious Questioner coughed and seemed to be waking up. Ilsan moved to help him.

Petyr pondered what to do next, but beyond chasing after the Quenikuhg, he could think of little else. He wouldn't know what to do if he found it.

Dyllan walked over and sat down next to Petyr. "So, that's what you wanted my help with?"

Petyr nodded.

"What demon spawned that thing?"

Petyr looked at his former friend. His soot covered face showed smears where he'd tried to rub at his eyes. "I'm not sure it's the spawn of a demon."

"Then what is it? I've never heard of anything like it."

"I think it might just *be* a demon."

Silence stretched between them. Dyllan appeared to be trying to come to terms with the idea. He opened his mouth a couple times to say something, but closed it again.

He looked away, surveying the carnage of the square. Petyr followed his gaze. Men still lay on the ground, dead. Ilsan had left the Questioner, who had rolled over on his side, to attend to those in the square that were still moving.

"I'll help," said Dyllan.

"What?"

"It's what you want, right? You want my help with this demon."

Petyr looked at Dyllan again and saw his old friend watching him. "Yes. And after?"

Dyllan shook his head. "I don't know, Petyr. I believe you, but..."

"It's a lot to deal with, I know."

"Do you have a plan for dealing with it?"

"Not entirely," Petyr said. "I have to somehow rescue Alura and my daughter..."

"They should be safe at my estate."

"For how long, Dyllan? How long will they be safe once the High Lords know you aren't bringing me home?" Petyr looked over at the Questioner, who looked like he might live. "How long will they be safe once they don't hear from their Questioners or their Tracker?"

Dyllan didn't respond. Petyr didn't have an answer either.

"Petyr," Alec said. Alec seemed to have mostly recovered. "Do you think it matters whether Bran was a Blocker?"

"Of course it matters."

"Why?"

"I couldn't seek the Quenikuhg. How can we find Carree if we can't find the Quenikuhg."

Alec nearly crossed his eyes. "Petyr, you don't need to seek the Quenikuhg. He's got Carree."

Of course. "Why didn't I see that?"

"You're exhausted?" Alec offered.

Petyr stood, but had to put his hand on Alec's shoulder to do so. His legs didn't want to hold him up. He despaired of having to run all that distance, and more.

He closed his eyes, and felt the world sway underneath him, and then grow still. *Carree.* He brought her into his mind, a vision of her. *Where are you?* He searched for the path, and even in his exhaustion, it came to him. He could feel her, walk straight to her, if his legs would carry him.

"I can find her," he said.

He opened his eyes again, and saw that Petyr and Dyllan had stood. *We need packs. The packs.* "The packs, Alec? Where are they?"

Alec pointed to a patch of land about twenty feet away. "I pulled yours away from the building while I retrieved the key."

"How did you know I'd need the key?"

"I saw the guards lying in the street."

Dyllan put his hand on Alec's shoulder, and Alec shrugged away. "Thanks, Ghost."

Alec looked around quickly. Petyr did, too. The only other who could have heard was the Questioner, and he didn't look like he was paying attention. "Quiet, Protector. I don't need people knowing that."

Petyr sighed. "I hope this isn't the way it will be between you two."

Dyllan shrugged, and Alec kept glaring at him.

A loud crash echoed through the square, and flames burst through a huge hole in the building. The roof had collapsed.

Petyr started walking over to the packs. "We need to get moving. I don't imagine we have much time."

"What's your plan?" Dyllan asked. He'd fallen into step behind Petyr.

"Plan? All I can think of is tracking Carree down and stealing her away." *I promised to do more, but I have no idea how.*

⚔ ⚔ ⚔

Petyr picked up his pack and turned to see Sim striding up to him, anger and fear warring on the merchant's face. "Why did you bring me back here?" he asked.

"I can find her," Petyr said, hoping to forestall any violence. "But I need to talk to you about Bran, first."

"I could have followed it. I could have tracked it to the Fringe."

Petyr felt too tired to deal with Sim, but he needed his questions answered. "You would not have made it through."

"What do you mean?"

Petyr looked around. People in the square were watching. "Follow me to Ilsan's. We'll talk there."

"You're wasting my time."

Petyr's patience finally gave out. He reached out and slapped Sim across the face. Petyr wasn't sure who was more surprised, him, Sim, Dyllan, or Alec. Other voices in the square went silent. "Listen to me, Sim. I have some things to tell you, and I need to ask you questions." He leaned in to Sim so he could lower his voice. "We can do it here, but do you really want people learning about what happened to Bran?"

Sim had that same fire in his eyes that he'd had two days earlier. The slap hadn't made it any easier to find a friend in Sim. Petyr didn't care. *Now isn't the time to worry about whether he will be a friend later.*

"Fine," Sim said.

Petyr lead the other three to Ilsan's home as fast as he could manage on his worn out legs. With all the injured being carried there, including the Questioner, Petyr feared they wouldn't find a room to themselves. He hoped they could hide in the sitting room.

Petyr looked down at himself. He'd have to change clothes while he was there. *It would be nice to bathe, too.* Deep inside, he felt there wasn't enough time for a bath and put the thought out of his head.

When they walked through the door, it was indeed as busy as Petyr feared. They had to slip past men sitting in the halls, as well as their wives and mothers who tended them. Fortunately, he'd also been right about the sitting room. It was empty.

The four of them slipped in and shut the door behind them.

"So," Sim said as the door shut, "what is this about?"

"It's about Bran."

"You said that."

"Sit down, Sim," said Petyr, motioning to the seat Ilsan normally occupied. Petyr took the seat next to it and stretched out his aching legs in front of him. He didn't allow the rest of him to relax though his body desperately wanted him to.

"Now, look at me. Was Bran a Blocker?"

"Why does that matter? And what about that Protector? You want him to know?"

Petyr grunted in frustration. "He's helping me, now. You know he can't go to the Empire with anything he learns here." Petyr hoped he wasn't putting words into Dyllan's mouth. Dyllan hadn't actually said he'd help beyond dealing with the Quenikuhg. "Don't evade the question, Sim."

Sim looked at Dyllan again before answering. "Yes, he was."

"The Mother," Petyr said.

"Why was that important?" Alec asked.

"If he wasn't a Blocker, then I thought maybe Carree could control him."

"What are you talking about?" Sim asked.

"It doesn't matter," Petyr said.

"It did matter. You asked me. Why?"

Petyr didn't really want to go into it with Sim. He didn't have the time. Carree was out there, he could feel her, getting farther away all the time. Petyr felt telling Sim that Bran was a part of the Quenikuhg could only send the man deeper into despair.

Sim leaned forward in his chair. "Petyr, tell me." He kept his voice low, controlled. "What does Bran have to do with saving Carree? Why would Carree need to control him?"

Petyr didn't want to say anything. *This can only end poorly.*

"Petyr, please?"

Petyr couldn't withstand the desperation in Sim's voice. He thought Sim already expected a horrible revelation. Petyr looked up to Alec, who was shaking his head.

Petyr decided telling Sim could break him, but holding out could also break Sim if he later found out. "Last night, Alec and I learned what happened to Bran. We learned about the Fringe, what it really is."

"Tell me."

"The Fringe is essentially a barrier to keep that giant trapped behind it. Usually, when people enter, they get lost and are either trapped forever in the Fringe, or get turned around and come out on this side of it. It takes people with certain talents to break through to the other side."

"Blockers."

Petyr nodded. "And when he went through, he made it possible for that giant to reach through the Fringe, to warp it and move it."

Sim practically snarled. "He wouldn't have done that."

"He didn't have a choice. The giant took your son, made him part of it."

"That's not possible. It's a lie."

Petyr shook his head. *This is taking too long.* "It's not a lie, Sim. I could show you, but I don't have the time. Carree is farther away by the minute, and we have to prepare to go after her."

"You're going after her? How will you find her? She must be lost for good by now."

"I can find her, Sim."

Sim stood. "I'm going with you."

"I don't think so. You can't help us, and your town needs you."

"I can help you. I know the forest. Roderick can take care of the town."

"Roderick's dead, Sim."

Sim's mouth opened a little, and he worked his jaw back and forth. The noise of the injured filtered through the door.

"I'll bring her back, Sim. I'll bring her back to you."

Sim sat down again, relenting. "Do you know why we were in the Square?"

"I don't. I was in the forest."

"We were looking for you. I don't know if she's safer with you than somewhere else, but I realized she wouldn't stay here."

Petyr drew his legs up under him and leaned over to Sim, putting his hand on Sim's knee. "I will save her from that giant, Sim. I promised her. I don't break promises."

"What about Bran?"

Petyr didn't want to hear the hope in Sim's voice. He had no idea if any of Bran could be saved, if the Quenikuhg could be driven out without killing Bran in the process. "I don't know, Sim."

Sim dropped his head for a moment, before pushing himself out of the chair. "I guess I had better get to work then. Save my daughter, Petyr."

Dyllan moved out of the way of the door, allowing Sim access to it. Petyr hadn't realized Dyllan had stood guard.

Sim opened the door, and the cries of the injured spilled into the room.

"I'll save her, Sim."

Sim stepped through, and the door shut behind him.

⚔ ⚔ ⚔

As soon as Sim left the room, Petyr pulled clothes from his pack and changed. He left the old set in a pile near the door.

I hope Ilsan doesn't mind the pile of clothes in here.

Petyr and Alec emptied out their packs, stacking Petyr's things in the corner of the room near a shelf, then they went to find food and other things they'd need. Dyllan went in search of a pack of his own.

They found Ilsan working on a man who had a long gash on his forehead. When asked about food, Ilsan didn't even turn around while saying, "Take what you need."

They stuffed their packs, then went outside.

They tracked down Sim and got him to help find some horses, as well as a sword or some other blade for Dyllan. The Protector would be of little use without a weapon. Before too long, Dyllan had his own sword back and they raced off through the open gate and out into the fields.

Petyr led Alec and Dyllan to the edge of the forest, right near where he and Alec had emerged earlier that morning.

"Where are we going?" Alec asked. "Is she this way?"

"No, she's not exactly this direction, but I want one more chat with Ulli. I want to try to convince her to come with us."

"Who is Ulli," Dyllan asked.

"You'll meet her."

The three of them dismounted and lead their horses down the trail. Petyr didn't try to find Ulli with his talent yet. He wanted to keep the link to Carree as long as he could.

Soon, quicker than Petyr had thought possible, they found the clearing where Ulli's daughter's skeleton hung on the tree.

"What's that?" Dyllan asked.

Petyr looked closer. This was his fourth time seeing it. He'd grown accustomed to it. Dyllan would be seeing this for the first time. "That's Ulli's daughter."

"Where are the arms?"

"The Quenikuhg did that to her."

"That giant we're chasing?"

Petyr nodded. "That's what Ulli's people, the Keekele, call it."

"Why didn't they take her body down?"

"They can't touch the spikes. It hurts them."

Petyr turned his thoughts inward and thought of Ulli, asking his talent to lead him to her. It came back, showing him the path. What surprised him was that he could still hold on to Carree's path as well.

Petyr looked one last time at the skeleton, reminding himself of what would happen to Carree if they failed. His eyes were once again drawn to the spikes. *They hurt the Keekele. Is that why the Quenikuhg chose them? What if...*

He ran over to the skeleton and acted on the unfinished thought by attempting to pull the spikes out.

"What are you doing, Petyr?" Alec asked.

"The spikes hurt the Keekele. What if they'll hurt the Quenikuhg, too."

"Why would they hurt the Quenikuhg? It had to handle them."

"I have no idea. But in several hundred years, the Keekele could not discover a way to kill it. What if they couldn't discover the solution because they couldn't touch it?"

Dyllan came over and pulled the spikes from the tree. The skeleton fell from the tree and exploded into a powdery plume of dust. "It can't hurt to carry them along, can it?" Dyllan asked.

Dyllan stuffed them in his pack.

Petyr led them out of the clearing and deeper into the forest, following the path to Ulli.

After a few minutes, they found her standing next to the tree that hid the entrance to her people's home.

"You knew we were coming?" Petyr asked.

"I did not have to guess." She shuddered and pointed at Dyllan. "Who is that man?"

"He's a friend of mine. Why do you ask?"

"He carries instruments of my daughter's death. I feel them. I do not wish to be near them."

Petyr looked to Dyllan. For his part, Dyllan seemed unfazed by the diminutive Keekele. *Of course, he's already seen the skeleton on the tree.*

"Ride my horse, then," Petyr said.

"Why ride? I can walk."

Petyr was surprised. "I thought it would be harder to convince you to come with us."

"I am not going with you for reasons you think. I go to my husband."

Petyr nodded as he realized she wouldn't be able to travel through the Fringe with them in any case.

He concentrated on the path to Carree, and it grew clear in his mind. He felt sure it would lead them through the Fringe. *I hope we have time, Carree.*

"When we ride, you will ride with me?" he asked.

"I will," said Ulli.

He tugged on the lead of his horse. "To the Fringe, then."

CHAPTER 24

After a short time, a path through the forest opened up before them, and they were able to ride. Ulli rode behind Petyr and directed him through the forest. She found paths and trails he would have missed. When asked how she did it, she said, "I have lived long, here."

Petyr knew that for truth.

"Ulli," he asked at one point, "why does the Quenikuhg not leave a trail through the forest?"

"When Quenikuhg stretches Protector, he does not move through forest."

Petyr didn't quite understand it, but he wasn't sure that Ulli would explain in a way he could understand. Instead of asking her to try, he posed a different question. This time, he wasn't sure she could answer. "How long does she have?"

"Your girl?"

"Yes. How long until he kills her?"

"I do not know. A day? Two? It performs a ritual, we know. Beyond that, we have only guesses."

Petyr cursed and urged his horse to go faster.

"You do not need to hurry so."

"Why not?"

"You will find her in time."

Petyr wondered at this. Ulli sounded so certain. "How do you know?"

"I am Dreamstrider. I dreamed it."

Petyr wanted to turn to look at her, but feared losing his head to an overhanging branch. "You mean you can dream of the future? You know how it will end?"

"Only in pieces. I do not know end. I do not know if you will save her. I know only that you find her alive."

Her tone did not invite other questions.

Her guidance through the forest had them near the Fringe just after mid-day, Petyr guessed. They would not have traveled as fast without her, and Petyr told her so.

"It is nothing. Forest knows what you attempt. It wants freedom from Quenikuhg just as you and I."

They came around a bend and the Fringe loomed up before them. He heard Dyllan swear an oath.

The Fringe roiled even more than it had the last time he'd seen it, when he'd touched it. It seemed angry.

The horses tried to shy away. They stamped their feet, and eventually refused to move any closer.

"Horses not go through," Ulli said.

Petyr had wondered if they could coerce the horses through, but knew the truth from Ulli's statement. He motioned for the others to dismount, then climbed down himself before helping Ulli to the ground.

He looked at the horses for a moment, contemplating whether to hitch them to the trees, but decided against it. He didn't know if they would be coming back, and he couldn't leave them tied up in the forest.

"Let them go," he said.

"What?" Dyllan asked.

"If we make it back, we can walk. I don't want to leave them here to die if we don't."

When they released the horses, the horses turned and moved quickly away from the Fringe, but they didn't go far. *Maybe they'll stay.*

The four of them approached the Fringe, coming to a stop with only a few paces separating them from the roiling wall.

"I will go first," Ulli said.

"But you will never come out," Petyr said.

"I will not be consumed. I will become a part. Remember I said only certain talents may pass through?"

Petyr nodded.

"You may pass on your own. Follow path to girl. Others will become lost if I don't join Protector. I will lead them through."

Petyr guessed, then, why his Seeking had led him to her. It wasn't entirely for her knowledge. It was for this. He needed her to provide a path for Alec and Dyllan.

It still doesn't tell me how to kill it, or rescue Carree.

She reached out and pulled on his coat, pulling him down to her. He knelt. "One more piece of advice I offer. Knowledge lies to east."

This confused him. The path he held in his head seemed to lead to the northwest. "I don't understand."

"Not help for Quenikuhg. For other quest."

"But we didn't..."

She smiled. "I am Dreamstrider."

"Thank you. How will I know where?"

"You will find it. Use your talent. Learn your talent." She turned to face the Fringe again. "Now, I must go. Long life, Petyr."

She stepped forward, almost running, into the Fringe. He couldn't tell for sure, but he thought she embraced it as she plunged deep into the mass and disappeared.

The Fringe swirled around where she entered. Petyr looked at the other two men with him: the big, bulky Protector who had been his friend for so long, and the smaller Ghost, who had proved a good friend over the past year.

"We're a pretty small force to go against that thing. Are you ready?"

"Do you believe her?" asked Dyllan.

"Every word, even if I don't understand it."

"That's not reassuring."

"Even more than believing her, I trust her," Petyr said.

Alec looked up at Dyllan. "Are you afraid, Protector? I thought you types weren't afraid of anything."

Dyllan looked down menacingly at the smaller Ghost. "I'm not afraid of you."

"So this is how it's going to be?" Petyr asked.

The two men looked at him. Neither said a thing.

"The Fringe won't kill you. Grab on to me if you must, but I trust Ulli. She wasn't lying to me. She thinks she can get you through.

"It probably would be better if we kept in touch. I have no idea how well we'll be able to see in there."

The two of them nodded. Petyr understood their reluctance. A strange energy seemed to come from the Fringe. Ulli had told him it was alive. He'd felt for himself that it was alive. But he hadn't entered.

He was reluctant to enter it himself, but Carree's plight demanded it. He'd promised.

"Come on," he said, grabbing Alec's arm and pulling him toward the blue wall.

Alec resisted for a moment, then went with him. He felt Dyllan's hand take hold of his other arm, and the three of them moved forward as one.

He slowed a little and shut his eyes as he put one foot through, then the other, carrying his body into the mist.

The consciousness that he'd felt when he'd last put out his hand to touch the Fringe was still there. It searched him quickly, but the malevolence it had held was gone. He knew it, it knew him, and they were not enemies. For a moment, he thought he felt something touch his mind that reminded him of Ulli, but he couldn't have described it in words.

He opened his eyes to find the mist surrounding him. He thought he could feel Alec and Dyllan, but he could not see them. The ground below had no markers, no brush, no trees, no stones. It was blue like the mist. He could have been floating in the air but for the solid feel of the ground beneath his feet. He understood how someone would get lost. He clutched at his friends, even though he could not see them. The mist blinded.

"Dyllan, Alec, can you hear me?" he asked.

Silence. He only had the feel of them. It would have to be enough. *Ulli said they would be allowed through. I hope you were right, Ulli.*

He closed his eyes again. He didn't need them in here. He fixed his mind on Carree, fixed his senses on the path, then started walking the path, pulling at the arms of his friends. He opened his eyes, and the blue mist continued to surround him. The sameness of it was disconcerting. *If I didn't have the path to Carree to follow...*

The others seemed to be coming with him. *I wonder what they're feeling. Did the mist search their minds, too? I wonder what it found.*

He kept walking. The mist didn't change. He started counting to himself, counting the seconds. *One...Two...Three...* He reached one hundred and started over. Two more times, his counting passed one hundred. *One...Two...Three...Four...*

His feet brought him out of the mist and into a land of stone, dirt, and ash. The sun, still high in the sky, held little warmth. He'd assumed he'd find forest when he reached this side, but the landscape in front of him bore no trees, no life at all. It was dead, barren. Hills rolled away into the distance. He brought his hands up to his face, and then realized that they hadn't been holding anything.

He looked to his left and his right. He spun around and saw the Fringe behind him, blue and implacable. Alec and Dyllan were nowhere in sight.

A wind picked up, carrying dust and ash, blasting it against the skin of his face. Some of it slipped through his tightly pressed lips and onto his tongue. It tasted of something he'd come to recognize over the past year. Despair.

Petyr spun around again, hoping he could find some trace that would lead him to his friends. He couldn't find even a footprint in the dirt to confirm their passing. *What am I going to do now?*

The path to Carree lead away from the Fringe, toward a low mountain range that looked to be a day's walk or more in the distance. He didn't think she was that far.

He looked up to the sun again, trying to gauge how much time he had left in the day. *A few hours of sunlight left, maybe.*

The desolate landscape gave him the chills, and he didn't think they were just from the cold. Some devastating catastrophe had occurred, removing or burning every bit of life.

He turned back to face the Fringe, trying to peer into its depths.

I can sit here and wait, or I can walk a way along the length of the Fringe and hope they came out somewhere else, or I can press on and try to rescue Carree by myself. He liked the last option the least. Dyllan carried the spikes in his pack, and they were the only thing he'd managed to think of that might have a chance of stopping the Quenikuhg. *If they were lost in the Fringe...*

Why was Ulli wrong? Why didn't they come through?

He sat down in the dirt and ash to wait. His legs were too tired to wander around aimlessly. Especially if it might not do any good.

Minutes passed. Occasionally, he thought he'd see the pattern in the mist change, and he expected either Dyllan or Alec to emerge, but neither did.

He checked on the path to Carree again. She hadn't moved. *If only...*

He stood up. "You're not too bright, Petyr," he said. His first words dissipated into the wind like he hadn't even said them. *First, Alec.*

He fixed Alec in his head. He wasn't sure finding someone *in* the Fringe would work, but it was worth a try. *Where are you Alec?*

The path came to him. It lead west along the Fringe. Alec didn't seem far, either. Petyr followed the path and soon came upon Alec's prone figure, face down on the blackened dirt. Petyr rushed over to him, bent down and rolled him over.

He was breathing. Petyr couldn't find anything obviously wrong with Alec, so he tried to shake him awake.

Alec's eyes fluttered open. "What…"

"I don't know," Petyr said. "I was holding on to you, and when I came out, you weren't there."

Alec sat up, blinked his eyes, and spit dirt from his mouth. "I couldn't see you or Dyllan. I couldn't see a thing."

"I couldn't either."

"How do you think we got separated?"

Petyr had been pondering that question when he wasn't worrying about where Alec and Dyllan were. "I think it's the nature of the Fringe. I don't think Ulli had as much influence over it as she thought she would."

"So where's Dyllan?"

"I don't know yet. Can you walk?"

"I think so. My head hurts, though."

Petyr put out a hand and helped Alec up.

Once Alec was standing, he took a look around. "What happened here?"

"I don't know exactly, but I have a guess."

"The Quenikuhg."

Petyr nodded.

"You think this is what awaits the rest of the world if it escapes?"

Petyr surveyed the landscape around him. The bleakness of it seemed to constantly sap his energy. *Is this really how it will be? If we don't stop it here, and it manages to escape the Fringe, can it really destroy the whole world like this? I can't be the only answer, can I?*

"I don't think we should let it escape," Petyr said.

"How are we supposed to stop it? Do you really think those spikes will do anything?"

"I don't have any other ideas. How many years did the Keekele try to find a way to kill that thing? I'm sure they never tried using those spikes."

"Why do you even think they'll work?"

"The Keekele can't touch them."

"But that thing can. It has to be able to, otherwise..."

"I know. I'm just hoping that driving one in will do something. Otherwise, we have nothing."

Petyr's words hung in the air until the swift wind returned and erased them with a cloud of dust.

After spitting out the dust that seemed to infiltrate his mouth despite his closed lips, he put Dyllan in his head, concentrating on his old friend. At first, the path refused to appear, as if Dyllan did not exist any more.

Petyr forced himself to remember every detail of Dyllan as he'd last seen him, right down to the smudges of soot that had remained on his face after escaping the fire.

He didn't know if the extra effort was responsible, but he found a path to Dyllan.

"I know where Dyllan is," he said. He started following the path, kicking up dust. Alec caught up to him, and they walked quickly through the wasteland.

The wind picked up as they walked, blasting them anew with dust and ash. The sky turned gray with it, blocking out the sun and dropping the temperature.

Petyr increased his pace. They had to hurry. He wanted to find some shelter and hide from the detritus of this dead land, but thoughts of Carree pushed him onward. They had little time to waste if they were to have a chance at saving her.

The wind grew stronger, and Petyr had to shut his eyes against the dust. He relied on following the path to take him where he should go and only opened his eyes a crack every few feet. He felt Alec grab hold of his pack. *He must not be able to see, either.*

Petyr pressed on through the gale. Dyllan seemed to be growing closer, but Petyr thought their progress toward him should have been greater. "We should have seen Dyllan by now!" he yelled over his shoulder.

Dyllan is moving. But if he's moving, where is he going?

He stopped for a moment so he could yell into Alec's ear. "Dyllan is moving!"

"Maybe he's looking for shelter!" Even with Alec's mouth to his ear, Petyr could barely hear him over the roar of the wind.

Petyr wondered if Alec was right. He hoped so. Some shelter from this wind storm would be nice, for a short time, at least. *But that won't find Carree.*

Petyr forced his feet to move faster. Carree's impending doom lay heavy on him, as did the prospect of searching for her at night. He had no way to gauge the time due to the storm, but there couldn't be too many hours of daylight left. He dreaded the idea of coming across the Quenikuhg at night, though a small part of him wondered if it slept.

The constant struggle against the storm wore on his already weary legs. They were now into the hills, and the struggle up each hill was only slightly relieved by the trip down the other side.

He wanted to sit down and rest, but his promise to Carree kept him going. *Why do I keep going? Perhaps she Coerced me.*

Whatever the reason, he put one leg in front of the other, and marked the distance to Dyllan as best he could. It was shrinking.

They topped another rise, and a blast of wind knocked him from his feet. He tumbled into Alec, and they both fell to the dirt. The wind had scoured most of the ash from the hill top.

Petyr did not want to get up. His muscles cried out for rest, and he wanted to give it to them. He could sleep here.

"Petyr! We have to get out of this!" Alec said.

Petyr agreed. He couldn't take much more of the constant struggle.

Petyr felt Alec stand. Then Alec started pulling at him. "Get up, Petyr!"

Petyr rolled over and pushed himself to his feet. He checked the path to Dyllan. They were close.

He felt Alec's hand on him once again, and Petyr started leading him down the hill toward Dyllan.

Step after step, down the hill.

Until his foot caught a rock, and he tumbled and rolled down kicking ash and dust into the already over-laden air.

He came to a stop, bashing his upper-arm against something hard, stone like. Pain shot through the arm. He cried out, and grasped at it.

Alec approached him and bent down. "Are you hurt?"

Petyr massaged the arm for a moment, probing at it. He wiggled his fingers a bit, then moved the arm around. It was sore, bruised probably. "I don't think it's broken."

Alec looked up. "What is this thing?"

Petyr looked for the first time at the stone that had broken his tumble and realized it wasn't just a stone. It was a column, probably eight feet high.

He got to his feet to better examine it. Through slitted eyes, he saw it only had three sides and was marked with runes. The runes were nearly worn away, and he had difficulty making out their exact details, but a couple of them he recognized, if he didn't know what they meant. He'd seen them outside the entrance to Ulli's cavern.

"Alec, look around the area for an entrance or cave or something!"

"Why?"

"The Keekele built this! It's got to be marking something!"

Petyr moved away, searching in widening circles for anything that might give them cover from the storm. Through slitted eyes, he could see Alec searching, too. *I know there's something here. Where is it?*

He didn't notice the hulking shadow approach until it was on him. When he saw it, he turned, pulling the hatchet from his pack, but it was too late.

The shadow reached out and grabbed his arm. "Petyr, it's me!"

Dyllan. Petyr had been so busy with trying to find the entrance he knew must be near he'd forgotten to pay attention to his search for Dyllan.

Petyr relaxed. "How did you find me?"

"I heard your cry. Follow me. I found shelter."

Alec approached them. "Where?"

"Not far."

Dyllan turned and lead them in the direction they'd been traveling before Petyr tumbled. His path brought them down into a valley, and then to the edge of a lake frothed by the wind.

They came upon a stone gateway, similar to what Petyr had seen outside the Keekele cavern, only this stood above ground. It also stood open. Dyllan lead them inside. The wind dropped off immediately, and Petyr wanted to fall to the ground right there, but Dyllan wouldn't let him.

"We need to go in further. You have to see this."

Petyr sighed, then followed Dyllan as the Protector lead them a down a tunnel that reminded Petyr of another tunnel. The one that had tree roots for an entrance. Everything seemed so familiar. The only difference was a dim light which lit this tunnel enough that he could see without the glowing ball Ulli had carried. *I wish I knew how to make that light.*

About the time he expected, they came to a doorway. Only this doorway was not closed. It had been smashed open and lay in pieces on the floor.

They picked their way through the rubble into the room beyond. It seemed a near replica of the room where Ulli had stored his chest, though rubble lined the walls instead of barrels and crates.

Petyr saw light from a doorway that he expected would lead to a central cavern. He pushed his way past Dyllan and made for the door. He felt certain this had been another Keekele home. He prepared himself to find the place in ruins, to find it choked with ash and rubble.

Instead, as he neared the door, his ash-clogged nose began to pick out the scents of flowers. He felt some moisture in the air.

He stepped into the doorway and gasped. The cavern was easily three times the size of Ulli's cavern. The floor was covered in vibrant plant life. He could see where the irrigation channels had been. Though they were grown over, they still carried water to support the life in the cavern. Whatever disaster had befallen the surface of this land, it had missed this place. *Perhaps some Keekele talent keeps it alive.*

He looked to his left, where he knew the ramp down to the floor of the cavern would be. Huge chunks of it were missing. About thirty feet along its length, it had completely broken away leaving a gap Petyr gauged as impassible.

"It's breathtaking, isn't it?" Dyllan asked from behind him.

Petyr nodded.

"I looked for a way down, but couldn't find one."

"How did you find this place?" Petyr asked.

"When I came out of the Fringe, I thought I saw footprints in the dirt, leading in this direction. Then the wind came up and wiped them away, but I decided to head in that direction. I thought they were yours."

"I was east of you, I think."

"I entered the valley and ran into the lake. I followed the edge of the lake until I discovered the entrance. I thought perhaps you had taken refuge in here, so I looked around and discovered this cavern. When I realized you weren't here, I headed back up to look around, and then I heard your shout."

Petyr continued to gaze out over the garden below them while he reached up the side of his pack looking for his water-skin. Seeing the water below had reminded him of how dusty his mouth felt. When he found the skin, the outside was damp and caked with mud. It felt near empty.

After scraping the muck from it, he took a sip, preserving what little was left.

"We need to find a way down," Petyr said, holding the skin up in front of him. "I'll run out of water before we're done, I think, and I'm not too interested in drinking the sludge from the lake above."

Petyr's need for water warred with his need to find and save Carree. The wilderness growing on the floor of the cavern below taunted him.

He rubbed at his head, pondering the situation. He felt the first bits of stubble reappearing.

"I have enough water," said Alec.

"My skin is full, too," said Dyllan. "We could probably make it last until we return here."

Petyr weighed the possibilities. The chances of being too late to save Carree versus the chances of never making it because they ran out of water, or because they fell to their deaths trying to scale the walls of this cavern to reach the water.

"What we don't know is how long this storm will last," he said.

"Or how far we have to go," Dyllan said.

Petyr cursed silently at himself. He hadn't tried to seek for Carree again since they'd found Dyllan. He had no idea how far away they'd traveled.

He placed her firmly in his mind, and the path came to him. To his surprise, she didn't seem to be very far away. He tried to remember back, thinking they were moving away from her when he'd switched to Seeking Dyllan. But somehow, they'd moved closer.

"She's nearby," he said. "I think you're right. We can wait to get water."

Something felt wrong about it, though. *How could we be so close?*

"I'm going to go check on the storm," Petyr said.

"Petyr, wait," said Alec. "Look down there." He pointed across to the far side of the cavern.

Petyr looked where Alec pointed, and didn't see anything. "I don't..."

Then he saw it. Something moving among the plant-life. Something distinctly human.

"You said you saw footprints, Dyllan?"

"I did."

Whatever moved on the cavern floor stopped and looked up at them. Human form, but not human. Taller than a Keekele, but with the same coloring.

What are you? Petyr hoped his talent would provide an answer. But he got nothing. Like he was blocked.

It smiled at Petyr.

A chill swept through him. "Oh, Mother," Petyr said.

"What?" Dyllan asked.

"The giant is not the Quenikuhg."

"What do you mean?" Alec asked. "Ulli said…"

"Ulli never said the giant was the Quenikuhg." Petyr couldn't take his eyes off the thing below him. "The giant is the Quenikuhg's offspring."

Petyr heard the grinding of stone upon stone behind him, and caught Alec running out of the corner of his eye. He turned and saw it was too late. What they had taken for a broken door was just concealment for the perfectly working door. Alec slammed into it as it ground shut, trapping the three of them in the room.

The Quenikuhg laughed. Petyr could hear its barking amusement echo through the cavern.

Petyr sank to his knees and cradled his head in his hands. "Can I do nothing right?"

Dyllan bent down next to him. "Petyr?"

"I trusted Ulli. I thought she knew everything there was to know about the Quenikuhg. But she didn't know this."

"What didn't she know?"

"She didn't know it could take human talents. We've just provided it with three more."

CHAPTER 25

The three of them sat on the ledge, watching the Quenikuhg work at something. It appeared to be gathering plants from its garden. It didn't seem to mind that they watched it. It moved methodically most of the time while it worked, as if it carried a great weight, or great age. But when it finished with its work in an area, it flitted from place to place almost as fast as Petyr's eye could follow. More than once, he lost it when it moved. As strange as the Keekele were, the Quenikuhg made them seem normal.

Carree was moving closer, the path in his head growing shorter. Petyr surmised the only tunnel large enough for the giant might involve a long circuitous route to the cavern. He'd found the opening to the tunnel—a large black maw off to their right.

Stuck on the ledge, unable to escape, he found himself thinking of Alura, safe at Dyllan's estate. And his daughter. *My daughter.*

"Dyllan, will they be safe if you don't return?" Petyr asked.

"Who?"

"Alura and my daughter."

"For a time, I should think," Dyllan said while continuing to stare out across the cavern.

Petyr understood. "Until they discover you helped me."

Dyllan nodded, still refusing to look at Petyr.

"They'll discover it, too. When you don't return, they'll send Trackers and Questioners looking for you, and they'll find Dunsriver."

"And if we die here," Dyllan continued, "they may never discover it. They'll put her somewhere they can use her against you."

"If we die here," Alec cut in, "you probably should hope they kill her."

Petyr looked at him and frowned. "I don't want to think about that." He stood up and moved back into the room, looking for anything he could find that might help. But everything in the room was rubble, everything except their packs, which they'd set against one of the walls. The gun stood there, too.

They'd dismissed the idea of using the gun against the Quenikuhg. It never came close enough to them to provide a decent target. The gun just wasn't accurate enough to hit it from their position, and they didn't have a lot of bullets. Petyr wondered if the Quenikuhg would hear the gun fire and move out of the way before the bullet arrived to hit it.

Not that they would do anything to the Quenikuhg. Bullets hadn't had any effect on the giant.

He picked up the gun and rummaged through Alec's pack for the powder and bullets.

"What are you doing?" Alec asked.

Petyr looked up to see Alec standing next to him. "Getting the bullets and powder."

"Why?"

"We have to try something. We can't just sit here. The giant will be here soon, and we should be prepared."

"Prepared for what? Bullets won't work on that thing."

Petyr's hands found the bullets and the powder bag. He removed them from the pack. "They might work on the Quenikuhg. At the very least, maybe we can lure it up here."

Dyllan came in and reached into his pack and pulled out the spikes. "And if we have to, we can at least try to prevent it from succeeding."

Petyr knew what Dyllan was getting at. Even if Dyllan was right, he didn't like it one bit. "We will not kill Carree. I need her. I promised her."

"You need her? She's a rogue Coercer, Petyr. I figured that much out. I don't want to be within a mile of her."

Petyr stood up and stuck a finger in his friend's chest. Petyr still wasn't sure whether their relationship would recover, but he didn't care. "She's had training, Dyllan. She's not a threat to us, and she's offered to help. I will not throw that possibility away."

Dyllan stood taller. "She's not a threat? How can you be sure you're not out here because she coerced you into protecting her?"

Petyr refused to back down. "I don't know that she didn't coerce me. Even if she did, aren't we doing the right thing, anyway? Sitting on the other side of the Fringe and hoping won't make the Quenikuhg stop trying to break free."

Petyr understood Dyllan's fear. Coercer's in general could be difficult to handle for anyone who was not a Blocker. In Genova, Coercer's were always paired with Blockers, and were rarely free to move about as they pleased. The idea of a Coercer using their talent on a Protector or other talented was frightening. *And if the Empire knew about my talent?*

They stood toe to toe for a moment, then Dyllan flicked his eyes away. "I'm not going to stand in your way on this. You're right. You need all the help you can get. I still think it's dangerous to bring her along."

Petyr put his hand on his friend's shoulder. "Thank you. I agree it's dangerous. But right now, it's dangerous just being me."

Petyr loaded the gun, then carried it to the doorway, trying to keep it hidden from the Quenikuhg. He didn't know if the thing knew what a gun was, but he didn't want to alert it before they had a chance to fire a shot.

He set the gun on the ground and sat down next to it. He looked through the garden again, but couldn't find the Quenikuhg. It had disappeared. *No. It's still there somewhere, perhaps a different room.*

Petyr felt the frustration rise up in him. The Quenikuhg was content to let them sit there. It knew they couldn't reach it.

Petyr looked down over the ledge. Thirty feet, forty feet below them, there was another ledge. Their own hung out several feet from the other in line with sloping walls of the cavern.

Dyllan sat down beside him. After a few moments, he asked, "Where did it go?"

"I don't know. Another room, perhaps."

"I saw you looking over the edge. What did you find?"

"There's a ledge thirty or forty feet below us."

"We have rope."

Petyr shook his head. "We don't have anything to anchor it."

"We have the spikes." Dyllan held them out in his hands.

"If we could find a way to drive them into stone, and if we didn't need them to kill the Quenikuhg and its giant."

"With all the damage done here, there's got to be a crack or something we can drive a spike into with the hatchet," Alec said.

"But we need them to kill these things," Petyr said.

"You don't know that. You're just guessing. It won't matter one whit if we don't find a way down."

"And maybe we don't need both," said Dyllan.

Petyr relented. It wouldn't hurt to know if they had the option available. "Fine. See if you can find a way to anchor a rope." *I'm going to sit here and watch for the Quenikuhg and see if I can't put a shot into it.*

The other two stood up, and he could hear them moving around, searching. Petyr kept looking for the Quenikuhg. It had to be somewhere near.

He started scanning the various dwelling doorways carved into the outer wall of the cavern. Every doorway looked broken in some fashion. He tried to imagine the horror that the Keekele living here went through as the Quenikuhg and its offspring invaded their home. Or, he hoped, perhaps they abandoned it before their doom fell on them.

I wonder how Carree is doing. I wish I could tell if she's hurt.

He couldn't tell, though. He only knew she was close, and getting closer. It seemed to be taking forever.

Out of the corner of his left eye, he caught some movement, and turned his head to face it. The Quenikuhg stood just on the other side of the gap in the walkway. It smiled when Petyr looked at it.

Petyr grabbed the gun, and fast as he could manage, he pointed the gun at the Quenikuhg and fired. The boom echoed throughout the cavern and made Petyr's ears ring.

The Quenikuhg flinched as if hit, but remained standing. Petyr then saw the hole the bullet had created in the Quenikuhg's chest, but it didn't bleed. The Quenikuhg reached up and fingered the hole, then held its hand out in front of its face and examined the finger.

It laughed at Petyr with the same bark of a laugh it had used earlier, only this time, Petyr thought there was something more sinister to it.

"You can not kill me," it said after it finished laughing. For a moment, the fact that it said anything at all paralyzed Petyr. He'd thought of it as a beast. He should have realized that it was more than that. It was the union of Keekele and something else, and because of Bran, it was now part human.

Alec and Dyllan came to Petyr's side, breaking him out of his paralysis. "I can try," Petyr said.

A roar echoed through the cavern, and Petyr recognized it. The giant, the Quenikuhg's offspring, approached.

The Quenikuhg laughed again. "Later, you can try. Now, I have work."

It turned and ran down the ramp to the floor to meet its minion. It moved so fast Petyr had trouble following it with his gaze.

When it reached the floor and started moving through the fauna, Petyr gave up trying to follow it and turned to face the hole where he expected to find the giant. Seconds later, it emerged carrying a limp Carree in its paw.

For a moment, Petyr worried she was dead, but realized it couldn't possibly be the case. He could still feel her position in his head. And the Quenikuhg needed her alive, for at least a while.

The giant carried her to a platform in the center of the cavern that Petyr hadn't seen before. The plant-life had obscured it. It laid her down on the platform, and then set its great bulk down to watch her with its back partly facing Petyr.

The Quenikuhg reappeared next to her. It bent down as if to examine her, and stayed bent for several minutes.

"Give me the hatchet," Dyllan said.

"Why?"

"I found a crack that might accept the spike. I'll need something to drive it in."

Petyr handed him the hatchet. He had little hope it would work. He kept his eye on Carree as Dyllan moved away. She lay on the platform, her golden hair spread out around her head like a halo. It was like staring down at Alura as she lay on the floor after her fall during his escape. He felt just as helpless now as he did then. He'd promised Carree, he'd promised Sim, and he'd promised himself. Her prone form indicated to him that he was about to break all those promises at once.

The Quenikuhg appeared, almost from nothing, at Carree's side. It ran a curved claw up her arm, and then almost as if it cared for her, along the side of her face.

The loud clank of metal on metal rang out behind Petyr, causing him to flinch a bit. He refused to turn and see what Dyllan was doing. He knew.

Below him, the Quenikuhg turned his way. It wasn't smiling this time. Petyr thought it seemed annoyed at being interrupted.

Maybe that will work. Maybe we can just make a lot of noise.

Another hatchet strike rang out through the cavern. Petyr watched the Quenikuhg intently, hoping to see more annoyance come to the surface, but it disappointed him by turning back to examining Carree. It appeared to have decided they could do little to interrupt its work.

Petyr also noticed with the second strike that the giant didn't move, either, and he realized it hadn't turned to look the first time. He watched it closely, and saw no movement. It almost looked dead.

More hatchet strikes. Neither the Quenikuhg, nor its giant, flinched. The Quenikuhg continued to examine Carree. Petyr thought it odd. He'd imagined the Quenikuhg would get on with its unthinkable ritual, but it seemed to be considering. Not having seen the ritual before, he had no idea whether this pondering was part of it, or was something different.

A thought struck him. *Could Bran possibly be alive in the Quenikuhg, somehow? Could it be pondering the fact that Carree is his sister?* Petyr hoped his thought might carry some truth, that the Bran part of the Quenikuhg could prevent what Petyr had assumed was about to happen.

The sound of footsteps came from behind him, and Dyllan sat down next to him. Dyllan had a coil of rope and the hatchet in his lap.

"What is it doing?"

"I'm not sure. It's just walked around Carree, looking at her."

"Did the noise bother it?"

Petyr shook his head. "It looked up on the first strike, then ignored the rest." He looked at the rope in Dyllan's lap. "Will that hold?"

"It should. I pulled on it with all my strength."

Alec approached from behind them, carrying the gun. "So what's the plan?"

I don't really have a plan. But he couldn't say that.

"As soon as we drop the rope over the edge, I'm sure the Quenikuhg will notice, so we should wait until its back is turned."

"Who goes down first?"

I don't know. Is the giant really immobile? "Does that giant look alive to you?"

Alec studied it for a moment before answering. Petyr joined him. It didn't even seem to breathe. "It almost looks like a statue," Alec said.

"Petyr, if you don't mind, I'd like to suggest a plan," Dyllan said.

Good. I've got nothing. "What do you suggest?"

"Let Alec go down first, carrying the spike. You follow him down with the gun. Alec, see if you can sneak up on the giant and ram that spike into the back of its neck. Petyr, you try to hide while covering Alec with that gun. Don't fire unless there's no other choice. You'll most likely have only one shot. Once you're down, I'll pull the other spike and jump the break in the ramp."

"I thought you said you couldn't make that jump," Alec said.

"I said 'we'. I can make the jump."

Petyr nodded. He'd seen Protectors make those jumps. It would be a close thing, however. "What about the Quenikuhg?"

"If Alec can manage to take out the giant, I'll try to jam the other spike down the throat of that creature."

"And if he can't?"

"I'll go after the giant myself. In either case, you get the girl and find your way out of here."

Petyr nodded. *It's not like I'm worth much in a fight. It'll be a miracle if I can slide down the rope without dropping the gun.*

The Quenikuhg looked up at them, almost as if it knew they were planning something.

Petyr panicked for a moment. *It can't know, can it?* Of course, it would only make sense for it to think they were planning something.

But Petyr's fears were allayed a bit when it moved off across the cavern, speeding through the brush, then disappeared into another opening in the cavern wall.

Dyllan threw the rope over the edge. "Now," he said.

Alec disappeared over the ledge and down the rope. Dyllan pulled out another piece of rope and tied it around Petyr's shoulder, then tied the gun to the end of it so that the gun dangled near his knees.

Petyr turned to Dyllan, suddenly unsure of the plan, of his ability to execute it. "Dyllan, I don't know…"

"Petyr, you brought us out here. This is our chance to not deal with both at the same time. Over the edge with you."

Petyr steeled himself, grasped the rope which was now hanging loose without Alec's weight on it, and let himself over the edge, hand over hand. It hung out away from the wall, so he wrapped his legs around it. The rope burned his palms a bit as he made his way down.

He started to spin with a slow motion, until he could see out over the cavern. The Quenikuhg had still not returned. He couldn't see Alec, who must have already started toward the still motionless giant.

Petyr hurried down the rope as fast as he dared, hands burning. He felt exposed hanging there. When his feet bumped the ground, he stood and released the rope. Soon after, the rest of the rope fell to the ground in a pile.

He looked out over the garden and could see very little over the tall reeds and other plants. The giant sat as it had, a statue amidst the fauna. He couldn't see Carree from where he stood. *I have to get closer.*

Before he moved, he looked up and saw Dyllan running down the ramp. *This is it.*

He started to move out into the brush, and the gun banged into his shins, reminding him of its presence. He brought the gun up from where it dangled and undid the rope that held it there. He felt a little better with it in his arms, even knowing that it couldn't do anything except distract the Quenikuhg.

He moved through the plants again and nearly stumbled into an overgrown irrigation trench. He worked his way around it, looking for a path to the center platform. He still couldn't see anything but the giant. *I wish I could see Alec.* Alec's talent would prevent that, however, even if he could see over the brush.

Petyr tried to remember the layout of the Ulli's cavern. If the pathways were similar, it might help, but he had no reason to suspect they'd be identical. This cavern was so much larger.

Stop, Petyr. You need to go get Carree before the Quenikuhg comes back.

Petyr pushed the 'what ifs' out of his head. A few more yards around the irrigation trench brought him to an overgrown path. He had to push his way through berry bushes and other tall plant life, wondering the entire time about the logic of a creature that blasted the world to ash and dust above, but left this underground cave to thrive.

His heart beat loudly in his chest as he walked. He feared the Quenikuhg would reappear, find him, and destroy him. He hurried as best he could, wishing he carried the hatchet instead of the gun, which seemed to catch on every vine he passed.

He looked back at the ramp, and could no longer see Dyllan. *He must be on the floor, now.*

Petyr knew he neared the center. The giant was close to him now, towering above him. He could see its face. Its eyes were shut, and it didn't even seem to breathe.

And then he passed out of the fauna and onto the platform. Carree lay quietly on her back, her arms and legs strapped to the low table with with leather thongs. Her chest moved with slow, shallow breaths.

Petyr raced up to her, rested the gun up against the table, and started loosening each of the ties that bound her. She didn't stir at his touch.

If I have to carry her, we won't get very far.

He glanced up at the giant. It still wasn't moving. He'd count himself very lucky if it never moved. If he wasn't so terrified of what he was doing, he might have chuckled. It would be the first time in a long time that anything went right.

Looking at the giant made Petyr wonder. *Where's Alec? He should have put a spike in that thing's neck by now.*

But maybe that isn't such a good idea. He wished he could talk to Alec and Dyllan about it, but they had both disappeared, Alec due to his talent, Dyllan due to the overgrown garden. He hoped Alec was having the same thoughts.

The last tie holding Carree down came loose, allowing her arm to slide off the edge of the table. Petyr grasped her by the shoulders and shook her gently, trying to wake her.

His efforts didn't appear to make a difference. He bent down to her ear. "Carree," he said. "Wake up, we have to get out of here."

Her eyes moved rapidly behind her eyelids, but her breathing remained steady.

He straightened up and looked around, but could not find Dyllan or Alec—or the Quenikuhg. The giant still slept.

Well, there's nothing for it. Petyr reached for Carree's arms and pulled her to a sitting position, then pulled her up over his shoulder. She felt lighter than he expected, but he wouldn't be able to carry her the entire distance back to the town this way. He stared for a moment at the gun where it rested against the table before deciding it would stay where it was. It was useless against the Quenikuhg, and he couldn't carry it and Carree at the same time.

Crouched over a bit to support Carree's weight, he started down the path by which he'd come to the center platform. He planned to take her to the edge of the cavern, then circle toward the tunnel the giant used to enter the cavern. He didn't want to follow that path, but it was the only other path he knew that lead out.

Step after step, he plodded down the path, Carree seemingly growing heavier on his already weary legs. He worried about even making it out of the cavern with her. It was almost certainly the middle of the night by now. He'd been running or moving since early morning, with little chance to rest, and no sleep.

He looked up and saw that he'd progressed about half the distance toward the wall of the cavern. Time passed slowly for him. It seemed far too long since he'd seen either Dyllan or Alec, or the Quenikuhg, for that matter. He glanced around him, trying to peer through the bushes, imagining the Quenikuhg coming for him at any moment, its long claws extended toward his throat.

A quick turn to look back at the giant, and he spotted Alec for the first time. He'd climbed up to the middle of the giant's back. Alec turned then, and their eyes met. Alec waved Petyr on, then turned back to finishing his climb. The giant seemed undisturbed by the man on his back.

He could only guess why Alec had waited so long. Perhaps he'd seen Carree asleep, and the giant doing its best to look dead. Perhaps he'd decided it better to wait until Petyr got Carree out of the way.

Petyr returned to carrying his burden away from her doom.

CHAPTER 26

Petyr felt Carree move on his shoulder, just before she started screaming. He set her down quickly, and she slipped to her knees. He bent down and placed himself so she could see him while desperately trying to cover her mouth and silence her. Her eyes were wild with fear, darting everywhere, until they finally settled on him and she began to calm herself.

She pulled herself to him and hugged him. He tried to comfort her as best he could, holding her tight until her screams became whimpers.

The position they were in gave him a view of the giant with Alec on its back, hanging precariously with one hand while he held the other high, wrapped around the iron spike as he prepared to plunge it into the neck of the giant.

But Carree's scream had already done its damage. The giant stirred under Alec, and rose to its feet. Alec had to put his free hand around its neck in order to keep from falling off. It started to turn toward Petyr and Carree, its angry eyes blinking and trying to focus.

Petyr pushed at Carree. "Get up, Carree."

She didn't seem to understand him. He stood, pulling her to her feet.

Dyllan plunged out of the brush and into the path between them and the giant. "Get her out of here, Petyr," he said.

Petyr turned to push her, and she must have caught sight of the giant. She started screaming again. The giant roared, and took steps toward them, Alec still hanging like a human necklace from the giant's neck.

"Run, Carree!" Petyr said, pushing at her. She took a couple slow steps, and he pushed at her some more. "Run!"

She still didn't move, frozen in terror. Petyr took her by the wrist and pulled her along after him. She moved with him, following behind, but still screaming. He looked over his shoulder.

The giant still gained on them, approaching Dyllan.

Alec, his purchase on the creature now more secure as it moved forward, raised the hand holding the spike, and plunged it into the giant's neck. It stopped walking toward them and howled in rage. It reached up with one immense hand and grabbed at Alec. It spun around in its effort to reach its attacker, but couldn't quite get at him. Petyr saw Alec holding on only by the spike embedded in its neck.

Was I wrong? he wondered as he pulled at Carree to run. They had a few more moments. If they could get to the tunnel, maybe hide in the darkness.

She finally started running with him in earnest, and Petyr didn't have to pull at her. They ran, side by side, until they reached the cavern wall. Petyr pointed to the tunnel entrance, directing Carree to head that way.

He paused a moment as they turned and looked at the giant. Dyllan had joined the fight, sword in one hand, iron spike in the other. Dyllan's ability to avoid the giant while dashing in and out between its legs and flailing arms entranced Petyr for a moment, until he caught other movement out of the corner of his eye—Carree, racing for the tunnel entrance.

Petyr raced after her. He couldn't fight that thing. His and Carree's only chance was to escape and hope his two friends could take care of it. While he ran, he wondered where the Quenikuhg might be. *It had to have heard the commotion. It has to know. It must be controlling the giant.* Petyr felt in his gut he had the answer there. But he pushed the thoughts aside, deciding he could reflect on them when he had more time. What mattered now was saving Carree.

He followed her into the tunnel. The light from the cavern extended into the tunnel only a short distance. He could clearly see Carree where she had come to a stop, waiting for him. She was watching the battle between Petyr's two friends and the giant. Petyr looked back.

Is it my imagination, or is it moving slower? Petyr couldn't be sure, but it did seem slower, more ponderous. It took a step, avoiding a slash from Dyllan's sword, and it stumbled a bit as its foot splashed into an irrigation canal.

"Petyr, where are we?" Carree asked. She held her arms close about her, as if she were cold, or perhaps trying to contain her fear.

Petyr could not answer her question for a moment. His mind blanked on just how to explain it. She didn't know about the Keekele, about the cavern, about her brother's role. *Can I even tell her?* Eventually, all he could manage was, "We're in its lair, on the other side of the Fringe."

All motion in her stopped. "How is that possible?"

"It's possible," said a hissing, scratchy voice, "because I brought you here." A shadow detached itself from the wall and resolved into the Quenikuhg.

Petyr grabbed Carree and tried to run. The Quenikuhg, using a burst of speed, caught them before they'd moved more than a step. It's sharp claws dug into Petyr's shoulder. Petyr could feel them piercing his skin through the padded coat he wore.

"Where do you think you're going?" It smiled, baring pointed teeth.

Neither Petyr, nor Carree, could answer it. Petyr struggled against it, trying to squirm away, but its grip held him fast, and it only dug its claws deeper into his shoulder. Petyr stopped resisting.

It turned them so they could watch the giant, and then it seemed to concentrate. Its presence withdrew from them a bit, and Petyr watched as the giant, which had seemed to be growing sluggish, returned to its fight against Dyllan and Alec with renewed vigor. Petyr's heart sank.

The giant reached up and finally plucked Alec from its shoulders, and threw him down where he was fortunate to splash into an irrigation ditch.

The giant started after Dyllan, who now struggled on alone against it. Watching Dyllan always filled Petyr with awe. His movements were so fluid, his strength incredible, his talent gifting him with an innate resilience and resistance to harm. But against the giant, Petyr didn't see how it could be enough. The spikes hadn't worked, and Dyllan would eventually wear out. Petyr did not think the giant would.

The two of them seemed locked in a crazy kind of dance. Every time the giant swung its long arms, Dyllan would leap out of the way, then rush in to swing with his sword, slipping through its legs, forcing it to spin to find him again.

Alec struggled to pull himself from the water where he'd landed. Petyr thought he looked hurt. He had an urge to go help Alec, and tried to shrug out of the grip of the Quenikuhg again, but the grip hadn't loosened despite the Quenikuhg's concentration elsewhere.

He looked over at Carree. She watched the uneven battle, a pall of fear on her face.

"I'm sorry," Petyr said.

"Sorry? For what?" Her voice shook.

"For failing you." *For failing Alura. For failing everyone.*

Her eyes grew soft as they looked at him across the visage of the Quenikuhg. He could still see pain and fear in them, but somehow, she set those feelings aside for the moment. "You haven't failed yet, Petyr," she said. "I'm still alive."

"Thank you, Carree, but..." Movement out of the corner of his eye distracted him. Dyllan had changed tactics, and had maneuvered the giant so that it had stepped into an irrigation canal and stumbled.

A quick jump brought Dyllan up close to the giant's enormous head. While seemingly hanging in the air, he rammed his sword into the giant's open eye to the hilt. A gush of brackish fluid spilled out of the wound and the giant reared back. Dyllan fell to the ground, sword still in hand, and rolled out of the way has the giant flailed around.

Petyr didn't see any more as the Quenikuhg wailed, threw he and Carree backward, and rushed out into the cavern, his captives forgotten.

Petyr got to his feet, found Carree, and pulled her up. "We have to go now."

She didn't resist. Together, they ran down the tunnel until the light failed, then they moved along its walls, hoping to find a way out before the Quenikuhg could find them again.

Petyr held back a sense of frustration. He wanted to go back and help Dyllan, help Alec. He knew he couldn't. He had no chance against the Quenikuhg. He'd never trained to fight. He had to hope his friends could kill the vile creature. He had to trust in them, and he couldn't protect them.

⚔ ⚔ ⚔

The tunnel walls and floor were smooth and hand carved, which kept Petyr and Carree's stumbling to a minimum. He could feel, under his fingers, pictographs in the walls. He suspected the walls were a giant history book, just like the room in Ulli's cavern.

The darkness in the tunnel felt oppressive. Petyr kept turning to try to see if the Quenikuhg, or perhaps Dyllan or Alec, were following them, but in the dark, he couldn't see a thing. The tunnel had long since curved up so that he could no longer see the cavern.

He could not see Carree, either. He only knew she was still with him from the sound of her feet on the floor, the sound of her breathing, and the warmth of her hand in his.

They didn't talk much. The darkness seemed to eat every word they spoke. Petyr worried too much sound would bring the Quenikuhg right to them.

The first time they came across a void in the wall, Petyr grew worried. In the darkness, he couldn't tell if it was another tunnel, or if the tunnel they were in made a rapid turn to the right.

Together, he and Carree were able to stretch across the opening and determine it was indeed a side tunnel, or some other opening. The opening was too small for the giant to have fit through, so they continued following their original tunnel.

An urgency grew in Petyr as they traveled through the darkness. Enough time had passed, he felt certain whatever fight had taken place was over. They passed more voids without coming to the end of their tunnel, and with every void, every potential side tunnel, his anxiety grew.

He used his talent to seek for Dyllan, and the path to Dyllan grew clear for Petyr. *He must still be alive. And if he's alive, maybe the Quenikuhg is dead.*

For some reason, he didn't believe it. Something in him drove him on down the tunnel, drove him to search for a way out. Something kept him from believing the Quenikuhg was dead.

Ahead of him, the path seemed to grow a little lighter. He started to think he could see the stone walls of the tunnel, but dismissed it as his imagination until Carree asked, "Is it getting lighter?"

Petyr reassessed what he could see, and had to agree. It was indeed getting lighter, and ahead of him, he could see the outline of the tunnel entrance, bathed in moonlight.

"That's the tunnel entrance," Petyr said.

She sighed. "We made it."

Petyr shook his head. "Not yet. We still have to get you across the wasteland and through the Fringe."

"Wasteland?"

"You'll see in a moment. Come on," he said, and pulled her toward the opening as quickly as he dared. It was still dark enough to hide fallen stones that could trip them up.

They made it through the huge opening, which they discovered to be a large gash in the side of a hill. The moonlight spilled down on them from a clear sky, illuminating broken pillars and the rubble from massive doors. The tunnel had been an immense entryway at one time, Petyr suspected, much like the Colonnade in Genova. He wished he could have known the Keekele before the Quenikuhg had destroyed them.

Beyond the rubble, the land was just as barren as he'd expected it. He felt like cursing the clear sky. The stars and moon would illuminate them as they passed across the desolate terrain. Without trees or bushes to hide behind, he knew they would be exposed every time they crossed a ridge or crested a hill.

"Let's get out of the entrance of the tunnel," he said.

Together, they worked their way down into the valley below the entrance.

While they picked their way, Petyr used his talent to seek out Sim. As he feared, Sim lay behind them, beyond the cavern, beyond the entrance they had originally used to enter the cavern. The Quenikuhg would only have to wait there for them and watch for them to pass by.

I'll have to try to make sure our path goes nowhere near that lake. It wouldn't be a problem if I had any idea where we are.

Petyr led Carree along the length of the valley, heading in Sim's general direction, until they could no longer follow the valley and maintain their direction. They climbed the hill in front of them, and carefully approached its summit. Petyr went to his belly in the ash and surveyed the surrounding land.

He didn't see anything moving. Of course, he didn't know what the Quenikuhg could and couldn't do, and in this landscape and the moonlight, its skin color could help it blend in.

He crept back down to where Carree waited.

"I don't think there's anything we can do except go over quickly and hope the Quenikuhg is not watching."

"You think it's still following us?" Carree asked.

"I think it's foolish to assume anything else."

She nodded.

Together, they skittered over the top, staying as low as they could, until they were on the downward slope of the other side of the hill.

Much of the next few hours they spent in the same fashion, traveling valleys until they had no choice but to climb and expose themselves. Petyr managed to keep them away from the lake and its inherent dangers. What he couldn't do, though, was keep either of them warm.

The empty sky leached the heat from the already cool air, and Carree had not been wearing a coat when the Quenikuhg's minion had snatched her. Petyr gave her his coat which helped her regain some warmth, but he soon found himself shivering from the cold. It wasn't until he started to see silvery frost on the ash and dirt that he began to worry. There was little wind to speak of, but he knew that if they didn't get to the other side of the fringe soon and find some shelter, one or the other of them, or perhaps both, would not survive the night.

Weary as he was, he pushed himself and Carree to move faster, hoping the exertion would keep them warm. It helped for awhile, until his exhaustion started to take its toll.

As they approached the crest of another hill, he stumbled and fell to the ground. His legs ached from the cold and exhaustion. He wanted to lay down and sleep, but he knew he couldn't. Knowing wasn't enough to keep him from closing his eyes.

"Petyr, what's that?" Carree asked. She had moved to the top of the hill while he lay resting. "Is that the Fringe?"

The Fringe? Get up, you fool. Petyr rolled over and pushed himself to his knees. They didn't want to help him stand, but he forced them to. *You can't fail her like you failed Alura!*

Petyr trudged up to the top of the hill and stood there for a moment, not quite seeing anything, except a blue light.

Blue light.

He forced his eyes to clear up and focus. Yes, blue light, just over the next hill. "Can it be that bright?"

Carree smiled at him, but it quickly turned to a look of concern. She took off the coat and put it over his shoulders.

He struggled to refuse, but she wouldn't let him. "Petyr, you'll freeze and you won't be any good to me dead," she said. "I'm warm enough now."

Petyr gave in and accepted the coat.

Once he took it, Carree ran down to the valley below, leaving Petyr to struggle to catch up to her.

Minutes later, they crested another hill, and found that indeed, they could see the fringe in the distance. Petyr didn't recognize the landscape, not that there was much difference between one patch of land and another on this side of the Fringe.

He checked his path to Sim and found they were still on it. The tunnel must have taken them a good distance out of the way.

They stumbled down the hill to a plain below them and started crossing it.

"When we go through, you will need to hold tight to me. Don't let go, or you could get lost in it forever," he said.

She nodded. "And you know your way through?"

"In a manner of speaking."

She looked at him with a questioning lift of her brow.

"I can find people, and I use them to find my way through."

"I thought you were a Questioner, not a Tracker."

"I'm neither, but I can imitate either."

The howl of a beast, not quite wolf, but not quite anything else, ripped through the air around them. It sounded far off, but he had no idea how sound might carry in this barren wasteland.

And as far as he knew, no beast lived here.

"What was that?" Carree asked.

"I think that was the Quenikuhg."

"That smaller creature?"

Petyr nodded. "And even if it isn't, we probably shouldn't take any chances. It's time to run for the Fringe. And remember, do not enter until you are holding on to me, tight."

She acknowledged him with a nod.

Together, they ran toward the Fringe, still hundreds of yards off. Petyr struggled to keep up with Carree. He had almost nothing left. He hadn't eaten or slept since the previous morning. He'd run long distances more than once. It was all he could do to continue to put one foot in front of the other.

He kept going though.

He turned around once, and saw a shadow on the hill behind him, loping along at an amazing speed, until it started down the hill.

"It's following us!" Petyr yelled. *And we don't have much time.*

He pushed himself harder. He ran until his breath burned in his throat. He pushed his dead legs to move, step after step toward the giant blue wall.

They were only a hundred yards or so from the Fringe, bathed in its glow, when Petyr looked behind him again. The Quenikuhg had gained ground on them. Petyr despaired of making it to the Fringe before the Quenikuhg could stab its claws into them again.

The breath Carree exhaled turned blue in the light of the Fringe. She'd put some good distance on him with her fresh legs. She neared the Fringe and came to a stop just within reach of it, but she didn't go in.

She turned to face him, to watch his race against impending death. "Run, Petyr!" she yelled.

She had to see it behind him. He didn't dare turn to look again. He ran straight toward Carree.

He could hear it behind him, growling, howling. And then he ran right into Carree, carried her into the Fringe, just as something, a claw, snaked out and sliced itself through his coat and shirt, down his back, leaving a line of fire behind.

But they were in the Fringe, and he could feel Carree. He hoped the Quenikuhg couldn't follow so easily.

He fell to the smooth blue ground, carrying Carree with him. He closed his eyes and tried to breathe.

CHAPTER 27

'Petyr, you must move.'

The voice came to him, but not from his ears. He recognized it. *Carree?*

'Not Carree. You must not rest. Quenikuhg searches.'

Ulli.

'Yes. Move. Stand up, Petyr. Hold girl.'

Petyr did as he was told. The aches in his body had somehow lessened. He no longer felt cold. The fire along his back where it had sliced him still burned, however.

Petyr pulled Carree up with him. He couldn't see her or hear her, but he could feel her still. *Is she still with me?*

'Do not worry. We will not let you lose her. Follow.'

Petyr saw a light, if it could be called that in this place of light, a brighter spot, and it moved away from him.

He followed, pulling Carree with him. *Where are you taking me?*

'We lead you through.'

I already know how to go through.

'Yes, but you must not go there. Trust us.'

Why shouldn't I go there?

'If you return to town without killing Quenikuhg, it will take her again, and nothing you can do will stop it.'

But I can't kill it!

The light stopped moving.

'Step out, Petyr. You must kill it, or all will end. You have seen what it has done to our home. All world will be this, if you fail.'

He felt something push at him from behind, and he stumbled out into the forest, pulling Carree with him.

"That was strange," she said.

Petyr ignored her and turned to face the Fringe. He shouted with all his lungs had left, "I can't kill it!" The Fringe continued to swirl in its cryptic patterns.

"Who are you shouting at, Petyr?"

Petyr shrugged and stumbled away. "The Fringe", he said finally, after settling himself on a log. It felt warmer on this side.

"Why are you shouting at the Fringe?"

"It's alive, Carree. It was built as a barrier to the Quenikuhg from the lives of an ancient people. They just told me I had to kill the Quenikuhg, or the whole world would become like that wasteland on the other side. I knew that already, or I suspected it."

"So why are you shouting?"

"I don't know how to kill it. I thought those spikes would work against it, but they didn't work on the giant. Who is to say they'd work on its master?"

"But you don't know they wouldn't."

"It doesn't matter, Carree. Even if they would work, I don't have any. Dyllan and Alec had them, and now, they must be dead. I can't imagine that thing would leave them behind."

"You don't know they're dead." She sat down next to him.

"Dyllan would not have let it escape." Despair washed through him. He had little desire left in him to do anything but take Carree home. He didn't even want to try to seek for his friends. He didn't want to confirm what he suspected. It was easier not to think of them at all.

"So what now?"

"I'm taking you home where you'll be safe."

Carree made a show of planting her feet in the ground and placing her hands on her hips. "You know I won't be safe there, Petyr."

"You'll be safer than you are with me."

"How can you say that? That thing, whatever you called it, will come after me there."

"Carree, I have nothing left to fight with! All of my plans are broken, my friends dead, or as good as." *Alura!* "My wife and my child, I'll never see again. Once the Empire realizes that Dyllan is not coming back, they will be moved somewhere I'll never find them. How could you possibly want to come with me?"

She moved close to him, put her hands on his face. Her fingers felt warm, even in the cold of the night air. "Petyr, I can help you. Whatever happens, I can't stay in Dunsriver."

Petyr shook his head, denying her.

She turned and looked at the fringe, her fingers still massaging his face. The blue glow that bathed her face as she turned gave it a ghostly hue. "Petyr," she said, "there must be some reason why they think you can kill it."

"Let's just go," he said, and turned away from her. He started walking away from the Fringe, not following any particular path. At that moment, he didn't care if he got lost in the forest.

Moments later, he heard Carree's footsteps catch up to him. He kept looking straight ahead at the forest, the shapes of the trees illuminated by a mixture of the blue glow from the Fringe and the moonlight that filtered down through the forest canopy.

I should take her home and leave her there. But he rejected that thought. She was right, and he knew it. She couldn't stay there. *If only I knew how to free Alura without Dyllan.*

A bright blue flash lit up the forest, leaving tracers of blue in his vision.

"Petyr?"

Petyr turned around. They'd already passed out of sight of the Fringe, but he knew instinctively what that flash meant, what the other flashes had meant. The Quenikuhg was breaking through the Fringe, working to expand it.

"Ulli was right," he said.

"What? Who's Ulli?"

"She's part of the Fringe, now."

Carree looked bewildered.

"Carree, we have to run. The Quenikuhg is pushing on the Fringe, expanding it. It's coming after us."

"I thought you said the Fringe was meant to trap it there."

Petyr looked at her for a moment, trying to gauge what to tell her. He didn't want to tell her that the Quenikuhg had taken her brother, that it's ability to penetrate the Fringe was due to her brother and his talent.

The Fringe flashed again. If daylight had been blue, the flash was bright enough he would have thought the day had come.

"We have to go, Carree. We have to run. We're too close."

"What don't you want to tell me, Petyr?"

"It's not that I don't want to tell you," he lied, and hated himself for it, "we just don't have the time right now."

The need in him to run, to go anywhere, do anything but stand where they were, mastered him. He took her hand, like he had in the cavern, and started to pull on her. She resisted. "Petyr, tell me."

The Fringe flashed again, and this time, he noticed tendrils of fog snaking through the forest behind him.

"Carree, I promise, I'll tell you all of it if we survive, but it's a long story and the Quenikuhg is coming. Look behind you," he pleaded. "The fog..."

She looked behind her. When she turned back to him, her face held the fright he'd expected to see after the flashes. "You promise?"

"I swear to you, Carree. I will tell you everything you wish to know." *I wonder why she doesn't coerce me into telling her.*

Petyr watched the tendrils of fog as they crept closer. They didn't have much time. *How much of it needs to surround us before the Quenikuhg can touch us?* He didn't want to find out.

"Carree?" he pleaded.

Her resistance melted, and she started to move with him in the direction he'd tried to go. Away from the fog. "Let's go then."

Together, they ran through the forest as quick as they dared. The flashes of light had ruined much of his ability to see by the moonlight. It was slowly coming back, but for the moment, the trees looked more like shadows than solid things.

They found an animal trail and followed it, but it seemed to wind back toward the Fringe. For a short while, they could find no easy way off the trail. At points, he saw the fog growing closer to them.

"This way," he said when the underbrush grew thinner at one point, and he pushed his way through it. Carree followed him.

He regretted not having the hatchet with him.

Ahead of him, he saw the fog, as if it had got in front of him somehow, or they had turned around.

"Petyr? Where are we going?" Her voice shook with fright.

"I've been trying to angle away from the town," he said. "I don't want to bring the Quenikuhg there."

"It seems like we're going in circles. The fog always seems to be in front of us."

"I know."

I wish I had something to seek. Almost simultaneous with that thought, he had an answer. He could seek Sim and use him as a guide. *I don't have to follow the path to him.*

He concentrated on Sim, forged a path to him. Then he turned to keep the Sim to the front of him but off to the left. Sim would guide him.

"Come," he said, pulling on Carree's wrist, and he forged off through the underbrush again.

They left the fog behind. He had to push his way through some thicker foliage, and circle around it sometimes, but the path to Sim kept them headed away from the Fringe, even with the occasional sideways movements.

He'd begun to think they'd evaded the fog when they stumbled into a clearing that he recognized.

So did Carree. "Petyr, why did you bring us here?"

"I didn't," he said. But he had.

This was, unmistakably, the clearing where they'd found Uma, where he'd gone mad and destroyed the thing that had come out of her.

It was also where he'd thrown the spikes.

"Carree, search the clearing for the spikes. I threw them down somewhere."

"Why?"

"I don't know why I threw them away." He started circling the edge of the clearing. *Where'd I throw them?*

"No, not why did you throw them away. Why do we need to find them?"

He looked up at her for a moment and saw the fog curling up behind her in the forest, coalescing in a barrier. He looked around the clearing and saw that the fog had encircled them. "Look around you, Carree! We're trapped. The spikes are the only possible weapon we have against it."

Why do I feel like I was lead here? No matter. He kept searching. He saw Carree begin to search, too. The fog started to close in. He had to find them fast.

Where was I standing when I threw them? He tried to remember. He looked at the tree again, saw the dark, blood-stained splotches in its trunk where the spikes had been driven in to hold Uma up. The whole period of time after he'd destroyed the Quenikuhg's offspring felt foggy.

He moved to the middle of the clearing, tried to run through the events in his head as quickly as he could.

He moved over by the tree, where he'd stood while he'd hacked the things head apart with the hatchet. And then they talked, and then he'd pulled the spikes from the tree and her body had slumped to the ground.

And then he'd stepped back, held the spikes in front of him and stared at them, then tossed them to the edge of the clearing with his right hand, over there.

He looked where he thought they landed, and the area was

almost enveloped in the fog. He ran over, bent down, and started searching the ground with his hands.

He found nothing. Until he reached into the fog and put his hands on iron. He picked them up and started to stand.

He backed away toward the middle of the clearing, and the fog came with him.

But I've got the spikes. I hope I can figure out what to do with them.

"Petyr!"

He turned and saw that she was also pulling fog along with her. There was no escape from this. One way or another, he realized, it ended for them, here. The Quenikuhg couldn't be very far away.

Petyr showed her the spikes, and she nodded. Instinctively, they came together in the center of the clearing, back to back. Wherever it came from, it would not surprise them.

The fog enveloped them, settled around them, an amorphous prison. While they waited, Petyr glanced down and saw that Carree had a large stone in her hand. Petyr admired her. Much like his wife, she was a strong woman and would not go without a fight.

But he refused to think about that night, refused to link the two situations. To do so, he knew, would be to give in, to try to run again. He would stand here with Carree and fight, whatever happened. *I'm done running.*

"I am not sure which of you I want more," said the Quenikuhg from somewhere in the fog. Petyr could not see it yet.

"You can't have us," Petyr said.

It laughed and stepped into the clearing. "Your friends could not stop me. What makes you think you can?"

The Quenikuhg circled them slowly while clicking and rubbing its claws together. Petyr couldn't keep from watching them, their curved, quarter moon profile reflected the filtered moonlight and reminded him of the scored flesh down his back.

It passed out of his vision, and he turned around so he could see it. "You are protective of her."

Carree tensed. "Leave us alone," she said. "Stay out of our land."

Petyr knew she had just tried to Coerce the Quenikuhg. He also knew it wouldn't work. It couldn't work. Not after it took her brother.

It smiled in response. "You cannot affect me with your talent."

"It blocks?" she asked.

Petyr didn't answer. He was waiting for something, though he wasn't sure what. Instead, he watched, looked it over. The bullet wound they had caused was gone, but he could see it had taken other damage. It had a hole in its torso that looked about the size a spike might create. Dyllan, or Alec, had managed to punch one in. *But why didn't it die?*

While it continued to circle them, it reached out and caressed Carree's cheek. Petyr stepped in front of her, inadvertently raising one of the spikes.

"Your companions tried one of those already. I still live," it said in its hissing voice. But it seemed to back away a little, and it kept its eye on it as Petyr tried to hide it again.

It was *hurt by the spike! It must have managed to pull it out.*

The circling brought the Quenikuhg between Petyr and the tree where Uma had hung. Petyr held up a spike in front of him, thinking he could use the Quenikuhg's fear against it.

The Quenikuhg backed away a bit more, moving closer to the tree.

The idea came upon Petyr like a flash from the Fringe.

He held the spike in front of him and rushed the Quenikuhg, slamming into it. He drove the spike into its chest, just below the shoulder, and kept pushing until he'd wedged the Quenikuhg up against the tree.

It slashed at him with its claws, drawing bands of fire along his back, and arms.

"Carree!" he yelled. "The stone!"

He held the Quenikuhg up against the tree and drove the spike right through to the wood, but he could not drive it further. The thing writhed in pain. Petyr's own pain threatened to take him to his knees, but he refused. Dyllan and Alec hadn't succeeded, but they hadn't known, or had the opportunity. He had to make the spike stay.

"Carree!"

A hand came from his right, carrying a stone, and bashed the stone against the spike. Over and over. It caught Petyr's hand once, but he refused to let go despite the pain. The Quenikuhg would not get away.

He took the second spike and drove it into the Quenikuhg's chest just below the other shoulder, just like Uma, and the other girl he found, and the Keekele. Carree drove it home with the stone. Petyr saw her arms were slashed, too. But she continued to pound on the stake until its head sat right up against the Quenikuhg's flesh.

The two of them fell backwards, out of reach of the Quenikuhg's claws.

Petyr's skin was slick with blood. He could feel it running down inside his shirt. Carree had deep slices on her arms and a gash across her nose and cheek. Her face was red with blood.

He looked up at the Quenikuhg where it writhed against the trunk of the huge tree. It was trying to pull at the spikes, and despite its rage and pain, Petyr saw that if they didn't do something, it might succeed at pulling them out.

The reason why it had removed the arms of the girls seemed obvious to him now. The spikes kept them alive, and they might have managed to remove the spikes, killing them in the process.

"What do we do," Carree asked.

Petyr shook his head, which caused it to ache. He was growing dizzy from the blood-loss.

The Quenikuhg had managed to loosen one of the spikes a little.

Petyr tried to get up, he wanted to take the stone from Carree and pound the spike back in, then try bashing the thing in the head with it. He could think of nothing else. However, his legs wouldn't respond. He couldn't move them. He could barely move his arms.

A dark shadow came into the clearing, big—tall. From his position on the ground, looking up, with blood beginning to drain into his eyes, he thought the giant had come.

"We do this," the shadow said, and a sword came out. Dyllan!

Dyllan limped across the clearing, and swung the sword at the base of the Quenikuhg's neck. The sword sliced through it and caught in the tree. The Quenikuhg's head slid off its shoulders and toppled to the ground. Its arms went slack.

Petyr fell to the ground, laying on his back. He didn't care about the dirt getting into his wounds. He didn't think he would survive the night.

He saw Dyllan lean over him.

"How is Carree?"

"She's hurt, but she'll live."

Petyr sighed and relaxed as much as the pain would allow him. "How did you find us?"

"A friend of yours," Dyllan said.

Petyr blinked, and for a moment, he thought he saw Ulli. He knew that wasn't possible. Ulli was a part of the Fringe. When he blinked again, Ulli was gone and all he saw was the red of his blood.

He closed his eyes, settling into the pain, knowing he wouldn't live, but satisfied he'd kept his promise to Carree.

CHAPTER 28

He floated in a world of blue. The fire and pain that had run through him at the last was gone. He was warm, and felt rested. *Is this what it's like after you die?*

Something, someone, laughed in his head. *'You are not dead, Petyr.'*

How? Where am I?

'You are in Fringe, with us.'

Ulli?

'And my people. We are grateful to you.'

He tried to stand up, but in the Fringe, he couldn't tell which way was up. Not without a path to follow. *Why are you grateful?*

'You managed to do what we could not. You destroyed Quenikuhg.'

I didn't destroy him, Dyllan did.

'Without your insight, without your determination, Dyllan and his blade of steel would not have cut through Quenikuhg.'

But Dyllan or Alec had already driven a spike into it. I saw the hole!

'We believe spikes are paired, that their magic only works when two are present in body.'

But they kept the girls alive.

'Remember, part of Quenikuhg was Keekele, just as part was

human. We can only think Keekele part can not stand touch of iron. Made it vulnerable, made it mortal.'

Petyr decided to give up on getting solid answers. He decided they were guessing as much as he. Or maybe they were hiding something. It didn't matter. It was dead.

Where are the others?

'They are safe, but not here.'

Back in the town?

'Perhaps. We do not know.'

Can I go to them?

'When you wish, you may go.'

So what happens now, to the other side, to you?

'We will remain as we are. It was choice we made. There is no reversing choice. Old home will grow green again with time.'

Will you let humans through?

'Perhaps, when land is ready. When your people are ready.'

Petyr wondered what that meant, but the land wouldn't support people for a long time. It wasn't for him, anyway. His path lay elsewhere.

Thank you for saving me.

'We owe you much more than that. You are welcome to return when your need arises.'

Petyr nodded to himself. *It's time to go.*

'Yes, goodbye.'

Petyr used his talent to seek out Carree, and when he had the path in his head, he set out on it.

⋏ ⋏ ⋏

Petyr stepped out of the Fringe to find himself bathed in early morning sunlight. The air around him was cool. A slight breeze exposed every tatter and tear in his clothes, but he didn't ache, and for that he was grateful. In fact, he felt energized, like he'd slept and eaten a full breakfast. The weather could have been a continuation from the night before, but he thought days had to have passed. His wounds had been too extensive, his exhaustion too severe.

But now, thanks to the care of the Keekele, he felt good enough to run.

So he ran, going where his talent led him, and the forest seemed to open up to let him pass as he made his way through it. *The influence of the Fringe. Thank you.*

His energy hadn't waned until he'd reached the road, at which point, he slowed to a walk. The walk felt good. His mind felt clear. He'd trusted Alec and Dyllan, and they had come through for him.

And Alec had every reason to leave, and every opportunity. Dyllan, well, Dyllan might still try to bring him in and hope they didn't ask too many questions. But Petyr felt too good to worry about that. He decided to put off thinking about what Dyllan might do until later. Maybe Dyllan had already left.

And for the first time, he wondered if they even knew he was alive. Ulli hadn't said they knew, and he hadn't thought to ask.

He knew Carree was there. And then he realized he knew how to find out about the others. He concentrated first on Dyllan, then on Alec, and they were both near Carree. They hadn't left, which meant that he might have a chance after all.

He strode into the town only an hour or so after noon, and followed his mental path to Carree, to her father's home. People gave him strange looks as he passed through the town, and he put it down to his clothes, torn up and ragged as they were.

He knocked on the door, and after a few moments, Sim opened it. Sim stepped back, eyes wide, and stuttered a welcome.

"They said you were dead," Sim managed after Petyr entered.

"I thought I would die, too," he said. "Where are they?"

"But you don't even have a scratch!"

"What?"

"They said you were torn to pieces. It's not possible."

"What do you mean, Sim?"

"They only arrived an hour ago. Yet, you..."

Petyr's path to Carree led upstairs. He rushed up the stairs and followed it to her room. Petyr stumbled in and found Carree on the bed, Ilsan tending to her, and Dyllan and Alec looking on anxiously.

The three men looked at Petyr as he entered, but Petyr's eyes went to Carree. Her lacerations looked bad, but nowhere near as bad as his memory told them they'd been. The bed sheets were bloody, and she would have a scar across her face, but she would live, he thought. Perhaps the Keekele had helped her some. *Why didn't they help her like they helped me?*

"Petyr! How is this possible?" Alec asked.

Dyllan rushed over to him. "We thought you dead."

"I thought so, too."

Dyllan stepped back and examined him for the first time, then reached out and grabbed Petyr's arms, and turned them over and over. "You aren't even hurt. How is it possible?"

Petyr felt guilty, now, looking down at Carree. She'd helped as much as he had. "The Keekele healed me," he said. "I woke up in the Fringe, and I no longer hurt."

"But why? Why help you and do nothing for her?"

"They told me they owed me for destroying the Quenikuhg, and I think they helped her, too. I seem to remember thinking she wouldn't make it home before I..."

"Before you died," said Alec.

"How could that be?" Petyr asked.

Ilsan stood and faced them. "You may have been as near dead as it is possible to be without actually being dead. Who is to know? They healed you to full health, and you are here because of it. We have our talents. These Keekele, they must have theirs. Maybe you could bring one here to help her? Would they do that for you?"

Petyr shook his head. "They are a part of the Fringe, now. They cannot leave it."

"Well, it will be no matter. Carree will live."

"But she'll be scarred."

"It will only be a fine line of a scar. With makeup, perhaps not even noticeable."

"Petyr," Carree said. Her voice was tired, but not weak.

Petyr went to her and bent down.

"I think I know what happened to my brother."

Petyr cringed. He didn't want to tell her now.

"That thing got to him. I tried to Coerce it, but it blocked me. The only person I've never been able to Coerce was my brother."

Petyr didn't want to confirm it. He didn't want to hurt her any more than she was, but he couldn't lie, either. "He went through…"

"You don't have to tell all. I know enough."

Petyr reached up and brushed her bloodstained hair. She stared up into his eyes, and he didn't look away. She was searching for something, and he decided he'd let her find whatever she was looking for.

After long moments, she said, "I'm coming with you."

Petyr nodded. "Of course, if that's what you want."

"Thank you," she said, then closed her eyes.

Petyr stood and turned to Dyllan. "What about you?"

"I go where you go, for now, as long as you have control." Dyllan nodded at Carree, and Petyr knew what Dyllan meant. He still didn't trust her.

Petyr and Alec shared a look that Petyr didn't even have to interpret. If Alec hadn't left him yet, he wouldn't be leaving soon.

"What do you think will happen to the town?" Petyr asked.

"The man who instigated the little rebellion is dead. They'll be able to say that I left with you. We can take the Questioner with us."

"At least until we're well on our way."

"You don't trust him?"

"I don't know him."

"He could be useful if we need Questions answered where you are not welcome."

Petyr shrugged. "If he wants to come, then he can come."

He looked around the room. "Ilsan, are you coming too?"

The doctor smiled and said, "I don't think so. Dunsriver is my home, now. But perhaps we should discuss your plans before you leave."

Petyr looked around the room, then. The four of them. Possibly five. After what they'd just survived, he thought perhaps they had a good chance of rescuing Alura and his daughter, at least. At most? Maybe they could save the Empire from its own corruption.

It was a start.

ABOUT THE AUTHOR

Mark Fassett lives in western Washington with his wife, children, and cats. He's had extensive experience in the mobile game business and was involved with some of the top selling titles at the time of their release, including multiple Duke Nukem Mobile games and Guitar Hero World Tour Mobile. He's also played and written music most of his life, and was "this close" to actually making money at it.

FIND ME ONLINE

Blog - http://www.markfassett.com
Twitter - http://twitter.com/mark_fassett

Questioner's Shadow was written using StoryBox. StoryBox is software I developed specifically for writing fiction. You can try it for free at http://www.storyboxsoftware.com

www.ingramcontent.com/pod-product-compliance
Lightning Source LLC
Chambersburg PA
CBHW021514240626
47154CB00002B/629